THE CASE OF THE
BLACK PEARL

THE CASE OF THE BLACK PEARL

A Patrick de Courvoisier mystery

Lin Anderson

This first world edition published 2014
in Great Britain and the USA by
SEVERN HOUSE PUBLISHERS LTD of
19 Cedar Road, Sutton, Surrey, England, SM2 5DA.
Trade paperback edition first published in Great Britain and the USA 2014
by SEVERN HOUSE PUBLISHERS LTD.

Anderson, Lin
  The case of the black pearl.
  1. English–France–Cannes–Fiction. 2. Private
  investigators–France–Cannes–Fiction. 3. Missing
  persons–Fiction. 4. Motion picture actors and actresses–
  Fiction. 5. Detective and mystery stories.
  I. Title
  823.9'2-dc23

ISBN-13: 978-0-7278-8386-5 (cased)
ISBN-13: 978-1-84751-515-5 (trade paper)

Typeset by Palimpsest Book Production Ltd.,
Falkirk, Stirlingshire, Scotland.

For my friends in Le Suquet who inspired this series, in particular Christine Blanc and the real Pascal, not forgetting Oscar.

ONE

The *Heavenly Princess* floated on a midnight sea, her layered decks painted silver by a full moon. Designed as a luxury home for the mobile rich, she was equipped with a helipad, a forty-two-foot motor yacht, and a decompression chamber for those who liked to take risks while diving. For those who sought relaxation, the *Princess* boasted a waterfall that tumbled over the aft lip of the sky deck into a large Jacuzzi.

Currently, the view north from the sky deck was of the city of Cannes, playground for the rich, and currently host to the most famous film festival in the world. Being too large to tie up at the main jetty, the *Princess* was normally anchored in the west bay, although tonight she had moved a little nearer to the island of Sainte Marguerite, whose colourfully lit medieval fort had been used in a scene from the movie *The Black Pearl*, a thriller involving yachts, jewels and death, which had been shown at the festival.

Having a party on board therefore required ferrying the cast to and from the harbour, along with film stars attending the festival, international journalists, beautiful young actresses and the rich older men who intended bedding them.

One such actress now stood on the sky deck, the tinkle of the waterfall masking the chat and music that drifted up from below. It was Angele Valette, star of *The Black Pearl*.

A little over five feet five inches tall, her body was slim but curvaceous. Wearing an indigo gown, her hair spun gold, she appeared to embody the moonlit sky above her. Around her neck hung the other star of the movie, the pearl itself. She fingered its warm smooth surface as she waited, martini glass in hand, looking towards the sheer wall of rock on which the brightly lit fort stood.

Hearing a footstep she turned, searching the shadows, but whoever she sought did not appear. She drank the martini in one gulp and placed the delicately stemmed glass on a table next to the Jacuzzi. As she did so she caught the sound of an engine and, scanning the water, spotted the beam of a motor boat, heralding the approach of another group of festival attendees, looking to party among the rich and famous. While she watched them board below, she heard someone call her name softly from the shadows.

She turned as the figure of a man came into view. Moonlight glistened on the dark hair, aquiline nose and square-cut jaw of her handsome co-star, American Conor Musso, his Italian-Irish ancestry obvious in the bright-blue eyes and olive skin.

'What are you doing up here? Everyone is looking for you. They want to see the pearl.' Conor looked flushed under his tan.

'I was too hot. I needed some air,' she said in accented English. Conor joined her at the rail, standing close enough for Angele to catch the astringent scent of his cologne.

He slid his arm about her shoulders, drawing her to him. 'They want to see you too,' he said in a husky voice, moving his other hand to touch her breast.

She slapped him away and turned her attention back to the water.

When he spoke, his voice was petulant. 'Chapayev wants you downstairs. Now.' He turned and walked away.

Angele did not move. Let the fat little Russian wait. The movie had shown to great reviews. He had served his purpose. She no longer had to dance to his tune. She leaned over the rail, dangling the pearl above the dark glistening water, and smiled. She would soon be free. Free of Conor Musso and his busy hands, free of Chapayev and his flabby body and small mean eyes. Contemplating her freedom, Angele did not hear the soft nudge of a dinghy against the opposite side of the yacht.

By the time she turned, the figure was already behind her.

TWO

The woman paused to check the name on yet another yacht moored along the *quai*. Taller than the average movie star hopeful, with shoulder-length dark hair and long slim legs showing discreetly below a stylish blue dress, she was striking and classy. And, Patrick suspected, bringing trouble his way.

The thought pleased him.

Things had been quiet since March, when he'd dealt with a Swedish national who'd attempted to leave without paying six months' rent on one of Chevalier's properties at the top of Le Suquet, just next to the church and with a view to die for.

Since then, Patrick had spent his time doing repair work on his boat, *Les Trois Soeurs*, climbing in the Estérel Mountains, reading and indulging his desire to take risks at the nearby casino. By May he'd had enough of the quiet life and was looking for a challenge.

It appeared his prayers had been answered.

Having reached his boat, the lady was scrutinizing its name. *The Three Sisters* was not the usual type of yacht moored in the old port. A former French gunboat, heavy hulled, she stood out like a French bulldog among a line of poodles, or at least that's what he liked to think.

His visitor had decided she'd found what she sought and was looking up at him, Patrick de Courvoisier, seated on the upper deck, reading, or pretending to. Lying across his feet, Oscar, an actual French bulldog, snorted in his sleep as though he knew and disapproved of what was about to happen. Patrick wondered if the dog might be right. But there was something about trouble – a scent as enticing as his favourite dish at Le Pistou on the nearby Rue Félix Faure – that he could not resist.

'Monsieur de Courvoisier?' She observed him quizzically, although it may have been the sun in her eyes.

Patrick often made a decision on voice alone. If he agreed to work for someone, he had to be prepared to listen to them pouring out their troubles, pleading, lying, arguing, complaining and sometimes refusing to pay.

Her voice reminded him of a cocktail served up in the Irish bar across the road. The cocktail contained, or so he'd been told, Bailey's liqueur, chocolate milk and whipped cream. It was entitled, in the understated way of the Irish, an Orgasm.

Patrick stirred himself and answered the luscious voice.

'*C'est moi.*'

Her rendition of his name had suggested French or at least someone whose pronunciation hadn't been learned from a phrase-book or at school. Now he waited as she decided whether he was French or had simply acquired the name from a French branch of the family. She chose correctly, which impressed and offended Patrick at the same time.

'May I come on board?' she said in lightly accented English.

'Be my guest.'

He lowered the walkway.

She hesitated for a moment. Having found him, she was entertaining second thoughts. Patrick wondered if the story he was about to be told was in the process of being re-written.

Oscar roused himself and stood up, observing the attractive intruder with a baleful eye. When he gave a low growl, she responded by offering him a hand to sniff, which showed courage, as she wasn't to know that Oscar was far less threatening than he sounded.

Patrick waved her to the second chair under the awning, picking up her fragrance as she brushed past. Then a thought struck him.

'Or you might prefer to sit inside?'

Her relief, although masked, was tangible. Patrick indicated the open cabin door, and that she should go in first. He dipped his head and followed her down the steps into the instant gloom of the dark wooden interior.

He'd bought *Les Trois Soeurs* from a French couple who'd lived on board for half their married lives. Intensely private, they'd discouraged visitors, preferring to meet their friends at one of the numerous restaurants and café-bars that lined Le Vieux Port. Patrick had been permitted to board only after he'd declared his intention of buying *Les Trois Soeurs*, even if he never saw inside her, endearing himself to the female half of the couple, Madame Blanc.

The moment he'd stepped aboard, he'd felt at home. Madame Blanc had stayed true to the masculine interior, her only feminine touch being the addition of a couple of colourful cushions. The polished wood, clean lines and a galley he could cook in all pleased him. The double bedroom was more than fit for purpose – and then came the surprise. Madame had asked him to follow her through the old engine room towards the stern, where she'd opened a door to reveal the *pièce de résistance*: a sunken mahogany bath.

His reaction and delight had brought a small smile to her stern countenance.

It was a surprise Patrick had often used on visitors that he, too, wished to impress.

At this moment, his visitor was viewing the cabin discreetly. He formed the impression that she rather liked what she saw.

'May I offer you a drink?' Patrick said.

Again the slight hesitation, or perhaps she was internally translating his request into French. Her reply in English, when it came, surprised him.

'A Bloody Mary, if you have the ingredients?'

He smiled an 'of course' and extracted a bottle from the display on the bar.

'Russian vodka?' he said.

'Please.'

He extracted ice from the small freezer compartment and dropped it into a long glass. Choosing Stoli Gold, he added a good measure, some tomato juice and a dash of Tabasco.

When he handed it over, she thanked him, then took time to taste the mix before indicating that it was good. At close quarters her eyes were blue with a violet tinge. Patrick thought that he had never seen eyes quite that colour before. Eventually she spoke.

'I believe you are known as Le Limier?'

'Some call me the fixer; others use less flattering terms.'

By her look of acknowledgement she'd heard a few.

'I need you to . . .' She hesitated, searching for the right words. 'To fix something for me.'

'Something other than a Bloody Mary?'

She smiled and the effect was dazzling, even out of the sun. He was on dangerous ground. A beautiful woman was a thing to behold, but distracting to do business with.

'My name is Camille Ager.'

She held out her hand. It was slim and fine boned and cold to his touch from the iced glass.

Patrick waved her to a seat. She settled herself, took another mouthful, then placed the glass on the table. All of this was done slowly and deliberately, as though to compose herself before she spoke.

'I have been told I can trust you.' She eyed him candidly.

'May I ask by whom?'

'Does it matter?'

'It does.'

'Monsieur Paul Chevalier,' she conceded.

Paul Chevalier, or Le Chevalier as he was affectionately known among residents of Le Suquet, was a man Patrick held in high regard.

'And how do you know Le Chevalier?' he asked.

She wasn't sure of her answer and he anticipated why. If her dealings with Chevalier had been about his real-estate business, and therefore above the legal radar, it would be easy. If the connection was of an altogether different nature, her explanation might prove more difficult.

'We share . . .' She hesitated. 'A mutual acquaintance.'

Patrick waited.

'In Brigitte Lacroix.'

Now this was a surprise. As he'd viewed her approach along the *quai*, Patrick hadn't thought for a moment that she might be one of Brigitte's girls. Patrick studied his visitor in a little more detail. The women who worked for Brigitte were highly intelligent, well educated and stunningly beautiful. Camille Ager was all of these.

As though in answer to his unspoken question, she said, 'I do not work for Madame Lacroix, but I have a friend who does.'

Brigitte Lacroix was mistress of Hibiscus, the premier escort agency on the Côte d'Azur. Becoming one of Brigitte's girls was more difficult, it was said, than gaining a place at the prestigious Sorbonne. Those who passed the entry requirements could look forward to five years' work, after which they could comfortably retire on the proceeds, if they had not already married a rich client.

Brigitte, like Le Chevalier, had been born and raised in Le Suquet. She knew its inhabitants and their secrets as thoroughly as she knew the intimate desires of her well-heeled clientele. If Brigitte had sent Camille to Le Chevalier, then she'd assumed he would send her here to Patrick.

'How can I help you?' Patrick said.

She released the breath she'd been holding. She had been more nervous, Patrick realized, than she'd shown.

'I have a younger half-sister. Her name is Angele Valette.' She paused to clear an emotional catch in her throat. 'She is in a great deal of trouble, Monsieur de Courvoisier.'

The story turned out to be anything but pretty, unlike the girl in the photograph Camille handed him. It was a press shot taken on the steps of the red carpet. The midnight-blue dress Angele wore accentuated her slim body and elegant white neck.

'The dress is the exact colour of the black pearl from the movie. It was made especially for the film,' Camille said, her voice breaking.

Angele resembled her name. Transparently beautiful, her eyes widened by the flash of cameras, she looked stunned to find herself dropped from heaven into a mad world.

'Who is the man with her?' Patrick said.

'Conor Musso, her co-star. An American.'

Dark-haired, tanned and handsome, the guy looked every inch a movie star. Patrick wondered if he could act.

'And the one standing behind?'

'Sergio Gramesci, the Italian director of *The Black Pearl*.'

'Should I have heard of him?' Patrick asked.

She shook her head. '*The Black Pearl* is his first movie. Until now he has worked in Italian TV soaps.'

Slightly out of shot stood a shorter, broader figure.

'That is Vasily Chapayev, a Russian entrepreneur – according to Angele, the money behind the movie,' Camille told him. 'Angele thought it was Italian backed when she took the part. She never found out about Chapayev until he turned up on set.'

'And that worried her?'

'Not at first. It is the producer who must worry about the money side of things.' Camille took in his blank expression. 'You know nothing about how films are made, monsieur?'

He shook his head.

'It takes a great deal of money to fund even a bad movie.'

'And *The Black Pearl* is a bad movie?'

Camille gave a Gallic shrug. 'It contains a lot of sex and some violence. It will make money; if not in cinemas, then on DVD.'

'And what did Angele think of it?'

'She was excited by the chance to star in a movie. And when she learned Chapayev was launching the film at Cannes, she was ecstatic. It was all she ever dreamed of.' Camille reached for her glass, took a swift drink and composed herself before continuing. 'Two nights ago, Angele called to tell me that Chapayev was holding the launch party on the *Heavenly Princess*. He'd invited a number of film people, including some from Hollywood. Angele was so excited. She texted me from the yacht about midnight to say she was having a wonderful time. That's the last I heard from her.'

'Have you spoken to anyone else about this?'

'I tried asking Sergio where Angele was. He fobbed me off, but he sounded angry.' She halted as if afraid to say what she was thinking.

'Why do you think he was angry?' Patrick asked.

'Without Angele they cannot promote the film.'

'Is that all?'

As she composed herself, Patrick decided he'd at last reached the real reason for her underlying fear.

'Angele was wearing the black pearl when she disappeared,' Camille said quietly.

Her violet-tinged eyes met his own.

'And you think your sister may have stolen the pearl?'

'I do not know, monsieur.' Camille's hand, when she touched his, was ice cold. 'But I fear if she has, then Chapayev may kill her to get it back.'

THREE

The café-bar named Le P'tit Zinc stood guard at the entrance to Le Suquet, the medieval heart of Cannes. Unlike the gourmet establishments that lined the steep street of the Rue Antoine, which catered for festival attendees with money to burn, the more traditional Le Zinc was the watering place of Le Suquet's full-time inhabitants. There they sat with a modestly priced glass of local wine and watched disdainfully as the wealthier visitors passed by.

Patrick departed the gunboat and, walking the length of the *quai*, entered Le Suquet via the Rue Antoine. Already six o'clock, the various restaurants that stretched from quayside to the square atop the hill were busy constructing their outside platforms, and perching tables to line the narrow cobbled thoroughfare.

Le Zinc was also taking advantage of the increased traffic by claiming a corner of the Rue de la Misericorde, although its tables weren't draped in snow-white linen and set with sparkling glassware, but rather were Formica topped and supplied with an ashtray, most of which were in use.

At one such table sat Chevalier, a small glass of red wine, almost finished, before him. Catching his eye, Patrick gestured that he would fetch his friend a refill, and went inside.

Veronique, the proprietress, stood behind the long zinc-topped counter that gave the café its name, muttering as she poured a glass of beer. Her words were unintelligible, but definitely annoyed. When she spotted Patrick she told him exactly what it was that had incensed her.

Two tourists had bought fast food and, taking a seat at one of *her* tables, had proceeded to eat it. If they want a snack, she told him, *she* would provide it. Veronique gestured angrily to the small blackboard that advertised today's offerings, among which featured the inimitable croque-monsieur.

Patrick waited until she reached the end of her tirade, nodding in between at the righteousness of her wrath, then ordered a half carafe of house red and another glass. Veronique raised her shoulders indicating she would deal with him after the miscreants. Exiting behind her, Patrick saw Chevalier observing the ungracious delivery of the beer with an amused smile.

'They will be lucky to leave with their lives,' he pronounced, as Patrick took his seat.

The tourists had got the message. They hastily drank their beers and vacated the table, finding refuge in the continuing stream of sightseers climbing the Rue Antoine. Veronique called something after them, which Patrick roughly translated as 'good riddance'.

When the wine arrived, via the now placated Veronique, Patrick topped up Le Chevalier's glass, then filled his own. The two men took a moment to savour the wine. There was no hurry. Le Chevalier was well aware why Patrick had sought him out.

The day had been warm for May, a notoriously fickle month in Cannes, when the sky could produce a sudden downpour as easily as rays of sunshine. Today the sun shone down from a clear blue sky. Le Chevalier wore his spring outfit of colourful shirt, dotted bow tie, smart jacket and trousers. With his smooth black hair and neat moustache he reminded Patrick of a modern version of Hercule Poirot, although Patrick doubted if the Belgian detective would ever have climbed aboard the magnificent Yamaha TMAX currently parked on the Rue de la Misericorde.

Setting the glass on the table, Chevalier drew out a checked handkerchief from his top pocket and dabbed his moustache dry.

'I take it Camille followed my advice and came to see you?'

'She did,' Patrick said.

'And what did you think of Mademoiselle Ager?'

Had it been anyone other than Chevalier, Patrick might have construed this as a subtle enquiry as to his visitor's sexual desirability. Chevalier, however, was a perfect gentleman, who was only inter-ested in other gentlemen, despite evidence to the contrary in the macho motorbike.

'Intriguing,' Patrick admitted. 'And very worried about her missing half-sister.'

Chevalier contemplated his response for a moment, before pouring himself another glass.

'I suggest you talk to Brigitte. I believe one of her girls was also at the *Black Pearl* party.'

This was welcome news.

'A friend of Camille's?' Patrick asked.

'I don't believe so. Her name is Marie Elise.'

'Is that her real name?' Patrick said.

Chevalier raised an amused eyebrow. 'I shouldn't think so.'

'How can I contact her?'

Chevalier gave his signature shrug. 'Through Brigitte – how else?'

Madame Lacroix was renowned for the protection she gave 'her girls'. If Patrick wanted to speak to Marie Elise, he would have to set up an appointment at Brigitte's office. The alternative was to hire her for an evening and speak to her alone. Which would not come cheap.

Patrick had already negotiated a daily rate with Camille Ager, who'd insisted on paying him for two weeks' work up front, cash in hand. He'd deposited the substantial amount in the usual place on board the gunboat. Even if an intruder managed to bypass Oscar, Patrick was certain they would not easily find his secret stash of euros and American dollars.

The two men fell silent as they contemplated two young starlets who were attempting the steeply cobbled Rue Antoine in very high heels, while their male companions strode ahead, oblivious to their difficulties.

'Ask her for a meal on board *Les Trois Soeurs*,' Chevalier said. 'She will like that. And you can talk in private.'

Brigitte's girls were used to expensive dinners served on visiting yachts, or in the restaurants of the magnificent hotels that lined the Croisette. Patrick regarded himself as a good cook, but dining aboard *Les Trois Soeurs* didn't come into that bracket.

Chevalier appeared to read his mind.

'Nothing too fancy. She gets plenty of that. A *fruits de mer* platter will suit Marie very well,' he said with certainty.

'So you know this girl?'

'I know them all. As a gay father figure, of course.' He topped up Patrick's glass as Veronique appeared with a selection of hors d'œuvre. 'The choice of wine, I leave up to you.'

Patrick raised his glass in salute, recognizing this as a compliment.

Later, the carafe empty and the appetizers eaten, Chevalier indicated that he had an evening engagement. He wished Patrick good luck, then roared off on his motorbike, much to the amazement of some nearby tourists.

Once his friend had departed, Patrick rang the Hibiscus number.

The voice that answered was undoubtedly that of Brigitte Lacroix. Patrick revealed his identity and asked if Marie Elise was free for that evening.

'For what?' Brigitte demanded.

'Dinner aboard *Les Trois Soeurs*.'

There was a short silence, followed by a chuckle.

'You wish Marie Elise to go slumming?'

'I have an unique mahogany sunken bath,' Patrick countered.

'We all know about your bath, Monsieur de Courvoisier.'

Patrick wondered how, but decided not to ask.

'I will check with Marie Elise,' Brigitte said. 'If she wishes to take up your offer, she will call you back.' The phone went down.

The return call came five minutes later. Marie Elise sounded charming and not a little amused by the proposition. When she asked for a time, Patrick suggested eight o'clock. There was no mention of a fee. Much like the designer shops on the Rue d'Antibes, if you had to ask, then you couldn't afford to buy.

Patrick settled the bill with Veronique and went to order his seafood selection and select his wine, before seeking out the director of *The Black Pearl*.

A variety of festivals used the large auditorium of the Palais des Festivals, but none so famous, nor so frantic, as the film festival. Negotiating the Croisette during these ten days, especially if you were swimming against the tide, required a great deal of time and effort.

Patrick decided to avoid the throng hanging about the red carpet area and instead wound his way eastwards through the back streets, only cutting down near the Hôtel Majestic Barriere. Set back from the Croisette and fronted by a wide drive and terraced garden bar, its grand entrance was being policed by two security guards. To gain entry you had to provide evidence of being a bona fide festival delegate via a treasured pass, or be a recognizable film star.

Patrick was neither.

However, he did know one of the guards on duty, who had once hired him to sort out a personal problem. Bruno had a long memory and a generous heart. Not only did he wave Patrick through, he handed him a journalist's badge to avoid any problems once inside.

The large reception area of the Majestic was thronging with movie people and journalists, on mobiles or standing talking in noisy groups. As he threaded his way through, a door opened on a large press conference and Patrick caught a glimpse of a platform of movie stars and their director taking questions amid the popping flashbulbs.

He located a lift and, stepping into the sudden and welcome silence, pressed the third-floor button.

When Camille had supplied him with Sergio Gramesci's contact details, she'd indicated that as far as she was aware, Angele hadn't revealed to her film colleagues that she had a sister. Nor would Angele like the idea of her interfering.

'I just want to make sure she's all right,' Camille had said quietly.

With that instruction in mind, Patrick had put a call through to Gramesci. The director had been distinctly unhelpful on the phone, until Patrick mentioned the possibility of financing his next movie, whereupon Sergio had swiftly changed his tune.

Patrick stood outside room 301 for a moment, listening. Despite the solid door, he could hear sounds of an argument: a woman's high-pitched voice and the more guttural sound of a man. Patrick waited until they paused for breath, then knocked. A few seconds later the door was opened.

Sergio Gramesci was tall, sleek and handsome. Whatever anger had been present behind the closed door had disappeared from his perfectly tanned face. Patrick offered his hand and introduced himself in Italian as Gerard Dubois, a French investment banker.

'I should warn you I have very little time,' Gramesci apologized. He raised his hands in mock horror. 'Cannes at the festival.' He stood aside indicating that Patrick should enter.

The woman whose voice he'd heard stood beside a table on which sat an ice bucket with a bottle of champagne and two glasses. She was dark-haired and dark-eyed, and she was angry, but covering it less well than Gramesci.

Patrick met her frosty look and held out his hand, which she grudgingly took.

'Madame?' he enquired.

'Celeste Colbert.'

At his '*enchanté*' her expression softened, but only a little. Patrick realized that worry as much as anger lurked in those eyes.

He turned his attention to Gramesci. 'As I indicated on the phone, I'm interested in financing your next film.' He paused. 'On the understanding that it would again star Angele Valette.'

The woman concentrated on a champagne glass, her expression studiously blank.

Gramesci, on the other hand, eyed him with interest.

'You have seen *The Black Pearl*?'

'No, but I have heard very good reports from reliable sources in the industry, which is why I'm here.'

The smile that curved Gramesci's lips showed he wasn't immune to flattery. Behind him the woman had adopted a scowl, which grew deeper. Patrick got the impression she had moved from studied indifference to biting her tongue.

'I'd like to discuss this opportunity with your leading lady,' Patrick said.

A cloud swept over Gramesci, killing his sunshine smile.

'I'm terribly sorry, but Angele is unavailable at the moment.'

Patrick feigned disappointment. 'When will she be available?'

'She's a very busy lady,' Gramesci said.

'I have to be in the Cayman Islands three days from now,' Patrick interrupted his excuse. 'I'm keen to place the funds before that.'

A mixture of avarice and worry crossed Gramesci's features. The woman attempted to catch his eye, but was ignored.

'I'll discuss it with Angele and see what we can arrange,' he said smoothly.

As he was obviously buying time, Patrick decided to put him on the spot. 'What about this evening?'

Gramesci came back quickly with his lie. 'She's out doing a photo shoot in the mountains. I'm not sure when she'll return,' he apologized.

'So it isn't true that she hasn't been seen since the launch party?'

Gramesci's look of amazement was impressive. 'Who told you that?'

Patrick chose not to answer the question. Instead he said, 'When I get to meet Mademoiselle Angele, we'll talk further.' He handed Gramesci a card. 'You can reach me on that number. Night or day.'

They shook hands at the door. When it shut behind him, Patrick waited, listening for the reaction to his visit. The argument had started again, the woman's voice being the most insistent. It was being conducted in Italian, but the only words he could clearly make out were 'stupid bitch', which he took to refer to the missing Angele.

FOUR

Departing room 301, Patrick headed for the bar. Situated between the white marble foyer and the main restaurant, the room was reminiscent of the Belle Époque in its opulence and view of the outside terrace.

He settled himself in a chair and, when the waiter arrived, ordered a vodka martini. The place was bustling, populated by those who wished to conquer the world of movies. The French and American contingent were clearly distinguishable, mainly for their style or lack of it. Young men, carrying the bags issued with the delegate pass, had their ears perpetually glued to mobiles or their gazes fixed on interactive tablet screens.

He eventually spotted the guy he'd seen manning the small office for Black Pearl Productions close to Gramesci's room on the third floor. The sign on the desk had said 'Producer'. The money man, according to Camille. Tall, pudgy, wearing long shorts and a T-shirt with the words 'The Black Pearl – A Movie to Die For' emblazoned across the front, he entered the bar, took a swift look round, then went out on to the terrace.

Patrick picked up his glass and followed, waiting by the open double doors until the object of his attention had settled himself at an empty table, before striding over.

'Excuse me, monsieur. My name is Gerard Dubois,' he said in French this time. 'I wonder if we might discuss a possible investment in Black Pearl Productions?' When he was met by a blank stare, Patrick repeated his little speech in English.

'Hey, sorry man. *Je suis américain.* That's about all I can say in French.' His proffered hand was hot and clammy. 'Richard Polinsky, producer of *The Black Pearl*,' he said proudly. The accent was Californian, which showed how movie money crossed all frontiers, even Russian–American ones.

Polinsky waved Patrick to a seat just as the waiter arrived. He eyed the martini glass. 'Can I buy you a drink?'

Patrick shook his head. 'You know what they say: "One martini is fine, two is too many and three is not enough".'

Polinsky gave a small laugh and ordered himself an American beer. When the waiter departed, Patrick got down to business.

'I would very much like to meet your leading lady, Angele Valette. She really made *The Black Pearl* a sellable commodity.'

The delight dropped from Polinsky's face.

'She's still in Cannes, I hope?' Patrick said anxiously.

Polinsky gave a sorrowful smile. 'I'm afraid not.'

'Really? I understood she was staying on the black yacht in the west bay.'

Polinsky hesitated a fraction too long. 'She had an audition to attend – in Paris,' he added imaginatively.

'You mean she won't be starring in your next movie?' Patrick looked suitably shocked.

Polinsky, quickly realizing his mistake, tried to back pedal. 'Oh, we've already signed her up for that. Her and Conor. This is just an in-between she might do, while we're raising the money.' He looked expectantly at Patrick.

'I very much wanted to meet with Mademoiselle Valette before I commit myself.'

'I don't blame you.' Polinsky raised an eyebrow. 'She's a popular lady. Maybe she could get in touch when she gets back?'

'And when will that be?'

'In the next day or two.'

Patrick considered this for a moment before asking, 'Who was your main backer on *The Black Pearl*?'

The pudgy face screwed up. 'That's kinda private.'

'I understand the yacht where you held the after-show party belongs to Vasily Chapayev, a Russian entrepreneur.'

Polinsky gave a secretive little smile. 'Hey, you've got me there.'

'Will he be investing in the next movie?' Patrick tried to sound territorial.

'Nothing's settled yet,' Polinsky said swiftly.

'This money. I don't want it to sit around for too long.' Patrick inclined his head. 'French bureaucracy might force me to put it elsewhere. You understand?'

Polinsky understood all right.

'How does Angele contact you, when she gets back from Paris?'

Patrick handed him the card for Dubois International Investments Ltd's head office in the Cayman Islands. 'My number. Once I take Angele out to dinner, we'll talk.' He gave Polinsky a smile that indicated a male understanding of what the dinner invitation really meant and held out his hand. 'I'll look forward to hearing from Angele.'

As he turned to go Polinsky caught his arm. 'A little something while you wait.' He handed Patrick a DVD. 'Some promotional footage of Angele I think you'll enjoy.'

Patrick smiled his appreciation. 'I'll look forward to watching it.' He slipped the DVD in his pocket.

Once beyond the screen of flowering camellias that bordered the terrace, Patrick checked back to find Polinsky talking rapidly on his mobile – a call, he suspected, instigated by his visit. But was it a call to Angele? Somehow he didn't think so.

He made his way back to the security gate where he gave Bruno the thumbs-up. When he tried to return the journalist's pass, Bruno waved it away.

'Keep it. It'll get you into all the best parties.'

As he left the Majestic's grounds, he was passed by a big black limo, its occupants hidden behind smoked glass. Cheers of approbation met the car as it turned on to the Croisette. The screams grew louder as it approached the red carpet, rising to a crescendo as its occupants, a male and a female, climbed out and posed for photographers.

According to Camille this was the adulation her sister craved. Perhaps *The Black Pearl* would have propelled her towards Hollywood and that dream.

So why throw it all away by stealing from her benefactor?

Unless staying with Chapayev had proved a more frightening prospect than going. Patrick had yet to meet the Russian, but even from what little he knew of the man, he didn't believe ditching him would have been easy.

He glanced out to the sleek black shape of the yacht in the bay. As he watched, a motorboat took off from its side and headed towards the shore.

A visit to the *Heavenly Princess* was a necessity and soon. He fingered the journalist's pass clipped to his breast pocket. He could try out his new-found status as a movie journalist. If that didn't get him on board, he had other ways at his disposal.

FIVE

Once away from the Croisette, the crowds began to thin. Celebrities could be spotted further west in Le Suquet, but most fans simply hung around the red-carpet entrance to the Palais, unaware that the restaurants of the Rue Saint Antoine and the pizza restaurant by the old harbour were popular places for the famous to dine.

Patrick made his way along the harbour walkway, hoping the local dive boat wouldn't be currently out on a trip, but its berth was empty. He would have to catch up with its proprietor Stephen later in the Irish bar.

Oscar lay asleep under the awning on the upper deck of the gunboat, his sleek tan body stretched out in the shape of a frog. Patrick gave a low whistle and Oscar dragged himself up, somewhat reluctantly, from his heat-induced snooze and awaited orders. When Patrick told him to 'stay', Oscar lay back down and went back to his slumbers.

Continuing along by the harbour, Patrick made for the curved bay of the Plages du Midi. At this time of day in May, it was normally populated by the members of Cannes's elderly swim club, who took a dip whatever the time of year, whatever the weather. A few film festival delegates had swelled their numbers, looking worn and hot, and wishing they had brought the means to swim in their festival bags.

Patrick took off his shirt and sandals and left them in a pile near the water, then walked in far enough to perform a shallow dive before heading straight out of the bay. The end of June would see rafts anchored all along the coast, including here in the west bay, but for now only a few grey heads bobbed the water apart from his own.

A strong steady crawl took him to the first of a line of buoys in fifteen minutes. He trod water there, checking out his line of sight, estimating the *Heavenly Princess* to be up to an hour's swim away, depending on the current.

He headed eastwards, keeping to the line of marker buoys that marked the edge of the shipping lane, before cutting directly across, keeping his eye out for motor boats. No one racing along the coast in a flurry of spray would be on the lookout for a lone swimmer outside the line of buoys, unless round a moored yacht.

As he neared the *Princess*, he spotted a few figures larking about in the water at her stern. From the various decks came the sound of laughter, music and voices. Regardless of the stolen pearl, the Russian's guests were still partying. Patrick pulled himself on to the metal platform and sat there for a moment, as though he too was a guest who'd decided to take a swim to cool off.

He was joined almost immediately by a young woman, who stripped off her dress to reveal a pair of enhanced breasts and a tiny thong.

'Is it cold?' she asked, her eyes bright with alcohol, or some other substance.

'Refreshing,' Patrick assured her.

She poised, then dived, her slim brown body entering the water with barely a splash. He watched her surface a few metres away and join two men.

Patrick rose and climbed the metal steps. At the top, a waiter in a fitted white jacket and tight black trousers presented him with a tray of drinks. Patrick chose a champagne glass with a strawberry attached. Now he was one of them, he could take a look around.

Patrick could not help but admire his surroundings. Ostentatious the *Heavenly Princess* might be, but she had been built by true craftsmen. As to her price tag, he could only guess – and even the guess, he thought, would be too low. Chapayev had money to burn, that much was obvious. How he made his money was something Patrick had yet to discover.

He made his way through the partygoers. They all appeared either inebriated on the chilled martinis and champagne cocktails that were being liberally distributed, or on a powdered substance, not so obvious, but no doubt as abundant as the alcohol. The balance of men to women was about equal. The age range was not: the men looked considerably older than their female counterparts.

The higher he climbed through the decks, the more clothes people were wearing. By the sky deck he was beginning to feel conspicuous, until he spotted the Jacuzzi. Balancing his drink he stepped into the bubbling water, which was occupied by two young women and an older man. They sat either side of him, laughing at whatever he said. One of the women, red-haired and striking, shot Patrick an interested glance. When he didn't reciprocate, she turned her attention back to her erstwhile companion. They were conversing in Russian.

Patrick assumed an expression that suggested he didn't understand a word, and did his best to listen in. The talk was mostly sexual flirtation – no mention was made of the movie, the missing starlet or the stolen pearl, suggesting that perhaps no one outside the immediate circle knew about Angele, or the supposed robbery.

Five minutes later, Chapayev, dressed in a smart, lightweight suit, his ample girth structured by its good cut, appeared on the sky deck and was immediately surrounded by a swarm of women. Ignoring them, he gestured to a tall, heavyset man, also suited, and they moved towards the railing. As though by prior arrangement, the other occupants of the sky deck melted away, out of earshot.

The Russian was imposing in the flesh. Big and ugly, he commanded your attention, just as the more famous movie stars drew your eyes when on screen. The man with him had the body and face of a heavyweight boxer, complete with broken nose.

There followed an animated and disgruntled conversation which Patrick could neither hear nor lip-read, which involved a number of glances towards Fort Royal on the nearby island of Sainte Marguerite. He contemplated exiting the Jacuzzi and trying to get a little closer, but knew that that would only draw attention to himself. The short exchange over, Chapayev and the man moved towards the stairs, his guests parting before him like the Red Sea before Moses.

Patrick climbed out of the Jacuzzi and followed.

The reconnaissance did not last long. Chapayev made for the helipad and boarded a black helicopter with the letters VC on the side in red. The helicopter took off, heading, Patrick decided, for the landing at the rear of the Palais des Festivals.

Patrick took his time making his way down through the yacht, memorizing the layout, becoming an inebriated French journalist if challenged. Most of the crew ignored him, although at one point the suited man from the sky deck took an unhealthy interest until Patrick feigned a bout of nausea, leaning over the railing, and making retching sounds to the consternation of those below.

Having seen all he was able to gain access to, he checked his watch, then made his way back to the stern and negotiated the metal stairs to the dive platform. Any swimmers who had been there on his arrival had given up by now. The sun was on its way down and the warmth of the day was dissipating. Patrick sat for a moment on the dive platform, then slipped into the water, hopefully unheeded.

Making his way round the stern, he emerged on the opposite side of the yacht. Before striking out across the bay, he took a last look for any signs of surveillance from the upper decks. Seeing that none of the figures clustered there seemed remotely interested in him, he set out for shore.

This time the current was with him and he made good progress until he reached the mouth of the bay, where things became more difficult, the westerly flow seeking to carry him right past the entrance. Patrick stopped at the earlier buoy and trod water to regain his strength for the final lap to shore.

He emerged on the beach to find it deserted, apart from a gang of teenagers mucking about up by the rocks. Patrick quickly dressed and headed for the promenade. Conscious of the time, he walked swiftly along the Vieux Port to find Oscar no longer on deck. He whistled, expecting the dog's distinctive head to pop up and be followed by a rumbling bark of welcome.

When the bulldog didn't appear, Patrick pulled down the walkway and went on board, calling Oscar's name. As he entered the cabin, he was immediately hit by a fragrant scent. A woman he presumed to be Marie Elise was seated on the leather couch, cradling Oscar, who regarded Patrick with a jaundiced and unwelcoming eye. At a whistle he managed finally to rouse himself and come over to greet his master, albeit reluctantly.

'Marie Elise?'

She stood up. Tall, with ebony skin, her hair was cropped short and sleek to her beautifully shaped head. He suddenly realized he had seen her before in Le Suquet, in the market perhaps or in one of the many restaurants. She stepped forward to greet him with the customary kiss on either cheek. Patrick, his face and body crusted with salt, felt at a distinct disadvantage.

'I'm sorry, I seem to be a little late,' Patrick said, knowing he wasn't.

She shook her head. 'No, I am a little early.' She glanced down to where Oscar was staring up at her with worshipful eyes. 'And I have been thoroughly entertained by your manservant while waiting.' She laughed.

Oscar's ears pricked up at the compliment and Patrick could swear the dog looked smug.

'He normally doesn't allow strangers to board,' he said, a little puzzled by the domestic tableau.

'But I am not a stranger,' she assured him.

Patrick looked at her quizzically.

'When you travel, you leave Oscar with a friend of mine,' she explained.

The local vet, Georges Baptiste, took on a whole new persona in Patrick's mind. Did vets really make enough money to afford Hibiscus rates?

'We went to school together,' Marie said, as though reading his mind.

There was an awkward moment before Patrick said, 'Can you help yourself to a drink while I shower?'

'Of course. Can I mix you something?'

Patrick had briefly forgotten that Brigitte's girls were the Mediterranean equivalent of geishas. Schooled in all the arts, including the perfect cocktail.

'I'd love a vodka martini, shaken not stirred.'

She raised a delicate black eyebrow in what he translated as amusement. 'Naturally,' she said.

Patrick glanced at the galley area.

'Don't worry, I'm sure I will find everything I need,' Marie assured him. 'If not, I'll shout.'

'The bathroom's in the stern,' Patrick said.

'I know.' She smiled.

Patrick turned the shower to power and soaped off the salt. It seemed Marie had turned up early, knowing Oscar would let her board *Les Trois Soeurs*, even if Patrick himself wasn't there. Had she done that on purpose? And if so, why?

Perhaps she'd turned up early in order to check out the sunken bath. Patrick smiled at the thought. The manner in which Madame Lacroix had mentioned it during their phone call had suggested it was regarded with some humour in her establishment.

It had been Patrick's habit on occasion to vacate Cannes during the film festival, renting the gunboat out to delegates via Le Chevalier, for a high price. He suspected at least one of Brigitte's girls had visited the boat during that time and probably discovered the pleasures of his bath.

Now dried and dressed, he headed back to the cabin. In his absence Marie had put on some music – the soulful jazz voice of Madeleine Peyroux. She had also mixed martinis and set out the *fruits de mer* platter he'd collected earlier and stored in the fridge.

They sat for a moment, nursing their cocktails, listening to the music, discussing the singer and her road to fame. Marie Elise reminded Patrick of the American actress Halle Berry, with her close-cropped hair, high cheekbones and stunning smile. Eventually Patrick suggested they eat and she nodded in agreement.

He produced the wine for her approval and she told him a funny story about a visit to the vineyard that had produced it. She was entertaining, beautiful, intelligent and, he reminded himself, she was with him because he was paying for her rather excellent company.

Patrick was surprised to find the thought made him a little sad.

They sat on opposite sides of the table, the large platter of shellfish between them, enough to feed at least three. Patrick motioned to Marie to begin and she delicately selected a langoustine. And so it began: food, good wine and conversation, none of which featured *The Black Pearl*.

Marie waited until the coffee and brandy stage before she raised the subject herself.

'I understand from Chevalier that you asked me here to discuss the launch party for *The Black Pearl*?' Marie swirled the brandy round the glass and took a sip. 'What do you want to know?'

When Patrick tried to soften this by suggesting her company had been just as important, she interrupted him.

'I don't believe you're a man who needs to pay for companionship,' she said delicately. 'I came here tonight because I want to help. I am not on duty.'

Patrick contemplated what that might mean, exactly.

She laughed. 'Don't look so surprised, Monsieur de Courvoisier. I do go on dates, you know.'

Patrick liked the sound of that. 'And this is a date?'

'Perhaps.'

She moved to sit on the couch, taking her brandy with her. Oscar immediately offered himself as a lap companion, but she told him sternly to stay on the floor. The dog acquiesced with an alacrity seldom experienced by Patrick. Marie Elise, he decided, was formidable as well as beautiful.

He joined her on the couch and listened while she told her story.

'I met with Angele Valette in the ladies' powder room. The surface by the sink was awash with cocaine.' She contemplated Patrick for a moment. 'However, I do not believe that Angele was high on drugs that night. Maybe high on her success. The movie was very well received. She was good. Arresting, yet somehow vulnerable. Like a young Marilyn Monroe.' She paused. 'We talked of make-up and men.'

'Any men in particular?'

'She mentioned Chapayev, the film's backer. I could almost feel her recoil.' Marie said this as though it was something she had experienced herself. 'She didn't want to make another film with him, no matter how successful this one was. She had other plans.'

'Did she say what they were?'

'No. She smiled like someone with a secret, applied her lipstick and left.'

'And you saw her again that night?'

Marie shook her head. 'No. I was at work.'

Patrick hesitated, not sure whether he could ask the question prominent in his mind. Marie seemed to anticipate this.

'My companion was an American, keen to get into movies. He had money but, I suspect, little talent. His main topic of conversation was vampire movies. He knew a great deal about them.'

They lapsed into silence. Marie finished her drink. 'If that is all . . .' She rose.

Patrick found himself suddenly saddened by the thought of her leaving. It was a feeling that didn't often occur with the women he brought aboard *Les Trois Soeurs*, and hadn't done so for some time. He found himself saying, 'You don't have to go. We could have another brandy, talk some more.'

Marie smiled. 'Do you know what I would really like?'

'What?'

'To stroll along the harbour and have a crêpe next to the bandstand.'

They took Oscar with them. Delighted, he walked alongside Marie. Had the dog possessed a tail, it would have been wagging wildly.

They ordered crêpes with Nutella and a can of iced tea each. The evening was balmy, the plane trees lime green with new leaves. Behind them the men of Le Suquet played pétanque by spotlight, the click of the balls travelling on the night air.

When she'd finished eating, Marie wiped her chocolate mouth. 'I should get home.'

'Would you like me to walk you?' Patrick offered.

'Then you would know where I live. Madame Lacroix would not be pleased.' Marie laughed.

As she rose to go, Patrick heard himself asking, 'May we meet again?'

Marie Elise observed him with warm brown eyes. 'For a crêpe, maybe.'

He would settle for that and hope for more. 'How do I get in touch?'

'Le Chevalier.' She threw him a farewell smile.

He watched the tall, slim figure pass the covered carousel and disappear behind the children's boating pool. Oscar emitted a low sound that resembled a smothered howl. He looked up at Patrick, his eyes accusing.

'We'll both see Marie Elise again,' Patrick promised.

On his way home, he went by Le P'tit Zinc. There was no one there he knew, the tables commandeered by festival delegates. Patrick headed for the Irish pub, hoping to catch Stephen.

The outside tables were packed with smokers, but Stephen wasn't one of them. He'd quit some years before, but occasionally succumbed after a couple of pints of Guinness. Patrick and Oscar headed inside.

Once his eyes grew accustomed to the gloom, he checked out the tables and those standing at the bar. A fiddler was blasting out an Irish jig over the loudspeakers, accompanied by a bodhran player who turned out to be a pretty young woman. The fiddler was male and of a similar age. They were in another world, and paid Patrick no heed as he pushed past their tiny stage to reach the dark corner that Stephen preferred. His friend was seated with a ginger-haired bearded chap with a face roasted red by the sun.

'Ah, Patrick,' Stephen said in his inimitable Irish brogue. 'There you are. Come and join us.'

He gave Oscar the required attention, consisting of telling him how handsome he was while ruffling his ears. Vanity satisfied, Oscar plonked himself down under the table, while Patrick slipped alongside Stephen in the booth. As if by magic a barman appeared and asked about drinks. Stephen ordered three pints of Guinness without consulting his companions.

'You didn't come here to drink French wine,' he told Patrick, firmly.

Stephen indicated his companion. 'This red-faced man is my cousin, Colm MacColl from Cork.'

Colm from Cork said not a word in response and Stephen continued, taking delight in his introductions.

'My friend Patrick de Courvoisier, on the other hand, is from nowhere. Or at least nowhere he wants us to know about. From his accent and knowledge of whisky, I suspect connections to Scotland. From the fact that he speaks several languages fluently, I suspect a polyglot upbringing, possibly a parent in the military or diplomatic service. He is also an expert in a number of physical skills, diving being one of them. The rest I prefer not to know about. Currently he lives on the old French gunboat in the harbour.'

Patrick nodded at Stephen's ruddy companion who didn't look fazed by either introduction. Stephen continued in his inimitable fashion.

'Colm on the other hand is not a man of action but a man of words. He is an author and a playwright, no less. Famous from Cork to Dublin and all places in between. He is also, like yourself, a rather fine diver.'

His cousin accepted this mixed bag of compliments with good grace.

The pints of Guinness having arrived, the two cousins toasted one another, then Patrick, in Gaelic.

'If you want to talk about this man,' Stephen told Colm conspiratorially, 'I suggest we use the Gaelic. As far as I'm aware he doesn't understand Irish.'

'Apart from a few curses I learned from you,' Patrick said.

Introductions complete, Stephen got straight to the point. 'So, what are you here for?'

'Is it that obvious?'

'I saw you earlier with an attractive lady. Either she ruined your evening by turning you down, or you had other things on your mind,' Stephen said, astute as always. When Patrick didn't answer immediately, Stephen made a swift comment in Irish to Colm who nodded and vacated the table, taking his pint with him.

'OK, let's have it.'

'I'd like to take a dive near the black yacht in the west bay,' Patrick said.

'Why? There's nothing down there but sea grass and sand.'

'A young woman disappeared from that yacht two nights ago.'

Stephen whistled through his teeth. 'And you think she went overboard?'

'I don't know what happened to her, yet.'

'Have the police been informed?'

'Her sister doesn't want the police involved.'

'We're talking about the Russian's yacht? The one who paid for the movie?'

Patrick marveled at how little bypassed Stephen.

'You know about the *Heavenly Princess*?' he said.

'I know it has a decompression chamber and that they ended up having to use it for one of their stuntmen in the *Black Pearl* shoot.' Stephen made a dismissive noise. 'Amateurs.' He studied Patrick. 'So who is this missing woman?'

'The star, Angele Valette.'

Stephen made a *wow* expression. 'And the press haven't got wind of it?'

Patrick shook his head. 'Not yet.'

Stephen contemplated him. 'That's not all, is it?'

'She was wearing the black pearl when she disappeared.'

'Holy Jesus.' Stephen whistled. 'I bet the owner isn't happy.' He paused, something dawning on him. 'The Russian's looking for her too?'

'I presume so.'

'Then we'd better find her first,' Stephen said with conviction.

Les Trois Soeurs lay in darkness. Oscar ran ahead, sniffing the air. The closer he got to the boat, the more agitated the dog became. There was something or someone aboard that the dog didn't like.

Patrick's first thought was that Marie Elise might have returned, but he dismissed that immediately. Oscar would be delighted if it was Marie. His hair wouldn't bristle, and he wouldn't be emitting a threatening growl.

Patrick cautiously lowered the walkway. Oscar made to run aboard, but he stopped him with a sharp command. The little bulldog was in attack mode, his teeth bared. Patrick trod the walkway as quietly as possible, Oscar following. He stopped and listened, hearing nothing more than the lap of water against the hull, then flicked a switch, flooding the boat with light. Nothing stirred, yet Oscar continued to growl in a menacing manner.

Patrick lifted the hatch and descended the steps to the cabin. Almost immediately the nauseating smell hit him. Fresh blood, just beginning to turn in the heat. The mess lay on the table where he and Marie had eaten from the shellfish platter. The platter was gone, now replaced by something furry and dead, where langoustines, pink and juicy, had previously sat.

Oscar went mad, launching himself at the table, filled with blood-lust. Patrick dragged the dog into the engine room and shut the door. He stood for a moment, observing the dead rabbit, analysing what its presence in his cabin might mean.

To say the word 'rabbit' on board a boat was the same as uttering the word 'Macbeth' in a theatre. Bad luck of the highest order. To find the real item lying, throat cut, entrails strung out, on his dining table said much more than that.

Patrick fetched a refuse bag from under the sink and scooped the rabbit's remains inside, knotting the top. He deposited it in the nearest bin ashore, then washed the table, leaving the cabin door open to get rid of the smell. Oscar's mad scrabbling at the engine-room door had lessened once the corpse had been disposed of. Patrick let him out and Oscar rushed to the table looking for his prey, meeting only the strong smell of disinfectant.

Patrick went through the rest of the boat. Nothing appeared to be missing and there were no further 'messages' left for him to find. He poured himself a whisky and sat down on the leather couch, the memory of his earlier and more pleasant encounter there with Marie eviscerated.

It was then he spotted the envelope on the floor behind the cabin door.

Of high quality, embossed, his name beautifully written on the front, he knew immediately what it was, and who it was from.

SIX

Who exactly was Patrick de Courvoisier? He knew who he had been, and what he had left behind. Status. Recognition. A place in the hierarchy. Those in positions of power had deemed his withdrawal as inexplicable, irritating and quite unbelievable. After all, did he not know that London was the centre of the universe?

Those had been the parting words of his then superior. Even the term 'superior' had irritated.

Patrick's answer had been, 'I don't care.'

He still remembered Forsyth's expression. How do you marry arrogance and disbelief? Not easily. Forsyth lived in a bubble of the state's making. A bubble so certain of its omnipotence, necessity, endurance, certitude and righteousness that anyone questioning its existence had to be mad.

So in Forsyth's eyes, Patrick de Courvoisier was mad. And probably bad.

Patrick decided he liked that version of himself. It played truer than any of the previous ones.

There had been good reasons for his departure. The powers that be knew them, as did he. They just weren't up for discussion. His previous employers had taken his already impressive skills and honed them. Patrick was grateful for that, although he no longer wished to use those skills in the way they wanted him to.

Duty was something he now abhorred, because it had so often trampled on what he deemed to have value: ordinary people going about their ordinary lives.

Patrick lifted his whisky and went to sit on the upper deck, a now subdued Oscar at his heels. Oscar was loyal, but he wasn't subjugated, and he was unwilling to do what he didn't approve of. Patrick liked that about the little bulldog. It was something he was striving to achieve himself, but old habits die hard, especially if the powers that be had a hold over you.

Sitting under the awning, he read again the latest missive that had been delivered to the boat in his absence. A summons. Couched as an invitation, but a summons nonetheless. Patrick regarded the gold-rimmed card. They were calling him back. A siren call, which he'd already decided to ignore.

His life was here now. His patch was Le Suquet. The jobs he took on were the ones he chose. He said where. He said when. He said how much. It was a line from a Hollywood movie about a beck-and-call girl, but it echoed his own thoughts entirely.

Patrick tore the gold-rimmed invitation in two and turned his attention back to the job he'd chosen to take on: find the missing starlet.

His thoughts strayed to Camille Ager, and from there to Marie.

Contemplating the two women, another female face rose in his mind. For a moment he permitted himself to view it, then swept it from his memory. That's what gold-rimmed invitations brought with them. Memories that were best forgotten.

He swallowed his whisky and stood up, intent on heading for bed. He was physically tired from the swim out to the black yacht, but he wondered whether his brain was yet ready to shut down.

Below decks, order was restored. The scent of both blood and disinfectant had dissipated. If bad luck had been laid on him, he did not feel its presence – in the cabin or in his thoughts. Intrigued maybe, but certainly not cursed. Already the game begun by the arrival of Camille Ager had taken form on the chessboard. If anything, the dead rabbit was a diversion; a subplot designed to deflect him from what he should be considering.

If the Russian was aware than Patrick had entered the frame, would he try to warn him off in such a manner? Psychology was not, he thought, a tactic much used by the Russian. It involved time, and it might not have the desired outcome. Beating someone to pulp was much more likely to succeed.

So if it wasn't the Russian who'd delivered the gutted rabbit, then who was it?

He rinsed his whisky glass and set it to drain. Lying by the sink, he discovered a small silver ring and realized immediately that it must belong to Marie. She'd insisted on rinsing the plates after their meal. The sight of a beautiful woman washing dishes at that sink had amused him. Mainly because it had never happened before.

So Marie had taken off the ring before rinsing the plates. Had she simply forgotten it or had she left it there on purpose, offering a reason for him to contact her? He examined it in the light.

Comprising a delicate threading of silver strands, it also had a hallmark that identified its worth, but no engraving. Patrick sat it up on a shelf for safety. He would explain to Chevalier that Marie had left it, and ask for her number. It was worth a try.

The presence of the ring had transformed his earlier dark thoughts, just as her visit had done. Patrick allowed himself a few moments of anticipation, then headed for bed. His contemplation of who might have massacred the rabbit, he left for tomorrow.

He had hoped that the ring might provide him with sweet dreams, but instead his sleep was punctured by lurid images of entrails. Rabbit-sized ones and then the larger human kind. He saw a body lying on snow, turning the white to red. The face wore a grin, or was it a grimace? Drawing closer, Patrick recognized his own face in death.

He woke, gasping for breath as he always did when the nightmare revisited him. Annoyed with himself he rose, bathed in sweat, and went back out on deck.

This was the time he liked best. Too late for the night-time revellers, too early even for the fishermen or the marketeers. Le Suquet slumbered amid its maze of secret alleys and passages, intricately layered buildings with red-topped roofs that clung to the hill, climbing ever upward until they reached the castle.

Patrick had no love for the modern Cannes that stretched eastwards along the bay, nor for the elegance of the Croisette's manicured palm trees and flower displays. He preferred the Saracen town where life had begun. He loved the old town's resilience and the prickly nature of its inhabitants. Which is why he'd ended up on a French gunboat in Le Vieux Port. Oscar, hearing him come back on deck, had deigned to join him, despite the late hour.

The sound of an argument punctured the late-night serenity, causing Oscar to give a warning growl. Patrick identified a man and a woman on a nearby balcony, overlooking Place Massuque, their French as rapid and incisive as gunfire. Eventually they ceased and went inside and silence descended again. Patrick directed his gaze out to sea. From here he could just make out a row of lights he identified as belonging to the *Heavenly Princess*.

He had been right to think, when he spotted Camille Ager on the *quai*, that she was bringing trouble his way. He relished that feeling again, his skin prickling, the scent of rabbit's blood in his nostrils.

*   *   *

The sun rose just after six. Patrick stirred from his shallow sleep and went to fetch his dive suit from the engine room. He had his own air tanks, but in this instance he would make use of Stephen's supply. It was a short walk along a deserted *quai*. The occupants of the neighbouring motor yachts were fast asleep; the local fishing boats, *les pointus*, already departed.

Stephen was on deck. 'I have to be back for a class at nine thirty,' he reminded Patrick.

'No problem.'

The heavy, flat-bottomed boat chugged out of the harbour, wetsuits swaying on the overhead rail. Colm appeared from below with a flask of coffee, its strong aroma sharpening Patrick's senses as he poured out two cups. The Irishman's face looked less fiery in the dawn light, but he was as reticent as ever. Last night Patrick had assumed Colm had been unable to get a word in edgeways. Now it looked as though he was naturally taciturn, or only half awake. Or maybe he preferred to commit all his fine words to paper.

The sea appeared flat calm until they crossed the line of buoys where it began to exhibit a long, slow swell. The *Diving Belle*, by the nature of her hull, was an uncomfortable boat if you suffered from seasickness. Patrick had watched some of Stephen's tourist divers go green as they exited the harbour. Once in the calmer waters between Sainte Marguerite and Saint Honorat they usually rallied and, embarrassed by their display of weakness, tried to make up for it by taking chances underwater, much to Stephen's irritation.

They were fast approaching the *Heavenly Princess*. The decks were empty, the partygoers sleeping off their excesses of the night before. Through binoculars, Patrick could make out a few crew members moving about, no doubt clearing up the mess. No one seemed interested in the battered dive boat making its way sedately past.

Patrick joined Stephen at the wheel.

'How far do you want to go?' Stephen asked.

'She was anchored closer to the island for the launch party. A scene from the film was shot at the fort. They wanted that as a backdrop.' Patrick recalled Chapayev's studied gaze in that direction, when he'd been aboard the black yacht the day before. Both the Russian and his henchman had been concerned about something, but what?

Stephen dropped anchor as close to the rock face at Fort Royal as the depth allowed, then all three men got kitted up. Patrick had no idea what they were looking for, but if the *Heavenly Princess* had anchored here the night Angele had disappeared, then the area was worth checking out.

In his past life, Patrick had rarely dived for pleasure. Like a champion swimmer who entered the water only to train or perform, diving for Patrick had been part of the job. He occasionally came out with Stephen, but more often absented himself from Cannes to travel to more challenging diving locations around the world, to hone his skills, in case he might have to rely on them again in the future.

Today wouldn't prove to be a difficult dive; merely a reconnaissance mission in fairly shallow water. Nothing to get excited about.

Despite telling himself this, his entry into the water still brought a rush of adrenaline. Much like he experienced at the gaming tables of the casino, or when he'd spied Camille Ager walking towards him along the *quai*.

As he looked round the calm, quiet and weightless universe, a *castagnola* emerged from the rocks below. A vivid blue, the tiny fish approached Patrick's mask inquisitively, seeing its reflection there. Soon it was joined by others, darting around him.

Patrick noted the location of the anchor rope to orientate himself, before kicking off through the shimmering blue cloud. Below him, white sand drifted between great swathes of sea grass, punctured by the occasional stony limestone outcrop.

Had Angele chosen to leave the ship here, she could have gone ashore in a dinghy. Or perhaps swum as far as the tiny harbour west of Fort Royal, used predominantly by the ferries that ploughed daily between the old port and island of Sainte Marguerite. At night the ferries were docked at the Vieux Port, just west of the gunboat, and the only craft left here were small family boats tied up to the left of the pier, or anchored offshore in shallow water. Perhaps one of them had picked up Angele, and taken her somewhere along the coast? Alternatively, she could have come ashore at La Guerite, a small and exclusive restaurant to the east of the fort, reached only by motor taxi in the evening.

According to Stephen, Chapayev had a diver – or divers – in his entourage. If the Russian had suspected that his leading lady had fallen overboard, surely he would have sent a diver to search for her? If so, Patrick doubted whether such a search would have escaped the eagle eyes of the local fishermen. Yet there had been no talk of it, leading him to conclude that Chapayev believed his star hadn't departed the yacht by accident.

The water was glassily clear as he approached Fort Royal. This time Patrick shared the underwater kingdom with a shoal of larger, yellow-striped girelle. Occasionally, he saw flotsam from an anchorage, but when he checked it was nothing of significance. He criss-crossed the area, looking for a larger object secured to the bottom, or caught among the limestone outcrops on the sea bed.

Eventually he headed for the surface, noting the distant bubbles that indicated where Colm and Stephen currently were. Between the two of them, they had covered a fair area of seabed and, Patrick suspected, had likewise found nothing of significance.

Patrick was the last to pull himself aboard. Stephen and Colm had already taken off their gear and were sitting down to a breakfast of coffee, French bread and cheese. They indicated by their demeanour that they'd found nothing.

'So the fat little Russian didn't throw her overboard. Not here, at least,' Stephen said. 'If it were me, I would have kept her until I was well out to sea. Weighted down, the chances are she would never be found. That size of yacht will have a big freezer compartment, and an adequate hold. Lots of places to keep a body.'

Which is what Patrick had been thinking. 'I need to take a proper look round the *Princess*,' he said.

Stephen nodded his agreement.

'There's a dinner for some bigwigs tonight. François is supplying fresh fish for it,' he informed Patrick. 'If you like we can deliver it for him.'

Patrick approached the gunboat with some trepidation, which evaporated when Oscar rushed from the top deck to greet him. The dog's manner suggested there had been no visitors, welcome or otherwise, in his absence. Once aboard, a quick look round proved this to be the case.

Patrick rinsed out his dive suit and hung it out to dry, then took a long hot shower.

Dressed, he sat under the awning to contemplate his next move.

His dive trip had eased his concerns that Angele may have gone overboard, either accidentally or by design. He couldn't be sure, of course, but from Stephen's knowledge of the area and its currents, the Irishman seemed convinced that there was no body under the water, or likely to come ashore soon.

So, in Patrick's reckoning, Angele had left the yacht by some other means. Her sister seemed to think so too. Camille hadn't mentioned the possibility that Angele might have drowned. Her immediate reading of the situation was that Angele had left of her own free will and taken the pearl with her. Patrick had to assume Camille knew her sister well enough to make that judgement. Her main fear seemed to be that Chapayev would find her sister before she did.

Which brought him back to last night's warning.

Patrick went over the names of those who were aware that he was looking for Angele.

Camille Ager came top of the list. Since she'd employed him, he couldn't see why she would try to put him off the scent via a dead rabbit. Chevalier he also dismissed. He would trust Chevalier with his life. In fact, he had done so on more than one occasion.

Marie Elise? There was, as far as he was aware, no connection between Marie Elise and Chapayev. She'd revealed that she'd spoken to Angele that night and had sympathized with her opinion of her Russian benefactor. During their evening together, he'd had no sense that Marie was trying to get information from him, rather than the other way round.

Brigitte Lacroix? She'd supplied an escort for the party that night, but not directly to Chapayev.

He moved on to the production team from *The Black Pearl*. He hadn't revealed his true identity to either Polinsky or Gramesci, which didn't mean they wouldn't make a point of checking it. The card he had given them was bona fide, as was the company name, although if they dug too deep they would discover the company didn't do much business. If, on the other hand, they made local enquiries in Cannes, the likelihood was their visitor would emerge as Le Limier.

It seemed clear after his visit to the Hôtel Majestic Barriere that her director and producer were aware she was missing, probably with the pearl. He was also certain that neither Gramesci nor the producer had any idea where their leading lady was. Gramesci had appeared a lot more worried about Angele's disappearance than the American had. Though whether the Italian's concern was for Angele, or his own position with the Russian, Patrick didn't know.

However, neither Polinsky nor Gramesci struck him as the sort
to gut a rabbit, even if they had worked out who Patrick was, where
he lived, and wanted to stop him investigating further.

Which reduced it to two possibilities.

A local enemy, carrying out a grudge for some previous job he'd
undertaken, which meant it had nothing to do with Angele Valette.

Or back full circle to Vasily Chapayev, who'd issued a warning
to Patrick to stay out of his business.

Thinking about Polinsky reminded Patrick of the DVD the producer
had thrust into his hand as a parting gift. He went below deck to
check it out. The sleeve was blank, as was the DVD itself, with no
title or description of what it contained.

Patrick slipped it into his laptop and launched it.

It opened with an underwater scene. Patrick recognized the location almost immediately. There were two 'drowned' miniature
villages off the Côte d'Azur. The first was near Agay, west of Cannes,
and the second to the east, just south of the rock at Fourmigue, in
the bay of Golfe Juan. Both were semi-derelict due to diving souvenir
hunters.

Patrick studied the screen intently, trying to decide which of
the villages he was looking at. Then he spotted the grotto. Known
as the Grotte de Miro, it had originally contained a sculpture of
the Goddess of the Sea by the artist Miro, which had now been
replaced by a bust of Commandant le Prieur, inventor of what
French historians said was the first self-contained underwater
breathing apparatus.

Shoals of tiny fish darted among the concrete houses and swam
down the main street of shops, fashioned on Cannes establishments,
one of them Chevalier's estate agency. Patrick watched, intrigued.
When Polinsky had handed him the DVD, he'd assumed it to be
shots of Angele and, by Polinsky's expression, probably bordering
on the pornographic. Here he was, a minute in, and Angele had not
yet appeared.

And then she did.

The initial shot of the grotto had been fleeting. Knowing it well
he hadn't really registered anything different about it. On close-up
he now realized that, rather than Commandant le Prieur, the grotto
contained the Goddess of the Sea again, or rather Angele portraying
her. Even as he watched, her eyes opened and she looked straight

at him. Her blonde hair rippled in the water, but no bubbles escaped her lips.

The camera drew back and he saw that she was naked except for the black pearl that hung about her neck. She smiled as though at him, then thrust herself upwards, the camera following, showing tantalizing glimpses of her body as she moved towards the surface.

Then the screen went black.

Patrick tried moving forward but there was nothing else on the DVD except that sequence of shots. He sat back, perplexed. Was this an excerpt from the movie? He realized he had no idea what *The Black Pearl* was about, although Stephen had mentioned the use of divers, one of whom had got the bends.

He used his mobile to check out what was currently showing in the various cinema venues. Foreign films, with French subtitles, tended to show at Les Arcades. *The Black Pearl* was scheduled there that afternoon at three, which meant he could watch it before accompanying Stephen to the black yacht.

He called the number Camille had given him. It went immediately to voicemail. He listened to her husky tones requesting the caller to leave a message, but didn't. Camille Ager was an enigma to him. She had told him nothing of herself – not what she did for a living nor how she could afford the large sum of money she'd paid him on account. Patrick decided it was time he found out a little more about her.

He discovered Le Chevalier at his usual table at Le P'tit Zinc, reading the current edition of *Nice-Matin*. There were two glasses and a half carafe of red on the table. When Patrick glanced round for his companion, Le Chevalier shook his head. 'I'm a little early.' He didn't elaborate on who he was waiting for, merely waved Patrick to a seat.

Two chefs in immaculate whites emerged from the back door of a nearby restaurant on to the Rue de la Misericorde. They sat down, each on his own bollard, and lit a cigarette. It would be their last chance to relax before lunch, the most important meal in the French day. Chevalier too would be heading to one of his favourite restaurants soon, with whomever he was waiting for.

Patrick decided to pose his question, before Chevalier's lunch companion arrived.

'I wanted to ask you about Camille Ager. Do you know what she does for a living?' Patrick said.

Chevalier nodded.

'May I ask what?'

'She didn't tell you?' Le Chevalier inclined his head. 'Then maybe she thought it better you didn't know.'

'She paid me rather a lot of money.'

'Well, you don't come cheap,' Chevalier reminded him.

Veronique arrived to take his order and Patrick asked for a pastis, then tried again with Chevalier.

'Why don't you ask her yourself?'

Chevalier glanced pointedly over his shoulder and Patrick turned to find Camille standing directly behind him.

'Ah, Camille. Join us. I have already ordered the wine,' Chevalier said.

Today she wore a floral-print dress. She looked fresh and very pretty as she slipped in alongside Chevalier.

'We were discussing how expensive Monsieur de Courvoisier's rates are and whether you can afford them.' Le Chevalier was nothing if not forthright.

Camille helped herself to some wine and took an appreciative sip before responding. 'And have you earned your money, monsieur?'

'Well, I haven't found your sister, yet.' How could he tell her that he had searched for Angele's body off the island of Sainte Marguerite? 'But I am making progress.' Which was in essence a lie.

She sat back in her seat and composed herself.

'I am delighted to say I have heard from Angele,' she said. 'A few moments ago. She sent me a text.'

Now that did surprise him. 'May I ask what she said?'

'That she is in Paris auditioning for a stage part and will be back shortly.'

It was the story Polinsky had spun him. The one Patrick didn't believe.

The chefs disappeared in the back door of the kitchen as the lunchtime customers began filling the tables. The three of them sat in silence, Patrick unsure how to react to Camille's pronouncement. She sipped her wine, her mind elsewhere, her eyes revealing her discomfort.

'You're certain the text came from Angele?' Patrick said.

'It was from her phone,' she answered sharply, as though she didn't want him to throw doubt on this.

'So what would you like me to do?' he said.

She shrugged. 'I have found my sister. There is no longer need for concern.'

Patrick wanted to ask about the pearl, but didn't think it appropriate at this time.

'I'm happy to return the advance,' he offered.

'That won't be necessary.' She rose. 'I have to go, I'm afraid.'

Chevalier looked perplexed. 'You won't have lunch?'

Camille apologized. 'We are so busy with the festival. Movie stars always want to buy diamonds. A girl's best friend,' she added.

It seemed to Patrick she was merely keen to get away.

'So.' Le Chevalier sighed at the image of Camille disappearing into the passing crowd. 'We men must eat alone.'

When they entered Le Pistou, the average age decreased by at least fifteen years. Among the present company, Chevalier looked young, Patrick a mere slip of a boy. Le Pistou served excellent French cuisine and the discerning and more mature population of Cannes knew it. The restaurant on Félix Faure, so handy for the Palais, was not a natural choice of those attending the film festival. One glance inside would dissuade even those attracted by the menu. No obvious movie stars, directors or their eager followers sat at the pristine tables. Only those who understood and appreciated good French food.

Chevalier immediately headed for a table with a reserved sign on it. As they took their seats, Henri arrived with the pre-ordered aperitifs. Two glasses of Kir Royal.

'You are, for the purpose of this meal, Camille Ager,' Chevalier informed him.

Patrick was fine with that. He wanted to know more about Madamoiselle Ager, despite the fact she'd just sacked him. What she chose to eat would be a start.

The wine arrived shortly after. A half bottle of something Chevalier and the waiter discussed in reverential tones. This was soon followed by a *carafe d'eau* and the first course.

Patrick was aware that trying to discuss the recent events – in fact, anything about Camille – with Chevalier would have to wait until coffee. Chevalier took his food seriously. Patrick would be permitted to introduce a topic of conversation between courses, if time allowed. Otherwise he would have to wait.

There was little chance until coffee was served. One course followed the other, was savoured and pronounced delicious. Chevalier dabbed his moustache between times, his comments to Henri when his plate was removed were carefully considered, even if a little critical at times. By Henri's reaction, anything Chevalier said about food was obviously worth listening to.

When the coffee arrived, Chevalier sat back in his chair contentedly, then spoke.

'You must not stop looking for this girl, whatever Camille says.'

Patrick stirred his espresso for no other reason than to watch it circulate the tiny cup. He had felt the same himself. Something was wrong. It had been wrong on the black yacht. Wrong when a disemboweled rabbit had been deposited on his dining table. Wrong when Camille said she'd heard from her sister.

'Camille owns Bijou Magique.' Chevalier referred to a jeweller's shop on Rue d'Antibes. *And therefore can afford you*, he left unsaid. Chevalier observed Patrick with an open look. 'Why did you not believe her when she said her sister had been in touch?'

'Anyone can send a text. And the producer of *The Black Pearl* spun me the same story and he made it up on the spot.'

A shadow crossed Chevalier's face. 'What about Lieutenant Moreaux?'

'He won't appear unless we find a body.'

Chevalier considered that. 'You truly believe there's a chance Angele may be dead?'

Patrick had a sudden image of Angele underwater, no bubbles rising from her mouth. 'I hope not.' He glanced at his watch. 'I must leave. I have a movie to watch.'

When he offered to contribute his share of the bill, Chevalier waved it away. 'Mademoiselle Ager paid in advance. I will leave an appropriate tip.'

Les Arcades was a few minutes' walk east from the restaurant. Unlike UK cinemas, Les Arcades did not exist for the purpose of selling its clientele large quantities of Coca-Cola, hot dogs and popcorn. They also didn't run adverts prior to the film. The showing time was exactly that. Hence, Patrick was summarily ejected for being ten minutes early. He took himself into a nearby café and had another shot of caffeine, using the time to check his messages and to put a call through to Lieutenant Martin Moreaux of the Police Nationale.

There was a moment in which Patrick imagined the policeman studying his name on the screen and deciding whether he wished to speak to his nemesis or not. Moreaux and he had been involved in a number of cases together, not through desire, but necessity. Moreaux had found himself in the position of needing Patrick's help on occasion, which the detective had disliked intensely. The feeling was mutual.

'Monsieur de Courvoisier.' The voice was clipped, the manner uninviting. 'How can I help you?'

Five minutes later, Patrick had established that Moreaux knew nothing of a missing starlet and did not wish to know. As far as he was concerned the rich came and went during the film festival. What problems they generated while in Cannes they could take with them when they left.

Patrick rang off, confident that no body had been discovered in the harbour, or washed ashore along the Côte d'Azur. However, he had alerted Moreaux. Patrick had been discreet, talking about drunken starlets disappearing for a few hours, but Moreaux was no fool.

It wasn't what Patrick had said, but what he'd omitted to say. He'd kept Chapayev's name out of the discussion, talking about a minor actress in a minor film whose sister was looking for her. He had not fooled Moreaux. The short, suave, iron-haired lieutenant would already be checking with his sources. Cannes and Le Suquet were his patch and nothing much passed him by.

Before he rang off, Moreaux asked after Oscar.

'He's well, thank you,' Patrick said.

Oscar was the only thing Moreaux approved of with regard to Patrick, mainly because he was involved in the dog's origins. His wife Michelle bred French bulldogs and Oscar had come from one of the litters.

Martin Moreaux and his wife had been wed for thirty years, although for many of those years, according to Chevalier, the couple had indulged in other relationships. Michelle was currently playing the role of cougar to a twenty-four-year-old chef on a cruising yacht, while Moreaux had been seen with Madame Lacroix in the courtesy bar of Le Cavendish, a classy boutique hotel adjacent to the police station.

The fact that a serving police lieutenant was a 'friend' of a Madame, however upmarket her business, didn't seem to worry Chevalier, or anyone else for that matter.

Patrick paid for his coffee and entered the cinema. This time he was given a ticket and offered a pair of 3D spectacles. Apparently the underwater scenes were better if he donned them. Looking at Angele Valette in 3D didn't seem a big cross to bear. The blurb in the foyer read like the producer's T-shirt. *The Black Pearl – A Movie to Die For*. Patrick hoped that wasn't true in reality.

The cinema was three-quarters full, which wasn't bad for an indie movie showing at Cannes. Les Arcades didn't show trailers, neither during or outwith the festival. Patrick settled himself two rows from the back as the lights dimmed.

The movie opened with a stunning shot of a small fishing craft chugging through the blue waters of the Mediterranean. In the background was a deserted beach, with a backdrop of the blood-red Estérel Mountains. As the camera moved in, Patrick recognized Conor Musso as the young fisherman. As he retrieved his lobster pot, he caught sight of something on the shore. He took the boat closer, realized what it was and jumped into the water, swimming powerfully towards what was undoubtedly the figure of Angele, half-drowned and naked, apart from the black pearl hanging around her neck.

Regaining consciousness, Angele could not remember who she was, or how she had come to be there. Cared for by the fisherman, who became her lover, she was haunted by dreams of what may have happened in the past. One such dream featured the underwater scene Patrick had viewed on the DVD. Then a large black yacht appeared offshore and two men came in search of her. Terrified, she begged Conor to hide her. The two escaped into the mountains, but those who wanted both Angele and the pearl back had no intention of giving either of them up.

One hour and fifty minutes later, Patrick emerged with the feeling that what he'd said to Polinsky had been entirely true, despite having made it up. Angele had turned *The Black Pearl* into a highly saleable international commodity. The movie might also make Angele into a star.

He checked his watch before heading for Rue d'Antibes and Camille's place of work. Having now seen the film, Patrick was convinced that Angele, desperate to be a movie star, would not have disappeared by choice. By rights she should be giving countless interviews to promote the film and herself. *The Black Pearl* was her big chance and Patrick just didn't buy the idea that Angele would willingly pass it up. Not even for a possible mythical theatre job in Paris.

Five minutes later he stood outside Bijou Magique, which proved to be small, discreet and very classy. The current colour scheme of the window displays was lavender with a backdrop of Provençal artwork. One window housed the diamond collection, unobtrusive and expensive. The second window held a more avant-garde collection of pink-clouded stones in a variety of settings – intricate gold and copper bracelets, and a pair of unusual rings that immediately caught his eye. One was gold, the other silver, each setting resembling an ancient coin. The silver displayed a sky with a half moon and a single star; the gold a bright sun. Evidently designed for a match made in heaven.

As Patrick appeared, a young woman emerged from the back as though on cue. Patrick enquired if Mademoiselle Ager was available. The young woman gave him a steely eyed stare and asked who he was. Patrick offered his correct name and wondered by the flicker of recognition if she had been warned he might turn up.

'Mademoiselle Ager has gone to Paris to see her sister.'

'When do you expect her back?'

The young woman shrugged. 'She did not say, monsieur.'

Patrick thanked her with a warm smile which wasn't returned, then exited, immediately heading round the corner to the Rue Buttura to glance in through the window. The young woman was engaged in a rapid mobile phone conversation, the words of which he couldn't decipher, but he was pretty sure it was about his visit.

He left her to it and headed back towards Le Suquet. He had been discharged by Camille Ager and therefore had no reason to pursue the matter any further, yet he, like Chevalier, was concerned enough not to let it go.

He took out the photograph of Angele given him by Camille. Both women were beautiful, but they did not resemble one another in the slightest. That wasn't unusual when people shared only one parent. There could of course be an entirely different explanation. One that he hadn't considered until that moment. What if Angele Valette did not in fact have a half-sister?

If that was the case, what was Camille Ager's role in all of this?

SEVEN

A second and more worrying thought occurred to Patrick as he walked back to the boat. What if Camille was working for Chapayev? What better way to find out the whereabouts of the missing starlet – and more importantly the pearl – than for Chapayev to send Camille to Le Limier and have her profess fear for her sister?

If Chapayev had managed to locate Angele himself, then he, Patrick, was no longer required. Hence the true reason why Camille had dismissed him.

Patrick didn't like any of the possibilities that were presenting themselves, but the last thing he believed was that Angele was auditioning in Paris.

Reaching the *quai*, he ducked under the barrier at the fishermen's zone, where a line of six small boats, each uniquely numbered but unnamed, were tied up. Stephen and a fisherman Patrick recognized as François Girard sat enjoying a pastis under an awning. Beside them a crate held the catch of the day, which was headed for the black yacht's kitchens and tonight's dinner party. It seemed sea bass and langoustines were on the menu.

Stephen invited Patrick to join him and, finding another glass, poured him a pastis, while François loaded the crates.

'I want to come with you,' Stephen said in a low voice.

'I prefer to go alone.'

'Come on, Patrick. I promise I'll stay in the kitchen while you take your look round.'

Patrick finally succumbed to the Irishman's pleading look and nodded. Stephen was generally good in a crisis and had a fierce left hook, but Patrick suspected that the Russian contingent might offer an altogether different level of violence.

'You'll stay in the kitchen,' he ordered.

'Scout's honour,' Stephen said solemnly.

'You were never in the Scouts.'

François, or Posidonie as he was known locally, his beard resembling the tendrils of sea grass prevalent in the bay, said nothing as he directed the small blue fishing craft out of the harbour. Meanwhile Stephen supplied a few more details.

'His daughter is helping the onboard cook. The second in command in the kitchen was sacked the night of the launch party,' he told Patrick.

'Do we know why?'

'He didn't turn up for work.'

Leaving the bustling harbour behind, they chugged out into open water. Behind them, dusk was bathing Cannes in a warm rosy glow. Ahead, the upper decks of the *Heavenly Princess* were a blaze of coloured lights, although the sound of voices was at a much lower level than on Patrick's previous visit.

'François says the dinner party is only for twelve. None of them film people.'

That was interesting. 'Who then?' Patrick asked.

Stephen made a superior face. 'Important people from Cannes.'

That could mean many things. Local dignitaries. Prominent businessmen. The rich who had their exclusive villas in Super Cannes or Californie.

Tied up now to the yacht, all three men climbed the metal stairs, Patrick keeping his head down, in case one of the crew should recognize him from his former excursion. Carrying the crates, they made their way to the galley, where they found François's daughter, Monique, who didn't resemble her father in the slightest. Her petite and curvaceous body encased in a fitted white jacket, her jet-black hair rolled into a knot, her lips painted bright red, she observed Patrick with interest.

Stephen, catching that look, introduced them.

'Monique, Patrick de Courvoisier. The reason for our visit.'

Monique's dark eyes glittered. 'I'm intrigued, monsieur, but I should warn you my employer is not a man to cross.'

'I'll make sure we don't meet,' Patrick assured her.

She made a dismissive sound, then said, 'The crew are having their meal at the moment. You have thirty minutes to take a look around before dinner is served in the stateroom.'

Patrick nodded his thanks, then indicated Stephen. 'He stays here.'

Monique smiled. 'I can always use an extra pair of hands.'

She handed Stephen an apron and pointed at a large pile of dishes and pots next to the sink. The Irishman's expression was a picture. This wasn't how he'd seen his night's work.

For Patrick she had a waiter's uniform. 'Don't serve anyone,' she ordered.

Patrick had no time to thank her, as the chef was heard approaching the galley already shouting orders in bad French. François's daughter made a dismissive sound.

'And he thinks he can cook. *Salope!*'

Patrick swiftly removed himself and looked for a quiet place to don his jacket, eventually locating a laundry cupboard. A boat of this size needed a large crew, but it was common practice to hire locals to help out during the film festival, especially when entertaining on a lavish scale. If he kept a low profile, it shouldn't be a problem to take a proper look around.

The layout mirrored most super yachts. On the lower deck the swimming pool lay at the stern, followed by five en-suite guest cabins, then the engine room amidships and the crew quarters. The first of the empty luxury cabins was being used by a large male, judging by the clothes. The next three Patrick found made up with sheets and towels, but were seemingly unoccupied. The final one he was sure had been Angele's. The cupboards were full of clothes that looked to be her size. On the dressing table was a selection of make-up, perfumes and a jewellery box. Seeing her belongings made Angele seem suddenly more real than any discussion he'd had about her. It also increased his concern about her whereabouts.

On the bedside table was a photograph of Angele on the red carpet, a copy of the one Camille had given him. The fact that her belongings hadn't been disposed of suggested Chapayev expected her to return. Either that or he was keeping up a pretence of it.

On the main deck were a salon, a stateroom, a dining room and the galley, together with what he assumed were Chapayev's quarters, which were firmly locked. Patrick could hear the buzz of conversation coming from the second stateroom below the sky deck. When he reached there he found waiters putting the finishing touches to the dinner table, while the guests chatted in the open air.

The table was polished mahogany, the glasses cut crystal, sparking in the light of three candelabras. Four bottles of red wine, a rare Chateau Pétrus, stood uncorked and taking the air. The aroma from the galley promised the equivalent level of French cuisine, despite François's daughter's concerns.

Chapayev was sparing no expense on his guests, whoever they were.

Defying Monique's instructions not to serve, Patrick acquired a tray of Kir Royal and carried it outside for a closer look at the assembled party. The atmosphere on deck was muted, the guests behaving much more sedately than those he'd encountered at the launch party. He suspected the important business of money, power and prestige was being discussed here.

The party stood around in small groups, with only three of the guests being women, who looked more like same-age partners than younger arm candy. There was a handsome black couple. The man was tall and dressed in a European suit, his wife more traditionally in a colourful robe and headdress that looked West African in origin. Passing them by, Patrick heard them speak French but with a definite accent.

The rest of the guests looked French. The women were chic, the men well groomed. As he hovered in the background, Patrick picked up a mix of French and English conversations, but recognized no one. If, as Stephen said, these were important people from Cannes, then they didn't mix in the same company as himself.

Chapayev stood alone talking to a short, grey-haired man whose back was turned towards Patrick. As Patrick approached, the man turned. Almost immediately Patrick swiveled on his heel, to no avail.

'*Garçon!*'

Too late now to heed Monique's warning, he turned to face Lieutenant Martin Moreaux. Moreaux selected a glass and thanked him, the only sign of recognition being a delicately raised eyebrow. Patrick nodded, his face blank.

When Chapayev barked at him in Russian, asking for his name, Patrick feigned puzzlement and explained in French that he didn't understand. He declared himself a Cannois, hired for the evening.

His explanation brought a hidden smile to Moreaux's lips, but the detective didn't out him.

Patrick retreated and quickly dispensed with the tray. Whoever he'd expected to find on the *Heavenly Princess*, it had not been Lieutenant Martin Moreaux. He removed the waiter's jacket and headed for the galley, where Stephen eyed his arrival with undisguised relief.

Patrick nodded his thanks to Monique, who indicated she wanted to speak to him. She ushered them both into the corridor outside the galley.

In a low voice she told him, 'The word is that the woman you're looking for left the boat with the second chef, Leon Aubert.' She raised an eyebrow. 'Of course that could be kitchen gossip. They also say she took the black pearl with her when she went.'

'Is that why Moreaux is here?' Patrick said.

'Lieutenant Moreaux?' Stephen looked aghast.

By her expression, Monique hadn't been aware of the detective's visit. 'I don't know if he's here because of the pearl, but I do know that our police lieutenant likes to move among the monied and you don't get any more monied than Chapayev. I hear the fat Russian's buying a villa in Cannes worth five million euros.'

There was a clang followed by an explosion of curses from the galley.

'I'll have to go. If I find out anything else, I'll tell my father,' Monique said.

She headed off, before turning back, having suddenly remembered something else.

'Leon Aubert has a room somewhere in Le Suquet. You could check there.'

As the little fishing boat chugged away from the super yacht, Patrick thought he caught sight of Moreaux watching their departure from the upper deck. If the policeman had been unsure what Patrick was up to, he wasn't any longer. The question was, why was a lieutenant in the Police Nationale being wined and dined on a Russian's magnate's yacht?

EIGHT

Lieutenant Martin Moreaux and his wife, Michelle, lived in a large villa on a rocky promontory on the Estérel peninsula, ten minutes west of Cannes. It had a swimming pool in a walled garden with a wonderful view over the bay to the island of Sainte Marguerite.

Upmarket for a policeman, but rumour had it that Michelle's family had money. Either that or Moreaux was earning over and above his police pay. If he was, Patrick had never been able to discover how, just as Moreaux had tried and failed to find out Patrick's history.

Moreaux didn't like him, that Patrick knew, but the detective had aided him on occasion, when it was to his advantage, and Patrick had returned the favour in full. He had hoped to keep Moreaux out of this job, but their meeting tonight on the *Heavenly Princess* had rendered that impossible.

His mind filled with such thoughts, Patrick turned down Stephen's suggestion that they head for the Irish bar. He wanted time to think, and to eat. Neither would be possible in Stephen's company, agog as the Irishman was over their trip to the black yacht.

Patrick murmured his thanks for Stephen's help, ignored the disappointed look and headed into Le Suquet. The Rue Saint Antoine was packed, its cobbled route narrowed even further by the occupied tables set out on either side. Patrick didn't bother checking the menus, most of them *gastronomique*, but continued to the top and into the square, where a row of small cafés and restaurants, serving the locals, overlooked a park and the local school.

Los Faroles was a favourite of his. It served excellent fresh food at lunchtime, mostly to locals, although an occasional tourist stumbled upon its menu. At night it operated only as a café-bar.

He skirted the outside tables, fully occupied by beer and wine drinkers, and entered the small space within, making for a corner table stacked with menus. Fritz, the current waiter, was German. A retired school teacher, he lived in a tiny studio flat in the nearby Rue Louis Perissol and was currently writing a history of Le Suquet. When he saw Patrick he came over to him.

'Whatever you have left over from lunchtime,' Patrick pleaded. Fritz nodded. 'Keep an eye on the outside while I fix it.'

Fritz slipped behind the kitchen counter and Patrick heard the hiss of the gas. He headed outside to fulfil his duties. One of the beer drinkers, a very large man dressed in a light suit and Panama hat, asked for two more beers in bad French. His companion was much younger and dressed in a similar fashion to the *Black Pearl* producer, in long shorts and T-shirt.

Patrick removed their empty glasses and brought replenished ones and another bowl of potato chips. As he turned back inside, a couple strolled past to sit at a table at the top restaurant on Rue Saint Antoine.

Marie Elise looked stunning in a long pink dress that revealed her shapely shoulders. Her companion was a tall handsome man with white-blond hair. The contrast in colouring was drawing admiring glances from everyone, including the beer drinkers he'd just served. Marie Elise didn't appear to notice. She had eyes only for her companion, chatting easily to him in Swedish.

Patrick stepped quickly inside.

He was spared working out why he didn't want to be seen when Fritz gestured to a plate of eggs and sautéed potatoes on the corner table. Patrick gave him the thumbs-up and set to work on it. Eating wasn't the only reason he had come here tonight, however. Fritz was an authority on current residents of Le Suquet, both itinerant and long established.

Patrick got his chance to ask about Leon Aubert fifteen minutes later when Fritz announced he was closing. The surprised clientele, used to late-night Cannes, looked somewhat bemused as Fritz stacked chairs around them. Finally persuaded that he was indeed closing, they headed off to find an alternative drinking establishment.

Patrick rinsed glasses while Fritz secured the metal shutter. As it descended, so too did the noise of Cannes.

Fritz waved a bottle of cognac in Patrick's direction. 'You have time for a drink?'

Patrick nodded. 'I have something I wanted to ask you.'

'I suspected as much.'

Fritz put two tumblers on the table and poured a generous measure in each glass. He sniffed his and gave a small satisfied smile before sampling.

'A Camus,' he informed Patrick. 'Good.'

Patrick gave Fritz time to savour his cognac, before offering him the name Leon Aubert. Anger instantly suffused his face and he muttered a curse which Patrick translated as 'a walking piece of shit'.

'He came here looking for a job. Said he could cook. Lasted a week. When he went, we were missing at least a dozen bottles of good wine. I wanted to contact the police but He would have none of it. (He being the boss and owner of Los Faroles.) I went to his room on Rue du Pre. His landlady said he had a job cooking on a yacht in the harbour. God help them.' Fritz rolled his eyes.

'Monique Girard says Leon didn't turn up for work the other night,' Patrick said. 'That's why she's helping out on the black yacht.'

Fritz considered this. 'Did the owner find something missing?'

When Patrick didn't answer, Fritz said, 'What did he take?'

Patrick contemplated what, if anything, he should divulge. He didn't know for certain that the black pearl was missing. And he had no proof that Leon Aubert had anything to do with its possible disappearance.

Fritz accepted his reticence. 'The old woman he rents from said he had a girlfriend. Sylvie or Sophie, something like that. She works at the Crystal Bar. You could ask her where Leon is.'

Patrick nodded his thanks and finished up his cognac.

They exited the café together. When Fritz headed up the steps towards La Castre, Patrick took a left, but not before he checked out if Marie Elise and her companion were still at dinner.

The blond and dark heads had disappeared, replaced by two men with festival badges hanging round their necks. Patrick chose not to surmise where Marie had gone, and what she might now be doing. He cursed himself for not getting in touch with her sooner, and vowed to do so as soon as he met up with Chevalier again.

Rue du Pre was deserted. Few visitors ventured over the hill, not realizing they could access the western beachfront by walking down the backstreets of Le Suquet. Here, the late-night grocery shops and fast-food restaurants catered mainly for local inhabitants, many of them Algerians or itinerant workers from other African countries.

Leon's room was in a block at the foot of the street where it met the busier carriageway of Rue Georges Clémenceau. Patrick rang the buzzer and an elderly female voice answered. When Patrick said he was there to see Leon Aubert, she let him in.

She was waiting for him at an open door on the first floor. Behind the short rotund figure swathed in black, he could see the flash of a television set with an accompanying rattle of words in Arabic.

The woman peered at him through wrinkled folds. 'He's not here. Hasn't been for two weeks and he owes rent.'

Patrick pointedly reached for his wallet. 'I'd like to take a look at his room,' he said.

She didn't ask why but swiftly accepted the fifty euro note, slipped it somewhere among the black folds, checking over her shoulder as she did so. Shuffling out, she inserted a key in a nearby door, pushed it open and flicked on a light, before heading back to her own place.

Patrick stepped inside and shut the door.

The room was tiny, with scarcely space for the metal bed, single wardrobe and desk and chair that occupied it. On the wall was a calendar displaying super yachts available for hire. The address was a company with an office next to the Irish pub.

Patrick went through the scarce contents of the wardrobe, checking trouser and shirt pockets, before pulling the wardrobe away from what proved to be a blank wall. There was nothing under the bed or in the desk drawer either. It didn't take him long to realize he had paid dearly to view an empty room. Patrick wondered just how many visitors the landlady had scammed in their search for Leon.

As he made to leave, the calendar caught his eye again. Patrick took it down and flipped through, and was finally rewarded. On the back of the May page he found a faintly scribbled phone number. He tore out the page and slipped it in his pocket.

Finally, he checked the small window above the bed, through which he could see the illuminated Musée de la Castre. It opened easily and a cool breeze carrying the scent of the sea swept into the stuffy room.

Standing on the chair, he had a good view of the neighbouring rooftops. He stuck his head out to find a flat surface with a drying line where a number of items of clothing fluttered in the breeze. Patrick pulled himself up and out on to the roof space. A metal seat to the left of the window, with two empty beer bottles below it, suggested Leon had used this area as his balcony.

Beside the chair was what Patrick was looking for. Under a fringed blue throw was a metal box with a padlock. Leon's private safe.

The padlock was a cheap combination model, made in China. Patrick pulled on the shackle and, keeping the tension, started on the outer tumbler, easing it round until it locked in place at 5. Seconds later, he had the full combination. He unhooked the padlock and pulled open the door.

Inside he found a cloth bag containing a loaded SIG SP 2022, a custom-tailored semi-automatic pistol, standard issue of the Police Nationale. Inside the bag was a thick wad of euros and a French passport. The photograph inside was of a man in his twenties, name of Leon Aubert.

Patrick pocketed the money and passport, and slipped the pistol into his belt, then re-locked the safe and pulled the cover back in place. Pushing the window closed, he decided to use the rooftop terraces as his exit point.

Ten minutes later, he was dropping on to the road directly behind the castle.

There was no one on the western side of the ramparts, the eastern panoramic viewpoint with its fabulous vista of Cannes being more popular. Patrick headed in that direction, passing the big double doors of the Church of Notre-Dame de l'Espérance, which were firmly shut at this hour, to head down the steep hill towards the bus station.

The Crystal Bar stood opposite the Gare Routiere, which itself lay between the municipal police office and the town hall. As he approached the old port, the sounds of Cannes at play grew more prominent. Honking horns and the irritating farting of scooters met him as he passed the gaudily painted wall by the bus stance, decorated with images of famous movie moments.

This part of Le Suquet was buzzing, the street tables of the Crystal Bar and its neighbouring cafés packed with festival-goers and film tourists. Patrick spotted a couple vacating an outside table at the Crystal, and swiftly took up the empty spot.

There were two women serving the busy tables, while a male behind the counter mixed the cocktails for which the Crystal was renowned. Patrick waited until the younger of the two women was in view and waved her over.

He ordered a beer and tried a name. 'Sophie?'

'Sylvie,' she corrected him, then recognition dawned on her face. 'Heh, you're the guy with the cute dog who lives on the old boat at the harbour.'

Patrick silently thanked Oscar for his invaluable ability to attract female attention.

'His name is Oscar and he's incorrigible.' Patrick smiled, before adding, 'And you're Leon Aubert's girl. How's his new job going? I haven't seen him since he went aboard the *Heavenly Princess*.'

Her smile disappeared. 'Who told you I was Leon's girl?' she said sharply.

Patrick pretended embarrassment. 'Sorry. He said you and he were dating. I told him he was a lucky bastard.' He threw her an admiring glance, which wasn't undeserved.

'Well, I'm no one's girl.' She met his interested look with one of her own. 'So where's Oscar tonight?'

'Guard duty aboard *Les Trois Soeurs*.'

She smiled, then waited as though expecting something more.

'When do you finish here?' Patrick tried.

'We close at one.'

About an hour from now.

Patrick made his pitch. 'Oscar and I should be on deck having a nightcap if you're walking that way. I'm sure he'd be delighted to see you.'

'Would he now?'

Sylvie lifted the two empty glasses from the previous occupants. 'I'll get your beer.'

His order arrived via the older waitress, who gave him the once over, suggesting Sylvie had divulged their conversation. Patrick wasn't sure by her expression whether he came up to scratch. Oscar was obviously more enticing than his owner.

Patrick finished up his drink and headed back to the gunboat. It was time for Oscar's evening stroll and Patrick wanted to be back and waiting on the top deck just in case Sylvie should decide to visit. She'd denied being Leon's girl, but he'd gained the impression that she knew Leon, perhaps better than she'd been prepared to admit.

Patrick gave a soft whistle as he approached *Les Trois Soeurs*, normally answered by a bark of delight. This time there was silence. His first thought was that Marie Elise might have returned and taken Oscar below deck, but that idea didn't seem likely after seeing her deep in conversation with the Swede on Rue Saint Antoine.

When a second whistle brought no response, Patrick eased Leon's gun from his belt, before pulling down the walkway.

*   *   *

Opening the cabin door, he dipped his head and peered down the steps. No metallic scent of blood this time and still no evidence of Oscar. He tried the low whistle again. If Oscar was sleeping in the engine room, which he sometimes did, he may not have heard his arrival.

Patrick descended the steps and stood listening for a moment in the shadowy cabin, gun at the ready. There was sufficient light filtering in from the quayside to convince him that the room was empty. Patrick sniffed the air, catching a scent he recognized as that worn by Marie Elise. So she *had* been here, and not long ago.

Maybe she'd taken Oscar for an evening stroll?

Patrick stuck the gun in his belt and switched on the light, before heading back up the steps to scan the various walkways that criss-crossed the harbour. Apart from the usual smokers outside the Irish bar there was no one in sight. Puzzled, Patrick went back inside for a better look. Oscar had been known to get himself trapped in remote corners of the gunboat, but his incarceration was usually accompanied by enough yelps and whines to wake the dead.

His senses back on high alert, Patrick headed for the engine room, checking all the nooks and crannies the dog might have squeezed into. That's when he heard it. Living on a boat had inured him to the sound of water forever lapping the hull, but this wasn't water lapping, this was water running and it was coming from under the door that led to the sunken bath. He drew the gun again and eased his way along the narrow walkway to the aft of the engine.

Reaching the door, he stood outside listening. Apart from the continuing trickle of water, there was nothing. He ran possible scenarios over in his head as to why the bath should have filled to overflowing. He'd used the shower when he'd come back from the dive, but he was sure he'd turned it off.

He pushed the door, forcing it against what was definitely lying water. A ripple washed through the narrow opening, surrounding his feet. The bathroom was in darkness, the only light a blink of red-orange via the rear porthole, which seemed at that moment like an evil eye.

What that eye revealed horrified him.

Patrick put his full weight behind the door and it lurched open, sending water to gush past him. Tossing the gun to one side, he sprang for the bath, sloshing his way through the overspill, grabbing one arm then the other to drag her head above the surface of the water.

The beautiful mouth hung open, the liquid brown eyes stared emptily up at him. Desperate now, he fastened his lips on hers, blowing air into her sodden lungs, knowing his attempts were useless. Marie Elise was cold and dead, and no breath from him would change that.

Seconds later, he heard the shriek of a police siren, as though on cue, and too much of a coincidence. Patrick gently released Marie Elise and she sank back below the surface. He could do nothing for her now and being discovered here with her naked body wouldn't help.

Retrieving the gun, he quickly re-traced his steps to the engine room and located his hoard of money and passports sealed in a waterproof bag, then waded back through the water. There was a hatch above the bath, from the time when the stern had been a store. He reached up, unfastened it and eased it open.

The police car screeched to a halt next to the gunboat just as Patrick thrust himself up through the open hatch. Keeping low and hidden by the cabin, he climbed over the handrail and dropped silently into the water.

Three yachts further on, he broke surface just in time to see Lieutenant Moreaux's iron-grey head cross the deck of *Les Trois Soeurs* and disappear down the steps to the cabin.

NINE

Silently treading water, Patrick considered his options. The choice was limited.

He could head for the harbour exit, swim around the point and come ashore on the west beach. Or he could swim across the harbour, keeping out of sight between the moored yachts, and emerge near the Palais des Festivals.

He decided almost immediately the latter was the better option. The more distance he put between himself and the gunboat, the better. The officers who'd accompanied Moreaux were already checking along the Quai Saint Pierre and he'd spotted one entering the Irish bar.

Only coming up for air when necessary, Patrick made his way around the numerous pontoons, trying not to get entangled in the guy ropes. The larger yachts were tied up at Jetée Albert Edouard, alongside the casino. Most were still brightly lit, with people moving about on deck, which might make it difficult to emerge from the water without causing comment.

On the outer flank of the harbour wall he spotted one large yacht in darkness. Patrick headed in that direction, keeping well out of the light. He waited at the stern, holding on to a rope, watching to see if a security guard was patrolling its upper decks.

Eventually he was rewarded for his patience. A black-shirted guy appeared to walk the length of the yacht and back again, before stopping to look enviously at what was obviously a party in full swing two yachts down.

Patrick chose that moment to swiftly climb a metal ladder attached to the harbour wall, before walking purposefully towards the party yacht. If the security guy shouted after him, he never heard, so quickly was he surrounded by the pounding music.

He lingered there for a moment to look back at the gunboat. *Les Trois Soeurs* was now a hive of activity, three police cars lined up along the *quai*, all with their lights flashing.

Patrick recalled his earlier ominous words to Chevalier, that Lieutenant Moreaux would appear only if they found a body. That declaration had returned to haunt him with a vengeance. Back then he'd been worried about Angele's safety. Never had he considered Marie Elise to be in danger, nor that by contacting her he might make it so.

With that distressing thought in mind, Patrick left the harbour and headed for the Croisette. A great swathe of the east beach was supplanted by a tented village for film festival delegates and movie companies. That area lay in darkness, although further along, the pontoons of the big hotels were still alive with partygoers.

Deciding now it was safe enough to double back, he departed the main thoroughfare and, keeping to the backstreets, made for the imposing red edifice that housed the daily market. A few yards further up Rue Forville, he approached a door and, slipping in his key, gained access to a courtyard.

Hôtel Chanteclair was in darkness apart from a single light above the closed front door.

Patrick entered as quietly as possible, shutting the door carefully behind him.

It didn't work. Pascal, light sleeper that he was, heard him and a sleepy face appeared at the bedroom door. A rapid conversation in French followed.

'What the hell are you doing here?'

'I need to use the room tonight.'

'What's wrong with *Les Trois Soeurs*?'

'Moreaux and his men are swarming all over it.'

'Why?'

'I have no idea, but I'd rather wait until morning to find out.'

Pascal noted his wet appearance, but did not comment further, as Patrick headed past him up the stairs.

He kept a room at the Chanteclair all year round, although he stayed in it only on occasion. Mostly in winter when the gunboat got too cold for comfort, or when his cash reserves were running low, when he would rent out *Les Trois Soeurs* for the various festivals.

The arrangement suited both himself and the owner, Pascal, very well.

Patrick hadn't been back since February, when a cold snap, brought about by bitter winds from the nearby snow-covered Alps, had rendered *Les Trois Soeurs* uninhabitable, which meant that the supply of clothes he'd left behind were mostly for winter.

He took a quick shower, then rummaged around until he located a pair of jeans and a shirt, plus shoes to replace those he'd kicked off in his flight. He also found the whisky bottle – a ten-year-old Islay malt from which he poured a generous measure before settling down on the bed, where he emptied the contents of the waterproof bag beside him.

As well as a gun, money and passports, he had three mobiles, each 'owned' by one of his personas. He checked the Courvoisier one to find that Moreaux had attempted to reach him three times.

Patrick drank down the whisky and poured another, allowing himself to be consumed by the anger which had replaced his shock at discovering Marie Elise's body. He relived the moment when, pushing open the door, he had seen her lovely face floating below the water, the eyes frozen open in horror.

She had come to the gunboat, perhaps seeking his help, perhaps just to see him, and because of that she had died. Had he never contacted her, invited her on to the gunboat, questioned her, she would still be alive. Her connection with him had led to her death. Of that he was certain.

Patrick drank the whisky down and poured another. He couldn't bring Marie back, but he sure as hell could avenge her, by finding and executing the bastard who had taken her life. And to do that he needed to be calm, ice cold and calculating. A version of himself he knew only too well.

Patrick began to contemplate how best to achieve this.

Marie Elise had been discovered on his boat, which would render him a suspect. If he could prove that he had been elsewhere tonight, would that allow him to stay out of custody and carry out his own search for her killer?

The alternative was to mount his search with Moreaux on his tail.

The third whisky brought thoughts thick and fast.

Pascal could be relied on to vouch for his stay here. But why would he be staying at the Chanteclair instead of on the boat? And what of the missing Oscar?

An image of the determined little bulldog flashed up. Moreaux would want to know Oscar's whereabouts, and Patrick had no idea what had happened to his canine companion. Oscar would never have deserted Marie Elise willingly, particularly if he thought she was in danger, which left him with the terrible thought that Oscar too was dead.

He considered calling Chevalier, then decided against it. He would have to make up his own mind how he planned to play this, before getting Chevalier involved. He eventually dozed off and was awakened after a short and fitful sleep by an early morning sun streaming in through the half-open shutters. That and the smell of coffee.

Weather permitting, Pascal always served breakfast out in the courtyard. All the tables were occupied by delegates, badges round their necks, downing coffee and croissants, already answering phone calls. Patrick headed downstairs, and into the kitchen, where he found Pascal preparing the next breakfast tray.

Without looking up, Pascal said, 'What time did you get in?'

Patrick did a quick calculation. Marie Elise had left the restaurant by the time he'd emerged from Los Faroles at eleven. He'd spoken to Sylvie around midnight and hinted that she might like to come by the boat when she finished work at one. She would no doubt tell Moreaux that if he asked. And why would he invite her to the boat if he intended to sleep at the Chanteclair?

'Just after twelve,' Patrick said. 'We had a drink together, and I decided to crash out here.'

Pascal eyed him. 'The marketeers say the police found a dead body on your boat.'

News travelled fast, especially since the nearby Marché Forville would have been setting up from five o'clock, spreading the word.

Patrick feigned shock. 'What?'

'Word is it's a woman.'

'My God. So that's why the police were there.'

Pascal studied him intently. 'What are you going to do?'

'Call Inspector Moreaux, of course.'

Pascal seemed satisfied with his response. 'I'd do that right away.' He lifted the tray he'd prepared and headed outside with it.

Patrick took a deep breath, poured himself a coffee and carried it into the courtyard.

Pascal had enclosed the tables with a ring of shrubs, leaving one outside for those who wished a little privacy. Patrick left the hum of other guests and took up residence there.

Moreaux answered almost immediately. 'Courvoisier. I've been trying to reach you.'

'My apologies. I've just woken up.'

'Where are you?'

'The Chanteclair. I slept here last night.'

'You have heard?'

'Pascal just told me.' Patrick feigned deep shock. 'Shall I come down?'

'Please do,' the lieutenant said crisply.

Patrick rang off and finished his coffee, finalizing his story as he did so, reminding himself that a good lie should be as near the truth as possible.

The Marché Forville was buzzing. The locals took their food buying seriously; the tourists saw it as a unique French pastime that should be savoured. Film festival delegates passed it by, too intent on their mobile phone conversations and their first meeting of the day.

Patrick had a sudden and vivid memory of seeing Marie there laughing and chatting with a stall holder. He'd wondered back then who the stunning woman was and whether he might ever get to meet her.

He dispensed with that troubling image and tried to focus on the present.

The first hole in his alibi could well be Sylvie's version of last night's events.

The Crystal Bar was open, but there was no sign of Sylvie. Obviously those who did the late shift didn't have to turn out to work first thing.

The Quai Saint Pierre, always a popular strolling area, had been made even busier by the presence of a police incident van and the taped-off area round *Les Trois Soeurs*. Patrick gave a low whistle on approach, hoping that Oscar's tan head would bob into view. When it didn't, he decided to go with the story he had settled on.

His decision to co-operate with Moreaux had been a necessity. Hiding from the intrepid lieutenant in Cannes hadn't been an option. And he definitely wasn't leaving before he cleared this up. Besides, how the lieutenant conducted the imminent interview might prove both informative and interesting. Patrick hadn't forgotten Moreaux's initial denial of any missing starlet, then his rather surprising appearance on board the *Heavenly Princess* as Vasily Chapayev's guest.

Moreaux was waiting for him in the café next to the yachting agents, drinking a double espresso. Patrick indicated to the waiter he would have the same and took a seat on the other side of the small table. In the bright light of a May morning, Moreaux looked immaculate, but tired. The few hours' sleep Patrick had enjoyed had not, it appeared, been experienced by Moreaux.

The lieutenant waited until Patrick tasted his coffee before saying, 'Tell me what you know.'

'Just that the body of a woman has been found on my boat.'

Moreaux's eyes glinted like steel. 'That is all?'

Patrick nodded.

'The victim's name is Marie Clermand. I believe you knew her as Marie Elise? An associate of Brigitte Lacroix?'

Patrick's horror was real enough as he relived the scene in the bathroom the previous night. The weight of Marie's body when he'd lifted her free of the water. The touch of her cold lips on his.

'But I saw her last night in a restaurant on the Rue Saint Antoine having dinner with a Swedish man.'

'When was this?' Moreaux said.

'About eleven. I was at Los Faroles with Fritz. They were sitting at an outside table at Le Provençal.'

Moreaux asked for a description of the man, which Patrick supplied.

'Did you see her leave?'

Patrick hadn't, and said so.

'Where did you go after that?'

'The Crystal Bar, then the Chanteclair.' Patrick mentioned times.

'Was Oscar with you?'

'I collected him after the Crystal. We headed along the Esplanade, then up round by Rue Forville where he deserted me. There's a bitch in season . . .' Patrick didn't need to spell it out. 'I called in to see Pascal, we had a drink and I crashed out there.'

'You did not board the boat?'

'Not after I visited the *Heavenly Princess*.' That part of his evening Moreaux could vouch for.

'Ah, *le garçon Cannois*.'

Moreaux waited for Patrick's explanation, which he had ready.

'I was employed by Camille Ager to locate the whereabouts of her half-sister Angele, last seen at the launch party of *The Black Pearl*, a movie she starred in. I decided to take a look on board.'

'And did you find her?' Moreaux's black eyes glittered.

'I have since discovered that Angele is in Paris.'

'Really. You spoke to her?'

'She contacted her sister.' Patrick had no idea how much of this Moreaux already knew.

The lieutenant relinquished that line of enquiry and took a sip of his coffee. 'You were acquainted with Marie Elise?'

'We had dinner together the night before last on *Les Trois Soeurs*.' Patrick contemplated a lie, but suspected Moreaux already knew the reason. 'She was at the launch party. I wanted to ask her about Angele.'

'And what did she say?'

'That they talked in the toilets about men and make-up.'

'That was all?'

'Yes.'

Moreaux pushed his cup away. 'I will require a full statement as to your movements. And a description of the man you saw Marie with.'

'Surely Brigitte will have his details?' Patrick said.

'Marie told Madame Lacroix she was meeting you last night.'

Patrick looked as perplexed as he felt. 'We hadn't made any such arrangement.'

'Then why would she say it?'

'I have no idea.'

Moreaux brought Patrick back from his troubled thoughts with a start. 'You haven't asked how she died.'

'I assumed you weren't at liberty to say.'

'I sometimes forget how aware you are of the way we work.' Moreaux gave a little smile as though to confirm this. 'One thing puzzles me.'

Patrick waited, thinking how fortunate Moreaux was, if only one thing was puzzling him. 'You say you collected the dog from the boat just after twelve.'

Patrick nodded.

'Did Oscar give you any reason to believe something was wrong?'

Patrick remembered the dog's mad scramble to get on board when he'd caught the scent of the gutted rabbit. How would Oscar have reacted to a dead human being? And his favourite Marie Elise at that?'

'He was no more excitable than usual,' Patrick said. 'May I ask how you discovered the body?'

'An anonymous phone call.' Moreaux rose. 'We will expect you at the station.'

'Of course. I'll call in later today.'

Patrick watched the lieutenant cross the road and approach *Les Trois Soeurs*, where a team of suited forensic officers were at work. He recalled Moreaux's demeanour on board the *Heavenly Princess*, his friendly attitude towards the Russian. Moreaux was a master at manipulation. He may have been there as a confidant of the Russian, or as a police officer. There was no way of knowing. And throughout his conversation with Patrick, there had been no mention of the black pearl.

Patrick took out his mobile and made a call to the number written on Leon's calendar. It rang for a few moments before a woman's voice answered, giving the name of a yacht catering business in the Rue Félix Faure.

'I'm trying to locate the whereabouts of Leon Aubert,' Patrick said.

'Monsieur Aubert no longer works for us,' she said sharply before putting the phone down.

Patrick then tried Camille's number, but it rang out unanswered, before switching to voicemail. He left a message asking her to call him, saying it was urgent.

His next move must be to find Oscar. Oscar would have allowed Marie Elise to board *Les Trois Soeurs*, Patrick was certain of that. But what about her killer?

His brain constructed a possible scenario.

Marie Elise arriving, perhaps to tell him something she'd found out about Angele's disappearance. Oscar happy to see her. As she waited, someone else arrived. If Marie Elise had known and welcomed her assailant, Oscar would have allowed him on board. Alternatively the assailant could have boarded undetected, perhaps the way he himself had escaped.

And how did her dinner companion figure in all of this?

Somehow Patrick couldn't see Marie Elise taking a bath while awaiting his arrival. Their relationship hadn't got anywhere near that stage. So whoever killed her must have stripped her naked and put her in the bath to implicate him in her death. But where was Oscar when all this had happened?

Patrick paid for his coffee and headed back to the Chanteclair.

The delegates had all departed to deal movies for the day, leaving Pascal and his partner, Preben, to breakfast in the courtyard by themselves. Patrick joined them.

'Well?' Preben asked, worried. 'Who was it?'

Patrick saw no reason not to tell them. 'Marie Elise.'

'Brigitte's Marie Elise?' Pascal's eyes opened wide and he put his hand to his mouth in shock. 'Poor Marie. Who would do such a thing?' Pascal's eyes glistened with tears as Preben put a hand on his arm to comfort him.

'I have no idea, but I intend finding out.' The steely coldness of Patrick's reply appeared to worry Pascal even further. Sensing this, Patrick changed tack. 'I need you to find Oscar for me.' He watched as Pascal's fear transferred to the dog. 'I left him on board when I went out,' Patrick explained. 'I haven't seen him since.'

'Oh my God. He was there when . . .' Pascal contemplated what may have happened to the dog. '*Le pauvre petit chien.*'

Oscar's fan club wasn't just restricted to Moreaux and Marie Elise. If Patrick put the word out that the dog was missing, a search party would be formed. Pascal said as much.

'Leave Oscar to us,' he announced. 'You find who did this to Marie.'

Departing the quiet of the courtyard, Patrick headed for Le P'tit Zinc. Being almost lunchtime, he was hopeful that Chevalier would be having his aperitif. He hadn't heard from his friend all morning, although, judging by the excitement caused by the police presence on the *quai*, he couldn't conceive of Chevalier being ignorant of what had happened aboard *Les Trois Soeurs*. Having suggested Patrick involve Marie Elise in his search for Angele, Chevalier would have taken the news of her death personally.

Yet Patrick had not had a call from his friend.

Chevalier's usual table was empty with no reserved sign on it. It seemed he wasn't expected. Veronique came rushing out at the sight of Patrick and proceeded in rapid French to question him about Marie's murder. When he insisted he knew nothing, she dispensed with him with a wave of her hand. He thought he also caught a reference to 'a stupid goat' in her final retort.

His next port of call was Chevalier's agency. A young man sat at the front desk on the lower level. Fresh-faced and dark-haired, he stood up in anticipation on Patrick's entry. Obviously a new employee, he greeted Patrick with the open smile of someone keen to sell a property. Patrick quickly got to the point, telling him he sought Monsieur Chevalier and that it was urgent. The keen expression transformed into a poorly masked scowl.

'I'm sure I will be able to help. Monsieur Chevalier left me in charge.'

'Where is he?'

'Showing a client an expensive property,' he replied loftily.

'I'd like the address, please.'

Pierre, his name according to the sign on his desk, shook his head. 'I am not permitted . . .'

Patrick took a menacing step towards him and Pierre retreated, colliding with the chair, and sat down in a somewhat ungainly fashion.

'My name is Patrick de Courvoisier and Le Chevalier will likely sack you if you don't tell me where he is.'

Pierre attempted to retrieve his composure but an outbreak of sweat had marked his pristine shirt. 'If only you had mentioned your name when you came in, monsieur.' He looked unsure and offended at the same time. 'Monsieur Chevalier is at this property.' He handed Patrick a glossy brochure of a 'magnificent residence of character' located in the area known as Californie. The price was naturally on request, Californie being a Cannes neighbourhood popular with those who had no worry regarding the cost.

Outside the agency, Patrick turned swiftly towards Le Suquet.

Making his way past the market, now dismantled, the stall owners enjoying lunch at the adjacent cafés, Patrick headed back towards the Chanteclair. Opposite the door to the courtyard was a set of steps, leading on to the street of restaurants. Just prior to the steps was a store for the above restaurant, beside it a garage door.

Patrick used the remote to unlock the door and raise the shutter. Resting inside the cave was his much-loved Ferrari 330 GTS.

He stood for a moment, admiring the sleek blue lines and somewhat tight fit. Reversing out of the cave on to the narrow steep incline was a challenge – one he relished as much as driving the car, not in the inevitable crush of Cannes, but on the steep winding roads that radiated in all directions from the city.

Climbing in, he enjoyed the warm smell of upholstery and the lingering scent of the last female to occupy the passenger seat. Their liaison had been a brief but memorable day spent in a secluded hillside hotel, home to one of the best chefs in Provence.

He had met Estelle on a flight from Paris. The attraction had been instant and consuming. His suggestion as they left the airport that they lunch together was greeted with an enthusiasm matching his own. He had driven to Hôtel d'Or where he was well known, and his request for lunch and a room was easily accommodated.

The food had been exceptional, as were the hours that followed. Estelle had laughingly declined his offer of extending their stay to dinner and breakfast and had asked to be dropped back to Nice airport. She had accepted his Courvoisier number, but had not offered one of her own. Needless to say she hadn't called, which had disappointed him a little.

The following week Patrick had spotted her photograph in the Monaco section of the *Riviera Times*. Estelle Dupont was the wife of a prominent Monte Carlo businessman, twenty years her senior. In the photograph, she looked poised and happy. For her Patrick had been a pleasant way to spend an afternoon, but only one, it seemed.

He fired up the engine and sat for a moment listening to the purr, before hooting the horn, reversing without fear or favour and heading swiftly uphill.

Le Suquet, together with the Croisette and the nearby shopping quarter of Rue d'Antibes, occupied an area of Cannes known as La Banane – the banana – separated from the sprawl of Le Cannet to the north by the dual carriageway and the railway line that ran the length of the south coast.

Patrick used the slip road to join the line of traffic on the *voie rapide*, rapidly filling with marketeers, and headed east.

Twenty minutes later he found the place. It hadn't been easy. The interweaving lattice of access roads of Californie was designed to dissuade the curious. The surrounding walls of each property were high enough to maintain their privacy.

Patrick pulled up on the gravel some metres from the electronic gates and took a closer look at the brochure. Described as being set in a landscaped park of 14,000 square metres, it boasted not one residence but three: the main house, a guesthouse and a caretaker's lodge. According to the details, the main house had been built at the time of Napoleon III by an English lord.

Patrick quickly ran his eyes over the blurb. If he had to pass himself off as a prospective buyer, he'd better at least know what he was planning to buy. Satisfied he knew enough, Patrick restarted the engine and approached the gate indicating he wished to enter.

The camera on the nearest gate post rotated towards him.

Patrick looked directly at the lens.

'I have an appointment with Monsieur Chevalier and I'm late,' he said in a tone that brooked no argument.

There was a moment's hesitation before the gate, electronically released, swung open. Patrick made a point of roaring through, scattering stones on the white gravel drive.

The avenue of pines wound upwards, with brief glimpses of what lay beyond. Emerging from the trees he found the house at the top of a rise, facing the not-too-distant sea. A wide set of steps swept down from the forecourt to the obligatory aquamarine swimming pool with its manicured surrounding lawn.

As he swung into a spot beside Chevalier's motorbike and a smoked-windowed Mercedes, he spotted what looked like a roof terrace, complete with brightly coloured umbrellas and trellises of flowers, which undoubtedly commanded a remarkable view of the Côte d'Azur.

Parked now, he took a proper look at the other car. Who was Chevalier's prospective buyer? Patrick attempted to peer inside, but was prevented by the smoked-glass windows. One thing was certain, whoever owned this quality of car was unlikely to be put off purchasing this property because of its price.

Patrick approached the house. Finding the double front door open, he entered and stood for a moment in the grand entrance hall, admiring the superb frescos that adorned the walls, deciding the English lord who'd built this place had had an excellent taste in decoration.

The interior reminded Patrick of a Venetian palace without the crumbling mortar occasioned by the damp. In the hushed silence of the large vestibule, he finally discerned the murmur of distant voices. Tuning in, he made out Chevalier's distinctive tones and perhaps two others, one of them definitely that of a woman.

He wondered whether he should seek out the visiting party, or simply wait here and surprise them. He'd decided on the former and was heading for the stairs when a peel of somewhat forced feminine laughter drew his eye upwards.

Emerging from an upper room were three figures. Chevalier, as distinctive as ever in his trademark apparel and moustache, was followed by a woman with beautiful legs, her face hidden by her male companion, who'd turned for a final look at the room all three had just exited.

Patrick was halfway up the staircase before his approach was noted and all three faces turned suddenly towards him. Chevalier's reaction was muted. The woman's less so. Camille Ager's expression could only be described as one of horror and confusion, although it was Chapayev who definitely won the prize.

He stared at Patrick as though wishing to skin him alive.

'I understood this was to be a private showing,' he said sharply to Chevalier.

Patrick gave an inward sigh of relief. It seemed he wasn't immediately recognized without his waiter uniform, but being regarded as a possible rival for the purchase of the Villa Astrid.

'Ah, Courvoisier. I'm glad you could make it,' Chevalier said immediately. 'Let me introduce you to Monsieur Chapayev, a potential buyer for Villa Astrid, and of course you met Camille with me at Le P'tit Zinc.'

Patrick's acknowledging smile did nothing to ease Camille's worried expression.

Chapayev, confused by Le Chevalier's warm welcome, was re-evaluating the situation. Anger still burned in his eyes, but his expression became more cunning than aggressive as Chevalier continued with his smooth delivery.

'Monsieur de Courvoisier's family once owned this delightful villa. In fact, Lord Loudon who built it was, I believe, a distant relative?'

He passed the baton to Patrick, who picked it up and ran with it, impressed by Chevalier's ability to rise to such an occasion.

'And a fervent Francophile, which led to the establishment through marriage of my own branch of the family,' Patrick lied pleasantly.

Chapayev was studying him closely, recognition flickering in those mean little eyes, no doubt wondering how the man before him had mysteriously moved from status as a Cannois waiter on board his yacht, to being a direct descendant of an English lord.

Camille's hand fluttered to her face and Patrick saw that it was trembling. He wondered why she was here with a man she'd professed to fear.

There was a moment's silence when it seemed to Patrick that all took stock of the situation.

Chapayev was the first to respond. 'Since you know the house so well, monsieur, would you walk round with me? I would like to hear more of the man who built it.'

In the world of chess, it was a good move. Isolate your opponent before the attack.

Patrick smiled. 'Of course, I'd be delighted to.'

Camille, silent until now, interrupted them with a breathless, 'Can you please excuse me, gentlemen. I must get back to the shop,' while avoiding Patrick's eye.

'Of course.' Chevalier, ever the gentleman, offered to take her if she didn't mind a motorbike ride. He then turned to Chapayev. 'I will leave you in Courvoisier's capable hands. Obviously I hope you'll be in touch. Properties like Villa Astrid don't often come on the market.'

Camille glanced at Chapayev as though asking his permission to depart, and was met by a blank expression. The relationship between herself and the Russian was taking on a whole new hue in Patrick's eyes.

Chevalier took her arm. 'Shall we go?'

The Russian waited until the motorbike blasted down the avenue, scattering even more stones than Patrick's arrival, then turned to face him, jowls heavy with threat, eyes like two bullets poised to fire.

'Monsieur de Courvoisier. It seems wherever I am, you are there also.'

'Strangely, I've gained the same impression about you.'

Patrick met him eye to eye, at the same time wondering where the minder was. There had been no one near the Mercedes when he'd arrived, but he couldn't imagine Chapayev would drive himself here alone.

The Russian gave a sigh. 'You were hired to find the whereabouts of Angele Valette. Her sister has now made contact with Angele and therefore you are no longer required. Your time would be better spent talking to the police about the body found on your boat.'

Patrick pretended to concentrate on the frescos, when he was actually trying to work out where the minder was. He played for a little more time.

'You were the one who asked me to stay and discuss my ancestor and his artistic tastes.'

Chapayev emitted a choking sound, colour rising to his cheeks in a red sweep of diffused fury. Patrick was no less angry, though he strove to keep his voice steady. The mention of *Les Trois Soeurs* had flashed the image of Marie Elise once more in his brain.

'I intend finding out who killed Marie Elise,' he said coldly. 'And the whereabouts of both Angele and the black pearl.'

Chapayev glanced upwards and Patrick tensed, every muscle in his body preparing to spring. The minder was close by, perhaps with a gun, waiting for the signal to dispense with this irritant. Patrick decided to move first.

Launching himself forward, he propelled into the Russian, knocking the feet from under him and both went slamming to the ground. It wasn't an elegant manoeuvre but it achieved its purpose. In the resulting jumble of arms, legs and grunts of expelled air, Patrick smelled Chapayev's fear and heard his barked '*Nyet*'.

Patrick extracted himself and rose, taking care to maintain a position between the Russian's bulky body and the open door. Two backward strides and he was through and slamming it behind him.

His reverse turn on Rue Forville was nothing to the one he executed now. The shower of stones he threw up ricocheted off the windscreen and rained down on him in the open-topped car.

The gate would be the next problem, but as he descended the hill at speed, it anticipated his arrival and began to swing back. He took his chance and screeched through the half-opening.

As he wound his way past the walled enclaves of the rich, he contemplated what had just happened. He'd had no reason to believe that Chevalier would have placed him in danger by leaving him alone with Chapayev. Chevalier had been unaware of his visit to the *Heavenly Princess* and therefore didn't know that he had met Chapayev there. Chevalier also knew nothing of the gutted rabbit.

Would his friend have abandoned him so easily if he had? And what of Camille Ager? The fear on her face when Patrick had turned up had been hard to miss. And that look to Chapayev when she'd left. Maybe his interpretation of her actions was correct and Camille was just a pawn in whatever game Chapayev was playing.

To cap it all, he'd had no opportunity to gauge Chevalier's response to Marie's murder.

He took a ninety-degree turn, realizing he had missed the slip road for the *voie rapide*. Repeated glances in his mirror had convinced him that he hadn't been followed. If Chapayev had been intent on preventing his departure, he could have ordered the gate to stay shut.

Patrick hit the brake to avoid slamming into the queue building on the slip road. The *voie rapide* looked anything but quick, so he reversed in cavalier fashion, causing a blast of irritated horns, and chose an alternative route.

TEN

Avoiding the snarled-up dual carriageway didn't necessarily save him time: the backstreets of Cannes were equally busy. Although the bus and train services along the Côte d'Azur were cheap and frequent, people still preferred sitting in their cars, sounding their horns.

Patrick glanced at his watch, conscious it was already lunchtime and breakfast had consisted of only coffee. He headed for Boulevard Jean Hibert, on the western side of the old port, and was blessed with a parking space close by the beach restaurants. Tucked out of sight of the festival crowd, and serving non-stop, he was more likely to get a table here.

Hunger was preventing his brain from functioning. Either that or the fact that the sequence of events and behaviours he'd witnessed over the past couple of days made no sense at all.

He chose the O'key Beach where Jacky and Marcella ran a family business and knew their regulars. Offered a recently vacated table next to the beach, he ordered the day's special and a half pichet of rosé, then he called the Chanteclair.

It was Preben who answered.

'We've got him,' he said as soon as he heard Patrick's voice. 'He was found on the rocks near the entrance to the harbour, half-drowned, with a gash on his head, which is now stitched.'

Patrick was surprised at the strength of his relief. He was fond of the determined little bulldog.

'I'll be there shortly.'

'You'll be lucky if Pascal lets you have him back,' Preben said in a serious tone.

Patrick rang off as his lunch arrived. The sardines, freshly caught that morning, tasted excellent. The wine was local, fresh and un-assuming. Patrick ate with gusto, the one good piece of news regarding Oscar having sharpened his appetite.

Since his arrival, a second wave of diners had joined him on the deck.

On one side was a French family of parents, grandparents and two children under five, the children dividing their time between the table and the beach. On the other, two suited Americans conducted a lively conversation intermittently interrupted by mobile devices. One was definitely pitching a movie, which he proclaimed would be '*The Bourne Identity* meets *Pirates of the Caribbean*' and would star Johnny Depp. Patrick was intrigued, because the pitch sounded a bit like his own life at the moment.

When the waitress came for his empty plate, Patrick ordered a double espresso, then checked his mobile again. There was still nothing from Chevalier, and his message to Camille continued to be unanswered.

While sipping his coffee, he pondered the last forty-eight hours.

A frightened Camille Ager, having almost begged him to find her missing half-sister and the black pearl, before Chapayev did, now claimed her sister was well and in Paris. She had not however mentioned the pearl during that conversation. Now she appeared to be spending time in the company of the man she'd originally been frightened of, although judging by Camille's behaviour at Villa Astrid, that fear had not abated.

Patrick added in the threat of a gutted rabbit, the missing sous chef, the murdered escort and the half-drowned dog to the already complex equation. The possible duplicity of Moreaux, and evidence of Chevalier's connection with the Russian over Villa Astrid, rendered the water even murkier.

No further forward in his deliberations, despite a satisfied appetite, Patrick paid his bill and left. Returning the car to the garage, he let himself in at the Chanteclair and was immediately greeted by a tan bullet on somewhat wobbly legs. Pascal clucked along behind, trying to scoop up the small but hefty bundle.

'He will burst his stitches,' he said in alarm.

Patrick intervened, ordered Oscar to sit, and crouched beside him for a closer look. In the shaved area on top of his head was a stitched wound, red and raw-looking, about four centimetres long. Either the intruder had inflicted it, then thrown the dog overboard, or else Oscar had been injured once in the water. Knowing Oscar's propensity to defend those he loved, Patrick suspected the former was the more likely explanation.

Murmuring words of praise, he rubbed the dog's ears. That was sufficient for Oscar. He retreated to the rug laid out for him in the shade and went back to his drug-induced slumbers.

'You had a visitor,' Pascal said in an undertone, as though they were being observed from one of the various windows overlooking the courtyard. A dedicated fan of crime and thriller novels, it now appeared Pascal believed himself to be in one.

Patrick waited to hear who the visitor was.

'Madame Lacroix.' Pascal gave him a knowing look. 'She wants to see you.'

The Hibiscus headquarters were located on Rue d'Antibes, tucked between a prestigious bank and an expensive couturier, favoured by visiting movie stars. The entrance was a traditional heavy wooden door with polished brass handle, but with no nameplate.

If permitted to enter, visitors would discover murals imitating the erotic paintings of Bouchet and Fragonard lining the marble staircase leading to the upper level. Should they prefer to use the cage lift, they would find the metal bars fashioned in the female form.

Patrick chose the stairs.

Hibiscus was operated from Brigitte's apartment, which had once been owned by a prominent French politician who had used it to house a string of mistresses. It had been appropriated during the Vichy administration and operated as an upmarket brothel for collaborators and visiting Nazis. Fortunately, according to Chevalier, the interior decor had remained intact.

Brigitte's order to come up had been brusque and icily furious. She obviously blamed Patrick for what had happened to Marie Elise, thus assuming her death was something to do with his investigation. In that she wasn't far wrong.

As he reached the first landing, the door to the apartment was flung open.

Brigitte Lacroix was a stunningly handsome woman. Small, slim and elegantly dressed, she extruded a sensuality to rival the naked abandonment of those who lined her staircase. Her dark eyes and strong nose, high cheekbones and arched brows owed nothing to cosmetic surgery. Hers was a face that knew age and did not scorn it. Rather like a fine wine, she grew more flavoursome with the years. Patrick understood perfectly why Moreaux should favour her over a younger model for his mistress.

'Courvoisier.' She glared at him for a moment, registering the full extent of her wrath, then indicated that he should follow her inside.

Patrick had never been in the hallowed halls of Hibiscus before and found himself impressed, despite the circumstances. The interior decor rivalled the Villa Astrid in its sumptuousness. It too had frescos above each door in the large entrance hall, although he had no time to study them as he was quickly ushered into a sitting room. In here was cool and shadowy, the shutters closed against the noise of Rue d'Antibes.

Madame Lacroix lit a cheroot and took time to draw on it while observing him with flashing eyes.

'I did not arrange to meet Marie Elise last night,' he began.

'Then why was she on your boat?'

'I have no idea.'

The eyes became dagger points below the arched brows.

He strove to explain. 'I saw Marie Elise having dinner with a Swedish man at Le Provençal earlier in the evening when I was at Los Faroles. She had left by the time Fritz closed up. I went to the boat, collected Oscar and ended up at the Chanteclair where I spent the night.'

At his mention of the Swede, a look of puzzlement crossed Brigitte's face, suggesting any conversation she'd had with Moreaux had not included that part of the story.

'I told Lieutenant Moreaux all this when he interviewed me this morning,' Patrick said for good measure.

She paused to exhale her annoyance. 'What did this Swede look like?'

'Tall, blond, handsome, wealthy.' It might have been a description of any number of Hibiscus clients. 'Do you have someone fitting that description on your books? Or does your discretion go as far as protecting a killer?' he said pointedly.

Brigitte crossed her arms, the cheroot now pointing at him like a poison-tipped dart. The mention of the Swede had unnerved her, perhaps switching the reason for Marie Elise's death away from himself and towards Hibiscus.

'What did Lieutenant Moreaux say when you told him this?' she said sharply.

'He made no comment.'

'But you assumed he would contact me?'

Patrick nodded.

'Yet he did not.'

She chose a chair and sat down heavily. Her steel-like frame seemed to slump for a moment, then she re-erected herself.

'I thought meeting you had put her in danger.' She looked accusingly at him.

'I think that may yet be the case.' Patrick paused. 'What do you know of the Swede?'

She shook her head, puzzled. 'Nothing. She did not meet him through me.'

Patrick believed her. 'Could he have been a boyfriend?'

Brigitte contemplated such a possibility. 'If so, he must have been very recent. When a boyfriend is present, it is more difficult for the girls to be on call. Therefore I insist on knowing if they are in a relationship.' She met him squarely in the eye.

'Would Marie Elise confide in any of the other escorts?'

She considered this. 'Perhaps, although I would be displeased if such personal information was not related to me,' she said.

'Who might she confide in?'

Madame Lacroix took a long draw on her cheroot before answering. 'Anya Perova.' The name escaped in a cloud of smoke. 'And no, I will not give you her number. But I will ask her to call you, although I don't think she will.' She looked up at him. 'As far as my girls are concerned, you have become a jinx, monsieur.'

Patrick couldn't blame them, considering what had happened to Marie.

'What about Lieutenant Moreaux?' he said. 'Will you give him this girl's number?'

She eyed him. 'I may not even give him her name.'

The sharp nature of the retort surprised Patrick. Had Chevalier been wrong about Brigitte's relationship with the police lieutenant? Although, Patrick reminded himself, you didn't have to trust someone to become their lover.

Brigitte was back on her feet, stubbing the remains of the cheroot in a crystal ashtray.

'I expect you to find out who did this to Marie. Naturally I will make it worth your while.' She crossed to an ornate desk and, opening a drawer, extracted a fat envelope which she attempted to hand to him.

'That won't be necessary,' Patrick said.

'I prefer it this way,' she insisted.

The stand-off lasted several moments before he finally accepted the bundle and slipped it in his pocket, then followed her to the door.

He exited on to a busy Rue d'Antibes. Late afternoon was a popular shopping time, and it was obvious by the number of festival bags that film delegates were making up a large proportion of those thronging the famous stores.

Patrick headed inland to the train station, then up the ramp to Place du 18 Juin, occupied by the imposing headquarters of the Police Nationale. On entry, he was informed that Lieutenant Moreaux was otherwise engaged and that someone else would record his statement.

He was shown to a room that smelled of stale cigarette smoke, despite the prominent 'no smoking' sign, where he was left for twenty minutes to stew before a woman appeared and introduced herself as Officer Dubois. She was young, fresh-faced and apparently uncomfortable with the task she'd been given. Patrick had the impression that he might have met her before, but couldn't think where, and under what circumstances.

He duly dictated his statement, sticking to the story he'd told Moreaux, aware that if someone from the building opposite the *quai* had seen him board *Les Trois Soeurs* the previous night, then he was in trouble. He signed the lie nevertheless.

The officer thanked him, then asked in a seemingly genuine manner as to Oscar's well-being.

Patrick didn't mention the gash to the dog's head, or his half-drowned state. Doubtless that information would eventually reach Moreaux, which would likely cause him to question the version of events in Patrick's statement.

However, any delay was useful.

It wasn't until he was outside the building that Patrick realized where he'd seen the female officer before. As well as numerous restaurants, the Rue Saint Antoine had a couple of cocktail bars where the young and trendy inhabitants of Le Suquet met of an evening. His recollection placed her there during a visit with Stephen, who for once had spurned his usual after-work Guinness. She'd come over to talk to the Irishman about a possible dive trip to the original sunken village near Agay and they'd been introduced. Her first name, as he recalled, was Colette. Stephen had seemed quite taken with her. Patrick wondered whether the two had got together since. Someone close to Moreaux would be a useful contact.

He'd been disappointed by Moreaux's non-appearance, having nursed the hope of sparring with the detective again. Much had happened since their last meeting. Although Patrick had no intention of revealing any of it, he would have liked to gauge Moreaux's reaction to any subliminal message he might have chosen to impart. For instance, he wondered if the policeman had any idea that Chapayev was interested in buying the Villa Astrid, or that Camille Ager appeared to be working for the Russian.

Before heading for the Chanteclair, he took a walk along the *quai*, where *Les Trois Soeurs* looked longingly back at him from behind police tape. According to Officer Dubois, he was to be allowed back on board his boat tomorrow. Patrick couldn't wait.

The *Diving Belle* was moored nearby, a row of dripping wetsuits dangling on its rail, which meant that Stephen was probably in the Irish bar. Patrick swung across the busy road, dodging traffic, and went inside.

The place was buzzing. From the comments he overheard as he threaded his way through, it sounded as though Stephen's total diving contingent had headed in here after their trip. Patrick motioned to the barman, who indicated Stephen's presence in the back.

He and Colm were seated in the same booth as before, Colm registering his arrival with the slightest of nods. A man of few words indeed. Stephen, on the other hand, was his normal effusive self.

'I thought you were banged up for murder.' He whistled. 'Come, tell all.' He indicated Colm should shove along as a pint of Guinness arrived and was placed in front of the newly seated Patrick.

Patrick spun the same yarn as he'd told everyone else up to now, only adding that Oscar had been found, injured but alive on the harbour rocks.

'I bet he had a right go at whoever killed that girl,' Stephen said, in approval.

'And got hit over the head for his pains,' Patrick said.

'But he'll be all right?' Colm's deep voice, so seldom heard, was full of concern.

'He's fine. Pascal has him at the Chanteclair.'

'So,' Stephen asked, 'do you require an alibi?'

'I didn't kill Marie Elise.'

'Sure, we know that, but it doesn't mean you don't need an alibi. Let's face it, Lieutenant Moreaux isn't exactly a fan of yours, and you did spot him keeping company with the Russian.'

Patrick reassured him: 'Pascal will vouch for my stay at the Chanteclair.' Then he steered the conversation to what he wanted to ask. He explained about spotting Marie the previous evening with a Swedish man on Rue Saint Antoine. 'They'd gone by the time Fritz closed up. Marie must have come to the gunboat – with or without the Swede – later on, maybe around midnight?'

He could tell by Stephen's face that he would love to say he'd seen them, but was unable to offer anything.

'I saw them,' Colm said suddenly.

Stephen's expression was a mixture of curiosity and envy. 'Where?'

'They were coming down the steps by the fountain.'

The fountain Colm referred to stood in the Place Massuque behind the Irish bar. From it, a wide set of steps led up to the Suquet.

'When was this?' Patrick demanded.

'I was out for a smoke.' Colm took a guess. 'Maybe around midnight.'

'Did they board the boat?' Stephen broke in.

Colm shrugged. 'I went back inside.'

'I should never have given up smoking.' Stephen shook his head. 'I can ask around. See if anyone else saw them?'

'Moreaux should have been doing that already,' Patrick said.

'We've been out on the *Diving Belle* all day.' Stephen looked disappointed at missing out on so much of the action.

Patrick downed the rest of his pint. 'Find out what you can. About the black yacht, the Russian, and last night.' He stood up.

Stephen's eyes glistened with delight. 'We're on it.' He waved at the barman for a refill.

The outside air was cool and damp, indicating it had been raining somewhere in the hills behind Cannes. The previous two days had been warm and dry, but at this time of year, downpours weren't uncommon, even at sea level.

Patrick took a deep breath, glad to be out of the stuffy bar, then made for Place Massuque. He realized it had been here he'd spotted the couple arguing on a balcony, the day this had all kicked off.

He'd sat on the upper deck of *Les Trois Soeurs* and wished for trouble to come walking his way. He'd been excited by the prospect – welcomed it, because he was bored. What he hadn't known then was how much collateral damage it would cause. Marie Elise had come to him, concerned for Angele Valette's safety, and offered her help. She'd put her trust in him and he'd betrayed that trust, because he had seriously underestimated his opponent.

In the field, that would have meant his own death. It should never have resulted in the death of an innocent party.

Camille's demeanour when she'd spoken of Chapayev should have alerted him. He should have been more careful. He should never have involved an innocent bystander in his games. It was something he'd told himself before. It was the reason he'd said goodbye to the past, and come here.

It seemed he may have left the job behind, but not the arrogance that went with it.

Now at the top of the hill, Patrick entered the castle courtyard, where he stood looking down on the twinkling lights of Cannes, spread out like a fairytale town below him. This was what visitors recognized as Cannes. Festival city of the Côte d'Azur. Sunshine and blue seas, beautiful views, great food and good wine. All of this was true, but Cannes, like any city, had an underworld. A world the tourists rarely saw. A world of organized crime, made easy by the flow of money from all over Europe, east and west. Cannes offered an opportunity to launder that money, via expensive real estate and luxury yachts and movie making. Patrick suspected that Vasily Chapayev regarded Cannes as more than just a place to launch a movie, and men like Chapayev didn't countenance those who crossed him.

Patrick turned from the view and set off down the steeply cobbled street towards the square of Le Suquet, intending to call in on Fritz for any updates on the missing Leon. Within seconds, he had the distinct feeling that he was being followed. In the hush between the neighbouring buildings, he sensed rather than heard someone. Choosing not to alert his tail, he waited until he reached the Place du Suquet before he looked back.

It was a man of medium height, muscular, dark-haired, and recognizable as the owner of the passport he'd removed from Leon's flat. The man met Patrick's gaze with a look of hatred, then turned and, climbing three stone steps, entered a door on the left-hand side of Rue Panisse, slamming the door shut behind him.

It was most definitely a challenge.

Patrick stood for a moment to consider his response, then retraced his steps. The door was solid wood, three inches thick, a Le Suquet original, probably boasting an internal bolt as well as a lock. He imagined the guy standing behind the door, listening.

'I have your money and passport, Leon. You can't leave Cannes without them.'

There was a moment's silence while Patrick contemplated that he might have got it wrong, then he heard the thud as the bolt was pulled back. He checked on the gun in the back of his waistband as the door swung ajar to reveal a shadowy interior passageway with a narrow staircase.

Leon Aubert stepped into view. He was a good-looking guy. In another time or place he could have been the one starring in the movies. He had the sultry look of a brooding Brando, full of murderous thoughts, all directed at Patrick.

Without a word, Leon shut and re-bolted the door, then motioned Patrick to follow. The narrow spiral staircase led to a landing with only one door. Leon opened it and went inside. Even as Patrick crossed the threshold he sensed it was a mistake. The unseen blow met the back of his head with a ferocity that stunned him. As his body folded, the hard red tiles came up to meet him. He heard a crack as his head hit the floor, then it was lights out.

Sometimes consciousness can be elusive, advancing and retreating like the pain that accompanies it. Patrick strove to open his eyes, recoiling from the brightness of the light. Eventually the room swam into view and with it the memory of how he'd come to be here, trussed up on a chair. It seemed he had found Angele Valette. Or, more precisely, Angele Valette had found him.

She was standing by the shuttered window, smoking. At her feet lay the bloodied iron bar she'd struck him with. Her face as she took a draw had lost its angelic look. The eyes that bore down on him wished him nothing but bad things. At that moment, he felt the same about her.

She spoke in rapid French, full of expletives. She called him a variety of imaginative names for ruining her plans, for pursuing her. Patrick understood now why she was such a good actress. Any character could inhabit that face, any voice or emotion emerge from those lips.

'Where's the money and passport?' she said.

'Hidden on *Les Trois Soeurs*, along with his gun.'

'Bastard.'

Something hard and metallic swiped his temple, whipping his head to the right. Blood trickled into his eye, turning the room a swimming scarlet. Angele's voice rang out, ordering Leon to stop. After a moment's silence she addressed Patrick again, her voice venomous.

'When do the police leave the boat?'

'They haven't said.' He eyed the gun in Leon's hand, recognizing it as his own, rifled from his person, no doubt along with Brigitte's money.

Leon glanced at Angele, who motioned him to step back.

'As soon as the police free the boat, you can have everything back,' Patrick said.

She eyed him suspiciously. 'Who hired you? Chapayev?'

He shook his head, then wished he hadn't as a shaft of pain sliced through it. 'A woman called Camille Ager, who claimed you were her half-sister. She thought you'd stolen the pearl and were in danger.'

Angele gave a brittle little laugh. 'You have been conned, monsieur. This woman you speak of works for Chapayev.'

'Did you steal the pearl?' Patrick asked.

She observed him, her expression inscrutable.

'If you did, then you are in great danger.'

'Perhaps Chapayev is the one in danger,' Leon spat at him.

Patrick eyed the man. Was Leon stupid enough to think he could square up to the Russian and win? The likelihood of this brought a smile to Patrick's lips, provoking another blow from Leon. This time the room swam more energetically, inducing a nausea that brought bile to his throat. He coughed as though about to vomit and Leon jumped back like a frightened rabbit. Which made Patrick think of another rabbit.

'It was you,' Patrick addressed Leon, 'who gutted the rabbit and left it on *Les Trois Soeurs* as a warning.'

Angele looked puzzled. 'What are you talking about?' She glanced at Leon, who shifted uncomfortably.

'Your *boyfriend* thought it clever to try and warn me off with a dead rabbit.' Patrick laughed.

'Hey,' Leon said to Angele, 'you told me . . .'

Angele held up her hand to silence him.

'If that's true, it didn't appear to work,' she said to Patrick.

'I don't scare easily.' Patrick made it sound as though Leon did. 'Chapayev knows that,' he added for good measure.

Angele narrowed her eyes. 'Who are you exactly, Monsieur de Courvoisier?'

Patrick threw Leon a disparaging look before answering. 'A professional.' The words *unlike him* didn't need to be said.

Angele contemplated him for a moment, then ordered Leon to go outside.

He looked wounded. 'What for?'

'Bring wine and coffee.'

'But . . .' he began.

'And leave the gun.' She held out her hand for it.

Leon handed it over reluctantly, shrugging as though he didn't care, but his poisonous look towards Patrick suggested the opposite. A few seconds later, the front door slammed hard enough to shake the building.

Angele opened the shutter a little and looked out. Satisfied that Leon had left to do her bidding, she turned her attention back to Patrick.

'What, as a professional, do you propose?'

Patrick made his move. 'I help you sell the pearl and I dispose of Chapayev. That's the only way you'll be safe.'

'And what's in it for you?'

'Money. And revenge.'

'Revenge for what?'

'The murder of a friend.'

She studied him. 'The woman on the boat?'

'Yes,' he said coldly.

'You believe Chapayev was responsible for her death?'

'She was trying to help me find you.'

That sparked Angele's interest. 'Who was she?'

'Her name was Marie Clermand. She worked for the Hibiscus escort agency as Marie Elise.'

If Leon hadn't managed to discover that, he wasn't much use to her.

Angele's hand fluttered to her mouth and the shock on her face was real enough.

'You knew her?' he asked.

She gave a little nod.

'Marie was seen near my boat with a tall blond Swedish man just before she died,' Patrick said.

A shadow crossed Angele's face, and for a brief moment Patrick saw fear in her eyes.

'You know this man?'

'Maybe. There is someone on Chapayev's payroll who looks like that.' She lit another cigarette and Patrick noticed that her hand was shaking. She took a deep draw before continuing. 'He is a diver. They used him in the underwater scenes.' She exhaled then had another shot of nicotine before she asked, 'How did Marie die?'

'Drowned in the bath.'

She gave an ugly little laugh. 'That sounds like him.' She blew smoke, then turned and stubbed the cigarette out on the window ledge. 'During the filming, Gustafson took offence at a remark I made about his boss. He was in charge of my air supply and chose to remind me of that.'

'He's capable of murder?'

'He's capable of worse than that.' She seemed lost in some terrible thought, which Patrick chose not to intrude upon.

She was behind him now, releasing the binding on his wrists. When he eventually rose to his feet, she handed him his gun. He took it then checked his pockets.

'Leon has the money,' she said.

'How much was in the envelope?'

The question surprised her. 'Ten thousand euros.'

A considerable sum. Madame Lacroix hadn't skimped on her desire to see Marie Elise's killer brought to justice. Rough or otherwise.

'And Lieutenant Moreaux. What part does he play in all this?' he asked.

'I have never heard this man's name before.'

Patrick described the short, dapper and immediately identifiable detective. 'He was being entertained on the *Heavenly Princess* just before Marie was found. He and Chapayev looked like old friends.'

She shook her head. 'I do not think so. Perhaps he was engaged to look for the pearl.' She didn't add 'and me'.

Patrick switched tack. 'What about Polinsky and Gramesci? How much do they know?'

Angele gave a dismissive little 'poof' sound. 'Richard is terrified of Chapayev. He had no idea what he was getting into when he took the Russian's money. He thought, as I did, that the funds were Italian, because of Gramesci's involvement. If the movie doesn't make money, Richard is likely to pay very dearly for it.'

She shrugged. 'Sergio has Mafia connections. Small time, but they may save him. Chapayev understands the power of the Mafia, however far down the chain the connection is.' She lifted the cigarette packet, thought about lighting another. 'Watch out for Conor. He's a real bastard. He'd sell his own child for fame.'

Patrick recalled the character of the kind fisherman who'd found Angele washed up on the beach in *The Black Pearl*.

'I take it Conor wasn't playing himself in the movie?'

'Apart from his desire to have sex with me all the time, no.'

'And the pearl?' he asked.

Angele regarded him with calculating eyes. 'Somewhere safe.'

'Unless Chapayev finds you.'

Patrick expected his remark to frighten her, but there was more anger than fear in her response.

'The meeting I had with Marie Elise in the toilet was more than just coincidence. We knew each other in Paris, before she went to work for Hibiscus.'

Patrick recalled Marie's intensity when she'd spoken of Angele's safety and her concern about Chapayev. Now he understood why.

'You told Marie that night what you were planning?'

She nodded. 'I never thought I was putting her in danger.'

Patrick had no doubt the *Heavenly Princess* was riddled with security equipment, even the washrooms. When Angele disappeared, the recording of her with Marie would have come to light. That was the reason the Swede had wined and dined Marie that night. And probably the reason she was dead.

'Leon will be back soon,' he said. 'We need to agree a plan.'

She nodded and waited for him to go on.

'First, I take you somewhere Chapayev won't find you.'

'What about Leon?'

He could always leave Leon to the Russian's henchman. Then again, the sous chef would talk very easily and knew too much. At that moment they heard the sound of the front door opening. The subject of their conversation was back.

Patrick turned to the door, gun in hand. 'I'll deal with Leon,' he said.

ELEVEN

Two hours later Patrick returned the Ferrari to the safety of the garage and re-entered the courtyard. Seeing him, Oscar raised his head briefly from his sick bed, but didn't come to greet his master. The bulldog had a sorry air about him, as though the drugs had worn off and the pain had returned.

Patrick understood his feelings entirely: his own head was throbbing in unison. He walked over and gently ruffled the dog's ears.

'I know exactly how you feel,' he said.

At the sound of Patrick's voice, Pascal came quickly out of the hotel, muttering, 'The vet will be here soon to give him another shot.' When he saw Patrick's battered face, his mouth dropped open in shock. '*Mon Dieu*. What happened to you?'

'An argument with a woman.' Patrick attempted a smile. Pascal's reaction suggested it made him look even more like a gargoyle. 'I'm going to have a whisky. Would you like to join me?'

Pascal nodded, momentarily lost for words.

Patrick went upstairs to his room, unlocked the door and stood for a moment studying the interior, then decided it looked exactly as he'd left it. The chance of a visitor without Pascal's knowledge was unlikely, but you could never be too sure.

He lifted the whisky bottle from the bedside cabinet, locked the door and headed downstairs again.

Pascal had two tumblers waiting on a table while Oscar had gone back to his pain-ridden slumbers, occasionally emitting a small pitiful whine to remind them how much he suffered.

Patrick poured two good measures, drank his swiftly and replenished the glass. The kick of the spirit, followed by the afterglow, was good enough to repeat. As he tipped in the third measure, Pascal was only just sampling his first.

'I have some painkillers if you need them?' he offered.

Patrick held up the glass. 'This will do the trick.' In truth he was drinking the whisky as much in celebration as for pain. He'd found Angele Valette and would soon be in possession of the pearl. And he had his revenge to look forward to.

Patrick glanced across the table at Pascal, who was giving him a concerned look.

'Have you found out anything about Marie Elise?'

Patrick nodded, but didn't elaborate. The less Pascal knew from now on, the safer he and Preben were.

'Any visitors while I was out?'

Pascal shook his head. 'None.'

Patrick's mobile drilled as he lifted the glass to his lips again. It was Chevalier's name on the screen.

'Chevalier?'

'I'm at the casino. Do you feel lucky?' Chevalier's tone was normal.

Patrick answered in the same manner. 'As a matter of fact, I do.'

He downed his whisky and stood up.

Pascal opened his mouth to ask where he was going, then decided against it. They both glanced over at poor Oscar.

'Look after him for me,' Patrick said.

A short while later, showered and dressed in more suitable attire for an evening at the casino, Patrick set off.

There were four serious casinos in Cannes, suitably spaced out along the Croisette. One at the Majestic, Les Princes at the Carlton, the Palme d'Or and, nearest to Le Suquet, the Casino Croisette, his own and Chevalier's regular haunt.

Passing the Crystal Bar he spotted Sylvie waiting on tables. She looked tired and drawn. He waited for her to approach the bar to place an order, then entered though the side door. When she saw him, she glanced round as though she might run away.

'What do *you* want?' she said sharply.

He placed a hand on her arm. 'Are you OK?' he said.

'I'd be better if you stayed away from me.'

Patrick wondered if she'd spoken to Leon, whether she knew anything about him and Angele. If she did, then she too was in danger.

'Has anyone been in here asking about Leon apart from me?' Patrick said.

'I told you, I have nothing to do with Leon.'

She attempted to free her arm, but Patrick held on. 'Don't speak to anyone,' he warned. 'About Leon, or about me. Even the police. Do you understand?'

She nodded, her eyes wide, and Patrick released her.

Picking up her order she cast him a fearful glance, then headed into the crowded tables.

Composing himself, Patrick exited the bar and moved out of sight. He didn't want to frighten Sylvie, but felt he had no choice. If she had any connection with Leon, she needed to break it now. From Sylvie's initial reaction he deduced that the police hadn't yet visited the Crystal, although they would eventually. It was close enough to the scene of the crime to warrant talking to its staff. With luck, Sylvie would keep her mouth shut when she met Moreaux. But she might just decide to make contact with Leon.

Making his way through the gardens of the Hôtel de Ville, he set a course for the Palais des Festivals. The closer he got to the distinctive building, the denser the crowds became. Two large viewing screens had been erected on either side of the famous red carpet, so that those at the back could see the arrivals. From the excitement of the crowd, it seemed someone really famous had just drawn up in a sleek black limousine.

Patrick veered to the right, out of the swiftly moving throng, and entered the casino's grand foyer, just as screams of delight rang out from the crowd outside. Passing a line of Greek statues, and the huge aquarium in which lurked a beady-eyed shark, Patrick spotted Cleo on duty behind the reception desk.

Newcomers were required to show their passport on entry, but not the casino regulars. Cleo, sufficiently far away not to register the facial bruising, waved Patrick through with a smile.

The main hall with its slot machines was busy, all eyes remaining fixated on the screens as Patrick walked past. It was a type of gambling he thought tedious. Endlessly pressing buttons, lights flashing inanely. No opponent to size up. No intelligence to challenge.

Patrick preferred poker or baccarat, and was skilled at both, although Chevalier was probably the better player. Not that Patrick would ever admit that to him.

He exchanged a substantial sum for chips, pleased that he'd succeeded in removing his cache from *Les Trois Soeurs* before Moreaux had taken over the boat. He'd also persuaded Angele to return half the Lacroix payment. The rest she said he would get when he gave back Leon's money, passport and gun. Patrick trusted Angele about as much as she trusted him, which wasn't a great deal. He might yet tell her that he'd discovered on re-boarding the gunboat that Leon's belongings had been found and confiscated by Moreaux.

Everything depended on whether Angele chose to reveal the whereabouts of the pearl.

With this thought in mind, Patrick checked the various poker rooms until he found Chevalier already seated and at play in room three. Chevalier briefly acknowledged Patrick's arrival, then went back to concentrating on the game. It seemed whatever he wanted to discuss with Patrick would have to wait.

Two hours later and 3000 euros richer from his own poker game, Patrick spotted Chevalier heading for the bar. Retiring from the table, he followed him there. Chevalier ordered a bottle of champagne and two glasses and took himself off to a quiet table, where Patrick joined him.

Chevalier said nothing until the champagne was served and he'd sampled it. Pronouncing it acceptable with a brief nod at the waiter, who then departed, Chevalier turned his gaze on Patrick. A quizzical look indicated he had noted the unhappy state of Patrick's face.

'How was your game?' Chevalier asked.

'Suitably rewarding.'

'I too have been lucky. I sold an expensive property today and have just won five thousand euros. Hence the champagne.'

'I take it Villa Astrid is now in Russian hands?' Patrick said.

'It soon will be.' Chevalier looked pointedly at Patrick's face. 'How did things go after I left?'

'I got the impression your client didn't like me.' Patrick fingered his bruised temple as though it had been Chapayev's work.

'How unfortunate.' Chevalier took a sip of champagne. 'You must have been surprised to find Madamoiselle Ager in our company.'

'A little,' Patrick admitted.

'I invited her. My client desires some changes to be made to the decor and Camille is an excellent interior designer.'

Patrick accepted what he suspected might be a lie.

'How is the search going for her sister?' Chevalier asked.

'I've made some progress.'

Chevalier studied him. 'And Marie Elise?' Having finally raised the subject, his voice broke a little on her name.

'Collateral damage, for which I believe your buyer was responsible.'

There was a moment's angry silence, then Chevalier said, 'For which we will make him pay.'

The Chanteclair lay in darkness. Oscar was nowhere to be seen in the downstairs public room, which suggested he'd been taken in with Pascal for the night. Patrick half-expected the dog to register his arrival with a growl or bark. Oscar's sense of smell and acute hearing were legendary. When the dog didn't make a sound, Patrick put it down to heavy sedation.

Climbing the stairs to the second floor, he opened his own door. Closing and locking it behind him, he lay down on the bed. It had been an eventful day and he needed to assimilate all that had happened. Chevalier's shock at Marie's murder had been palpable, but it still hadn't convinced Patrick to reveal that he'd found Angele.

According to Chevalier, Camille insisted she was now in regular contact with her sister.

'And you believe her?' Patrick had asked.

'No more than you do,' Chevalier had said.

Angele hadn't verified that she had a sister, only that 'the woman' who'd hired Patrick to look for her was in fact in Chapayev's pay.

Patrick rose and opened the shutter. Below him the courtyard, its tables, parasols and plants still lay in shadowy darkness, although a few lights were on in the surrounding buildings.

Cannes would awake soon. In less than two hours the nearby Place de la Misericorde would thrum with the sound of marketeers' vans as the produce from the surrounding farms arrived and was unloaded.

Standing in the silence, Patrick allowed himself a few moments of regret that he hadn't anticipated his opponent well enough to prevent Marie's death, before vowing aloud that Chapayev would pay, in every way possible.

With this murderous thought, he lay down on the bed and was swiftly asleep.

Cannes, unlike Venice, didn't begin each morning with a competing chorus of church bells. That was not to say there weren't any. The magnificent Notre-Dame de l'Espérance that crowned Le Suquet provided the main call to worship for the faithful.

Patrick preferred the bell of the nearby Chapelle de la Misericorde, a modest and ancient building that marked the outer wall of the original Saracen hill town. It was the Chapel of Mercy's call to

·early Mass that woke him, although mercy was far from his mind as he rose to face the day.

His sleep had been deep, his dreams vivid. Sunken bodies had been the chief feature. Marie's face floating just below the surface of the bath water. Angele in the grotto, before she kicked to the surface. He too had featured in the nightmare, struggling for air, the suffocating weight of the sea pressing down on him.

He stood up swiftly and went to shower, ignoring the thought that the dream might be a warning. The plan he'd hatched held danger. But this time the danger would be his alone. He turned the temperature to cold and the sharp prick of the water needles blistered his skin with goosebumps as the blood rose to the surface.

His head clear now of doubt, he emerged and dried himself roughly with the towel. He would be back aboard *Les Trois Soeurs* today. He considered whether he should take Oscar or leave the dog in Pascal's capable hands for the moment.

When he stepped into the courtyard, Oscar rose from his mat and came to greet him. More spritely this morning, he gave his master an affectionate lick and had his ears rubbed.

Pascal threw Patrick a warning glance.

'The vet recommends absolute rest.'

'I'd like to leave him here for the moment, if you're happy to have him?'

'Of course.' Pascal cheered up. 'Breakfast?'

Patrick declined the offer, anticipating an interrogation to accompany the coffee and croissants. He bade Oscar goodbye and sent him back to bed. It was indicative that the dog hadn't fully recovered that he immediately complied.

Pascal shot Patrick a look that said 'I told you so' and went back to serving his guests.

Twenty minutes later, Patrick was steering the Ferrari west along the coastal route, weaving his way through the intervening villages and occasional small towns. By train it took no more than half an hour. By road, it depended on the traffic. August, when the French took their holidays and flocked south, was the worst time for driving Côte d'Azur roads. May was decidedly quieter. His penchant for frequent overtaking and high speeds brought him to the small settlement of Le Dramont as swiftly as the train.

Entering the town, Patrick turned left into the upper car park, which featured a well-cared-for American landing craft, commemorating the landing of 20,000 GIs in August 1944 on the small beach below. Le Dramont was no larger now than it had been back then, consisting mostly of a cluster of villas, built by the artists and writers of La Belle Époque, which dotted the hillside, each surrounded by a wall and high pines.

He'd chosen not to hide Angele in one of the villas, but instead had selected the much less ostentatious surroundings of a beach restaurant with cabins. Jean Paul, who owned the place, was an old friend with a chequered career, not unlike his own. There had been no other guests registered, which suited Patrick, and Jean Paul had been adamant that they expected none until early June.

If Angele had been taken aback by Patrick's choice of hideaway, she hadn't shown it. Patrick had deposited her there, promising to return when his plan had been set in motion.

Having descended the steep hill by the gravel track, he parked alongside the main building, then headed for the kitchen, where Jean Paul was busy at the stove.

He was the cook in this establishment, his English wife Joanne serving the food, with help from students at the height of the season. The aroma of herbs, meat and wine met Patrick on entry and he found his mouth watering in anticipation. Whatever Angele had sampled on the *Heavenly Princess*, here she would sample good Provençal cooking.

Jean Paul looked round on Patrick's entry and answered before he'd managed to pose his question.

'One surprise guest. An English lady. A writer, I believe. Come to admire the Île d'Or.'

Patrick wasn't too happy about that. 'You said there were no bookings.'

'She's harmless and she likes my cooking.'

Patrick observed the stubborn expression and reminded himself Jean Paul was doing him a favour.

'Anyone tries to harm the little lady . . .' Jean Paul made a slice across his throat with the knife currently in his hand.

Jean Paul's grandfather, a famed resistance fighter during WW2, had an alley named after him in Le Suquet. His father had been a member of the French Foreign Legion. Jean Paul, although now a restaurateur, had served in the French army. Patrick reminded himself that Angele was in safe hands.

When he asked where she was, Jean Paul motioned him outside.

Patrick found her sitting at a table on the decking above the beach, gazing out towards the little island that lay offshore. When she turned on his approach, he thought he was mistaken and it was the English lady. Patrick came to a halt, ready to apologize for his intrusion, then realized it was Angele, although only the smile she shot him was recognizable.

Her hair under the wide-brimmed hat was now dark. The heavily made-up face looked older. Even the body had changed shape, appearing thicker, the narrow waist no longer visible, her long slim legs hidden by dark-blue trousers.

'Will I do?' she said in a cut-glass English accent.

'If you don't smile.' Patrick was impressed and told her so.

She regarded him disdainfully. 'I am an actress.'

He took a seat across the table as she turned her eyes back to the island. A craggy outcrop of red rock, it had featured in Hergé's Tin Tin adventure *Île Noire*. In bright May sunshine the stone seemed to glow like fire. Privately owned, it was guarded by a four-storey circular stone tower, the iconic image used on the cover of the book.

'Leon?' she said.

'He's meeting me at the *Les Trois Soeurs* later.'

'And Chapayev?' She spat out the name.

'Progressing.'

He could see this displeased her. She would have to learn patience.

'Revenge is a dish best served cold,' he reminded her.

'Not too cold, I hope.'

She seemed to relax then, the tension in her neck and shoulders dissipating. She flashed him a wide smile. 'I'd like to become Angele for a while. At least while you're here.'

Patrick didn't see a problem with that and told her so. She stood up and held out her hand. Once inside the cabin, she locked the door, then went straight to the bathroom. Patrick heard the shower come on and the sounds of undressing. The louvred shutters were part closed and in the strips of daylight he noticed a bottle of champagne chilling in a bucket.

He poured two glasses, drinking his quickly, then refilling.

When she emerged, she was the mermaid of the film, water trickling between and over her breasts. He handed her a filled glass. She took it in her right hand, and unzipped him with her left. As she ran her tongue round the mouth of the champagne glass, her finger traced the same movement below. Patrick played along, enjoying the anticipation of what she would do next, before he took charge.

Later, he rose and showered the slick sweat from his body. Glancing through the open door, Angele appeared to be asleep, but actress as she was, she could be faking it, just as her passion had seemed rehearsed.

She'd played the part of his lover very well, but it changed nothing. The deal remained. He would have a share of the pearl and his revenge. Leon, Patrick guessed, had been easier prey, his narcissistic nature revelling in the sexual attention Angele had undoubtedly bestowed, although he was still unsure why Angele had chosen Leon as a partner in her enterprise in the first place.

The answer came after dinner, which had consisted of a rich savoury stew eaten outside on the terrace, with a bottle of local red wine. During the meal, Angele continued to play the part of coquette, licking her fingers suggestively, causing Jean Paul to raise an eyebrow as he'd replenished their plates.

Meal over, a glass of brandy before them, Patrick indicated to Jean Paul that he wished to speak to Angele.

Alone now, Patrick studied Angele closely.

'What?' she said, leaning teasingly towards him, her mouth a pretty pout.

Patrick ignored the 'come hither' look.

'It's time to tell me where you hid the pearl.'

Angele sat back, a look of annoyance replacing the pout. 'Kill Chapayev, then I'll tell you.'

Patrick caught her by the wrist. 'You'll tell me now.'

Her glance shifted from his face, to the island and back again, before she revealed Leon's part in the plan.

'I needed Leon to get the pearl back.'

'Whatever you needed Leon for, it is my job now.'

Patrick tightened his grip briefly, then released her.

Angele made a show of rubbing her wrist, contemplated Patrick for a moment, then appeared to come to a decision. 'Leon is a diver.'

Something Patrick had already figured out.

'Luckily, so am I,' he said.

She observed him coolly. 'OK, I'll tell you.'

The incident tape had gone from *Les Trois Soeurs*, and as far as Patrick could tell, there was no longer a police presence on the gunboat. An earlier text from Police Nationale headquarters had indicated they'd finished collecting forensic evidence and that Patrick was free to board.

He opened the hatch and climbed inside.

The normal scents of leather and wood had been overlaid with the stale smell of sweat and chemicals. Patrick stood for a moment surveying the cabin, his sense of violation overpowering.

The old gunboat was the nearest he'd come to a permanent home for some years, and the thought of Moreaux and his gang invading it sickened him. Then he remembered why they'd been there, and went through to the bathroom.

The bath had been drained. A black dusting indicated fingerprint testing on the mahogany surface. A momentary flashback of the place as he'd last viewed it brought a cold sweat to his brow and a stab of anger to his heart.

With that thought in mind he made his phone call.

'I want to speak to Chapayev,' he said in Russian.

'Who is this?' It was the gruff voice of the bodyguard he'd seen talking to Chapayev aboard the yacht, the day he'd swum out there.

'Patrick de Courvoisier. Tell him I know the location of the black pearl.'

Seconds later, Chapayev was on the line.

'Monsieur de Courvoisier. I believe you have my property. Come to the *Heavenly Princess*. We'll talk,' Chapayev said.

'Tonight at ten,' Patrick told him.

A background discussion ensued.

Eventually, Chapayev came back on the line. 'Unfortunately I have a prior engagement.'

Patrick knew exactly what that engagement was. 'That's too bad.' He made as though to hang up.

'My deputy Korskof will be here,' Chapayev offered.

'I only deal with you,' Patrick said firmly.

There was a brief pause, then Chapayev said, 'Come at nine. We'll discuss terms.'

'The terms are two hundred thousand euros.'

There was a grunt at the other end. The price was high. Maybe too high. Natural black pearls of quality were rare, particularly one the size featured in the movie, but they weren't in the same league as other precious stones. Patrick was simply goading the Russian, testing the strength of his desire to retrieve the pearl.

'I'll expect you at nine,' was the terse reply.

Patrick rang off, then went in search of Stephen.

The *Diving Belle* wasn't at her mooring. The advertising board on the *quai* indicated she was on a dive trip and would return around six, which would give Patrick plenty of time to make arrangements before his visit to the *Heavenly Princess*.

Back at *Les Trois Soeurs*, he took up residence on the top deck under the awning and waited for Leon. From here he had an un-interrupted view of the old port and its comings and goings.

The fast-food restaurants were busy, in particular the popular pizza place next to the Police Municipale, where the usual queue had formed outside. Festival-goers had no respect for normal French meal times, such as practised by Le Pistou. Patrick doubted whether they even tasted true French food during their sojourn in Cannes, preferring instead to eat exactly how they did at home.

The Irish bar looked quiet. Its clientele tended to surface late and party into the small hours. A glance seaward established the black outline of the *Heavenly Princess* still anchored in the bay, the water a little choppy from an onshore wind, although not too rough for a dive.

Patrick checked his watch, registering the fact that Leon was late. He wondered if Angele had been in touch with her former lover. How much had Leon been told of what had taken place since their meeting on Rue Panisse?

He suspected Leon would be dispensed with as soon as the pearl was recovered. Once it was back in Angele's possession, Leon would be surplus to requirements. As would he.

It was then the replay happened.

She was walking along the *quai* towards him, but this time she had no need to check the names of the yachts along the way. Camille Ager glanced up, spotting his presence under the awning. Without greeting her, he lowered the walkway. She hesitated for a moment before coming aboard.

'May I speak with you?'

He gestured to the seat beside him.

'In private, please.'

Patrick acquiesced and led her into the cabin.

She looked pale and frightened out of the sun. He said nothing, waiting for her to explain her visit. Eventually she did.

'Angele isn't my sister. Vasily Chapayev made me come to see you.' Her voice faltered.

'Tell me something I don't know,' Patrick countered harshly.

'I wanted to explain why I did what he asked.'

Patrick glanced pointedly at his watch. 'I'm not interested.'

She blanched and sagged. Patrick caught her before she crumpled to the floor, and eased her on to a seat. Her face was so white, he went and poured a brandy. She accepted it gratefully and drank it down.

He was keen for her to leave, but couldn't throw her out until she was at least able to stand. Despite his reaction, he was curious as to why she'd chosen to work for Chapayev, although whether she would tell the truth was another matter.

She regarded the empty glass as though wishing for more, so he took it and poured another shot. She grimaced as she swallowed it, but it brought colour to her cheeks.

'I owe him a great deal of money. He gave me a choice. The lesser evil was to come here and pretend to be looking for my sister. I had no idea it would lead to . . . all this.' She ground to a halt.

'You mean Marie's murder,' Patrick said sharply.

The colour drained from her face again, then she appeared to steel herself.

'I'm so very sorry about that.'

He ignored the expression of sympathy. 'How much do you owe him?'

Her answer was a whisper. 'Almost half a million euros.'

Patrick drew breath. It was a hell of an amount, by any standards.

'He financed the shop in Rue d'Antibes. The interest payments are very high.' She hesitated as though unsure whether to say more. 'There was a problem in sourcing the diamonds at one point and he stepped in to help.'

Now this was news.

'Chapayev supplied you with diamonds?' Patrick repeated to be sure.

Camille nodded.

'And where does Chapayev source these diamonds from?'

She looked embarrassed. 'I don't know.'

Patrick gave a grim smile, as at least part of the puzzle became clearer.

His best guess was that Chapayev was smuggling the diamonds into Europe, probably from North Africa, possibly via his yacht, and laundering them through an independent jeweller's shop on Cannes's high-class Rue d'Antibes. No wonder the Russian wanted to buy the Villa Astrid. He obviously required a suitable base in Cannes to carry on the good work.

The Kimberley Process had resulted in helping to stem the flow of blood diamonds from conflict zones, but there were plenty of places where it didn't apply, the most recent being the Marange fields of Mugabe's Zimbabwe.

Patrick cast his mind back to his visit to Chapayev's dinner party. There had been a tall distinguished black gentleman there. He'd been speaking French, but with an African accent.

It was all beginning to add up.

He wondered if Lieutenant Moreaux knew anything about the Russian's diamond deals and whether he was choosing to turn a blind eye, which might explain his being entertained on board the *Heavenly Princess*.

At that point there was a noise like someone landing on the deck. Seized by fear, Camille dropped the glass. It met the table and shattered like ice on the hard surface.

Patrick motioned her to silence and, checking for his gun, went to take a look.

Leon was upright, but only just. His face looked as though it had been put through a meat grinder. Pummeled and bloody, he staggered towards Patrick as a big black limo took off with screeching tyres along the *quai*. There was no one visible behind the smoked-glass windows.

Patrick caught Leon as he fell. Through his bloodied mouth, he made out the strangled words: 'They know where the pearl is.'

Patrick half-carried Leon down the steps and into the main cabin, where he laid him on the leather couch. Patrick did a quick body check. Experience told him Leon had a couple of broken ribs and a broken nose. Plus he'd lost a few teeth. His life wasn't in danger, but Patrick still asked him if he wanted an ambulance.

There was no doubt by the painful shake of his head that he definitely didn't. As for the police, Patrick didn't mention them. He set about patching Leon up, giving Camille instructions when he needed help. He swiftly realigned the nose and applied ice to the facial bruising, then stripped Leon's shirt off and took a closer look at his body. Patrick had been beaten enough himself to know what they would have done to extract the information they wanted.

Pulling down the bloodied trousers exposed the worst of the damage. It seemed Leon valued his manhood more than his good looks. The cigarette burns on his scrotum were various but superficial. Patrick had a more than adequate medical kit. He did what he had to, then covered Leon up and administered a strong sedative and painkiller.

Within a short period of time, Leon was out.

During all of this, Camille had remained calm, although her underlying terror was plain to see. Patrick knew what she was thinking. If whoever had beaten Leon and tossed him on the *quai* had known she was aboard *Les Trois Soeurs*, she might well face the same fate.

Patrick didn't mention what Leon had said about the pearl. There was still a chance Chapayev had sent Camille here with a sob story to try and extract the information they'd tortured Leon for.

'Go home,' he told her.

'What about Chapayev?'

'He offered you two choices. Maybe it's time to take the other one.' It was a cruel remark and he meant it. Camille had been the one to forge a financial alliance with Chapayev. Greed was at the heart of her troubles. Patrick had one goal and one only: to make Chapayev pay for what he had done to Marie Elise.

She left without argument. As soon as she disappeared from sight, Patrick made the phone call. Chapayev answered almost immediately. The supercilious way he said 'Courvoisier' only incensed Patrick further.

'Leon doesn't know the location of the diamonds, whatever he told you.'

There was a sharp intake of breath. 'Diamonds?' Chapayev strove to sound puzzled. 'I am looking for my pearl.'

There followed a rapid background exchange in Russian, from which Patrick translated 'the bastard knows'. It had been a shot in the dark, arising from his conversation with Camille, but it had been right on target. And it went a long way to explaining what the hell had being going on here.

'Any information Leon gave you when you burned his balls, it won't lead you to the stones.'

Patrick heard the background sounds of someone entering the room, then a rapid burst of angry conversation in Swedish. It was easy enough to work out what had happened. Sometime between torturing Leon and dumping him at *Les Trois Soeurs*, a dive had taken place. One that had not produced the result Chapayev had expected. Whatever Angele had given Leon to hide underwater, it hadn't been a bag of diamonds – or, Patrick suspected, the black pearl.

'Leon doesn't know where they are, but I do, because Angele told me.'

A short icy silence followed Patrick's declaration.

'What are your terms?' Chapayev barked in Russian.

'Tell the Swede to be prepared for a night dive. I'll be in touch.'

Patrick ended the call and switched off the phone, then fetched one of the other two mobiles and called Brigitte.

Cutting short the discreet opening she used on prospective clients, he said, 'It's Courvoisier. I need you to contact Camille Ager.' He gave her the number. 'Tell her I said she has to stay with you tonight. Tell her it's for her own safety.'

He was impressed when Brigitte didn't attempt to interrogate him as to who this woman was and why she should choose to give her protection. Brigitte simply repeated the number Patrick had given her, then hung up.

His next call was to Jean Paul, who confirmed that the English lady was currently in their kitchen chatting to his wife. Patrick, speaking in Cannois, used the code words they'd decided on, and Jean Paul replied that the hotel was shut until June, before ringing off to the background sound of female laughter.

Satisfied that Angele had the best bodyguard available and was not party to his plans, Patrick undressed and, steeling himself, went into the bathroom. He turned on the water and cleansed the bath of fingerprint powder before stepping in and showering as quickly as possible.

Before dressing, he called Stephen.

'I need you to do me a favour,' he said.

TWELVE

There was a party in full swing on Le Pantiero. A huge striped awning resembling an open-sided circus tent had been raised in case of May showers, although the sky was clear and bright with stars. Beneath it, beautiful people mingled in a flurry of scent, haute couture, champagne, live music and loud chatter. Beyond, in the bay, a thousand lights twinkled from anchored yachts, no doubt their revellers similarly occupied.

Cannes was doing what it did best. Having a party.

Patrick slipped through the side gate to the fisherman's section. The contrast here with the glitzy goings on nearby couldn't be starker. François sat under his faded awning, a glass of rosé and a battered tin plate piled high with *fruits de mer* on an upturned crate close by. He glanced up as Patrick appeared and only an amused glint in his dark eye acknowledged Patrick's immaculate tuxedo.

Their conversation lasted twenty minutes. François listened carefully to the details of Patrick's proposal, thought about it, then nodded. They arranged a time and Patrick left. Walking along the Allées de la Liberté Charles de Gaulle, he took stock of the plan. If he managed to pull it off, it would accomplish exactly what he wanted. Retribution for all concerned in Marie's death.

If not . . .

Across the road, under the shade of the early leaves of the plane trees, he caught sight of the carousel. It was in motion, twirling children smiling out excitedly at their parents. He had a sudden memory of Marie's tall figure passing that spot after they'd eaten crêpes together; of her laughing and wiping the chocolate from her mouth.

As he'd watched her disappear from view that night, he knew he would ask to see her again.

Something lost to him now.

Patrick slipped his hand in his pocket and checked for his wallet. Combining his own resources with the advances from Camille and Brigitte, plus Leon's money, had given him a high enough stake to set the wheels in motion. All that remained was Chevalier's support.

The casino was busy and a queue of casual visitors who required their identities checked had formed at the desk. Patrick nodded at the doorman and headed straight through. This time he avoided the lower hall, busy with the digital sounds associated with mind-numbing slot machines. An eruption of raucous cheers suggested gold had been struck in there somewhere, but he paid it no heed, instead making his way immediately to the lift.

The upper floor was hushed and decidedly more luxurious. As Patrick entered the bar he heard the beat of blades as a helicopter landed on the helipad. Double glass doors led to a roof garden, and through them he saw the manicured palm trees wave in the resulting breeze.

He ordered a bottle of chilled champagne and took himself out of sight of anyone entering from the helipad. Ten minutes from now, the game would begin. He raised a silent toast to Marie Elise then headed for the *salle privée*, his eyes bright with anticipation.

The chef de partie greeted him on arrival and removed the silken cord to let him through. The kidney-shaped table had ten places set, some of which were already occupied.

Patrick took a quick glance round his fellow participants.

Seat two was occupied by a young American male chatting intimately to a beautiful woman twice his age in the neighbouring place. Patrick thought the woman was the gambler and the man merely arm candy.

Seat five contained a distinguished grey-haired man wearing a crested pinkie ring on his left hand. An aristocrat, probably British, Patrick decided. At that point a short, plump, dark-haired man arrived, Italian by the brief exchange of words with the chef de partie. He took up his place at seat seven.

Patrick handed the croupier a blank card with the numbers 3, 5, 7, 8, 9 and 10 on it. The croupier nodded and set about filling the list before handing the card back to Patrick.

As his glass was refilled Patrick studied the names of his fellow players, only one of whom he recognized:

3 Anita Chevron-Barclay
5 Lord Rubert Osbourne
7 Severino Cassiopeia
8 Alexa Queen
9 and 10 Mr and Mrs Anthony Rogers.

As he scanned the card, Vasily Chapayev arrived and took his reserved place at seat six, directly opposite the seat which would be occupied by the banker. Patrick kept his glance averted while Chapayev squashed his ample girth into the chair. As Patrick raised his head intending to reveal his presence, his thunder was stolen by the arrival of the New York actress Alexa Queen, in a flurry of scent and silk.

She ran her beautiful eyes round the table, then settled her gaze on Patrick as she made her introduction, obviously expecting to be recognized. This wasn't surprising since her face had been looking down from every billboard on the Croisette, and her film was short-listed for the Palme d'Or. As she settled herself, Mr and Mrs Rogers arrived in a much less pretentious manner and nervously took their seats, suggesting this was a new experience for them.

Chapayev had spotted Patrick's presence by now and was eyeing him malevolently across the table. Patrick raised his champagne glass in salutation. At that point the banker walked in.

Le Chevalier welcomed the assembled company in French, English, Russian and Italian, even adopting a New York accent for Miss Queen, causing amused smiles from everyone, apart from Chapayev, who looked uneasy. Clearly, he had been surprised by Patrick's presence, but even more so by Chevalier settling himself in the banker's chair.

It had been a stroke of genius for Chevalier to come up with this part of the plan.

Apparently, he had bought the bank for the game from a Libyan syndicate, who were busy gambling oil money they'd spirited away in advance of the fall of the Gaddafi regime. Ironically, he had done so aided by the profit made on the sale of Villa Astrid. A substantial sum, he had informed Patrick, which he had every intention of increasing at Chapayev's expense.

Chevalier was a serious gambler and a very good one. But no one was foolproof, and at Baccarat the odds against the banker and player were more or less even.

Chevalier cut the shuffled cards, the croupier fitted the six packs into the metal and wooden shoe and announced the game was about to begin. The bank was declared at 10,000 euros, which caused a little consternation from some of the prospective players.

Chevalier patted the fat pile of plaques in front of him and pronounced the bank ready. In position one, Patrick was required to start play. He received his first card, then Chevalier his. This was then repeated.

Patrick took time examining his two cards, his face suitably impassive. In Baccarat, court cards and tens counted for nothing, an ace as one. When added together only the last figure counted. He had drawn an eight and a nine, which meant together he had seventeen, but only the seven counted. Since the aim was to get closest to nine, the preferred option would be for Patrick to stand. He could of course take one more card and hope it was a ten, two or three, but that would be chancing his luck.

The pulse in his temple beating rapidly, Patrick indicated he didn't want another card.

From this, Chevalier would now know the range of his cards. He would expect Patrick to hold a five, six or a seven. To be certain of winning, Chevalier would have to reveal an eight or a nine.

Chevalier examined his cards. A consummate gambler, there was no way of knowing what he held by his expression. He turned the cards with a snap. Two fours. Chevalier had won.

'*Huit à la banque*,' the croupier declared. '*Et le sept*.' He unceremoniously raked in Patrick's losing cards and slipped them through the metal slot leading to the canister.

A quick glance at Chapayev revealed his delight at Patrick's loss. Chevalier had already pushed forward the bank's plaques, which had been raised to 50,000 euros. Patrick declared *suivi*, exercising his right to follow up his lost bet, and added his to the pile.

'*Un banco de cent mille*,' declared the croupier with no hint of emotion.

Patrick was no luckier the second time. To a three and a two, he added a useless ten. Chevalier scooped him with a nine and a court card.

By now Chapayev's pleasure could not be concealed. His beady eyes glistened with joy.

Chevalier doubled the stakes. The rest of the table remained silent, eyeing one another, awaiting who might be brave enough to take up the challenge.

The Russian ran his glance round the assembled group, assessing their reluctance. For a moment Lord Osbourne seemed tempted, then wilted somewhat under Chapayev's look. The Russian finally fastened on Patrick.

'*Banco*,' he said, challenging him.

It was at this point the bodyguard appeared opposite Patrick. He must have been lingering among the interested spectators hovering outside the playing area. From the quick glance he exchanged with the croupier, Patrick briefly wondered if an attempt had been made to bribe him, then decided not. Chevalier knew all the croupiers by name, and by much more besides. If Chevalier wasn't concerned about the cards being doctored, then neither should he be.

Chapayev was waiting to see if Patrick would rise to his bait. When he didn't, the Russian gave a curt nod and was dealt his cards. After a quick glance at them, he flipped them over with a flourish, to expose a clear nine.

There was a combined gasp from the assembled company and Alexa let slip an expletive that betrayed her Bronx origins.

Next to Patrick, Ray Silver gave an exasperated little noise as though he had really intended taking up the challenge and been prevented somehow from doing so. He whispered something in his paramour's ear. Her expression remained blank, but her hungry eyes said it all, just like everyone else's around that table. *If only I had taken the chance.*

Patrick drained his champagne, glanced at his watch and stood up, excusing himself in a slightly embarrassed fashion, as though his funds were insufficient, or his nerve had gone. Neither Chapayev nor Chevalier paid his departure any heed. Only Alexa seemed disappointed. She caught his eye, looking for an excuse to go with him. When none was forthcoming, she pouted and turned her attention back to the game.

Patrick weaved his way through the gathered throng, feeling Korskof's eyes on his back, guessing the bodyguard would have preferred to follow him, but couldn't, without a direct order from Chapayev.

Which suited Patrick just fine.

He swiftly exited the casino and headed along the busy thoroughfare to the old port. It was up to Chevalier now what happened in the casino. Patrick had other fish to fry.

THIRTEEN

The car was parked alongside *Les Trois Soeurs* just as he'd requested. Stephen was sitting on deck, a pint of Guinness in front of him. There was no sign of Colm. Patrick checked the trunk and was pleased to see his orders had been carried out in full.

Stephen bestowed a large grin on Patrick as he approached.

'Himself is still out for the count. What the hell did you give him?'

Patrick didn't answer. Just said thanks and went below.

Leon lay where he'd left him, face to one side, drool running from his part-open mouth. He wasn't a pretty sight, but judging by his pulse he was alive.

As he re-emerged, Stephen downed the last of his Guinness and stood up.

'Where are we headed then?'

Patrick regarded his eager face. 'I want you to stay here.'

'You need a buddy on a night dive. What if—'

Patrick cut him off. 'I have one.' He observed the Irishman's hurt expression, but didn't change his own. 'Lock up and bunk down when you're ready.'

'When will you be back?'

Patrick shrugged. He had no idea when, or even if he would return.

The texture of the Mediterranean changed at twilight, becoming limpid, as reflections from the strong sun died away and the breeze dropped. He loved night dives, even when on a job. No matter how many he did there was always a ripple of excitement and anticipation. Tonight more than ever.

The coast road was quiet, the headlights like underwater torch beams in the darkness. Above, stars glittered in a blackened sky. In the open-topped car Patrick breathed in the sharpness of Mediterranean pine and the even stronger fragrances of scent-laden gardens.

The car park was empty, the beach below a ribbon of white sand, fringed with green. Moonlight played on the water between the shore and the red rock of the island. The surrounding sounds of small insistent swishes as each fragile wave broke.

This must have been how it had been when the Allies arrived in 1944. Frightened young Americans who had never been outside their small Midwest towns, who had never seen an ocean, suddenly wading ashore on a foreign beach into Europe's war.

Patrick at least knew what he was risking his life for.

Minus headlights, he eased his way down the gravel road towards the restaurant and parked behind the main building, well out of sight of prying eyes. The only light was on in the kitchen. Angele's cabin was in darkness. She was either asleep or still chatting with Joanne. Either way was good.

He carried his gear to shore and kitted up by moonlight. He'd made the call before he left Cannes. The Swede knew where the booty was. He need only retrieve it.

Patrick watched as the inflatable from the *Heavenly Princess* appeared from behind the Île d'Or. The skipper would line up via three onshore landmarks, the restaurant probably being one. There was only one point at sea where three objects were in the same position relative to one another. A good skipper didn't need a GPS reading to guide his boat to the spot Patrick had given.

Soon he heard the engine cut out and the plop as the anchor dropped.

They were there.

Patrick walked into the water west of the island and was soon submerged. He knew exactly where he wanted to be. He was familiar with the varying depths of water. He was clear where he'd instructed François to drop his line.

Patrick glanced at his wrist computer, checking the depth. Everything depended on whether the Swede dived alone (Patrick was certain he would) and how clearly he would follow the directions.

Turning on his torch, Patrick illuminated a bright circle in the darkness. Below him, ripples in the sand ran parallel to shore. He allowed himself a sweet moment of anticipation, before kicking off towards his goal.

Gradually, creatures of the night appeared. The ones that lurked in dark holes and crevices during the day now hunted for those asleep in their nests and burrows. Below were what François sought for the restaurants of Cannes – lobsters and crabs moving as in a dance. A rare ray fish glided past, skimming the sand, smelling prey buried beneath. Patrick's movement disturbed water around the western outcrop of the island, resulting in a firework display of phosphorescent creatures, instantaneously lighting up the sea, to disappear just as quickly.

He switched off his torch and was instantly plunged into a suffocating darkness.

After a few moments he saw the circle of light that was the Swede's beam. Only one, which meant he was diving alone. Patrick smiled, remembering Stephen's scorn when he spoke of the diver they'd used in the shooting of *The Black Pearl*. How he had required the onboard decompression chamber.

It seemed Gustafson, like Patrick, took chances.

He watched from behind a rock as the Swede approached. His beam eventually focused on the sunken village, centring on the miniature church, its tall steeple long gone, removed by divers as a souvenir. Patrick watched as the Swede finned towards it, hand already outstretched for the bag the steeple contained.

Centimetres from his prize, he came to a sudden and abrupt halt.

Thin taut fishing lines were the curse of the diver, especially at night. Unseen in the torch beam, they caught on your equipment, anchoring you. Gustafson was finning but suddenly going nowhere. Turning, he tried to see what held him, his torch dancing wildly in the darkness. Twisting had been a mistake. Realizing this, he turned back, but by now the line was caught round his cylinder.

He tried to free himself, a little more frantically this time, but only succeeded in making things worse. A buddy would have realized by now that something was wrong. A buddy would have come back to cut the line and free him.

But the Swede had no buddy.

Patrick watched as the panic built up. The struggle as Gustafson flailed and twisted the dropped torch, the regulator torn from his mouth as he breathed in a foamy mixture of seawater and air. Gustafson's hands scrabbled to find his second regulator, which, like the other, floated free in the darkness.

Patrick switched on his own torch and the Swede swivelled desperately towards the light. For a moment his eyes held hope, until Patrick removed his own regulator and mouthed the words, 'For Marie Elise.'

It was over in seconds.

Patrick replaced his regulator and finned towards the inert body and took a closer look to make certain. Then he turned and finned swiftly away.

When he'd accomplished his final task, Patrick headed for shore, where he changed back into the tuxedo behind the restaurant, then headed for the car.

The drive back to Cannes was as fast as it was invigorating. Screeching into the underground car park by the casino, he entered by a side door. In the upstairs bar he ordered a bottle of champagne, then chose a poker table in full view of anyone emerging from the Baccarat room. Bolstered by adrenaline, he played well enough to make back most of what he had lost earlier.

Forty-five minutes later, the door opened and Chapayev and Korskof appeared. Korskof, like a good bodyguard, noted his presence. Patrick, engrossed in his game, pretended not to see him.

Chevalier followed ten minutes later. Patrick acknowledged him with a small nod, gathered his winnings and excused himself from the table. They both adjourned to the bar, where Patrick ordered more champagne.

Chevalier looked tired, but content. He accepted the glass of champagne gratefully. Examining Patrick's expression, he appeared to find there what he sought.

They touched glasses.

'For Marie Elise,' Chevalier said. 'May she now rest in peace.'

FOURTEEN

I t had been a long night, but Patrick had no intention of sleeping. Not yet. Parting from Chevalier, he walked towards Rue d'Antibes and Madame Lacroix.

Shuttered shops lined the empty street. His footsteps echoed from the metal shutters like jackboots. The Nazis had loved Cannes. The sun, the food, the sea. They'd used it for recreation, for wine, for sex. Just as the rich like Chapayev did now.

The inhabitants of Cannes had survived invaders before and would do so again. It would give those with money what they wanted, and use the payment to prosper. Patrick had a great admiration for the town's survival instinct. It matched his own.

The window overlooking the street was in darkness, but he suspected, tonight of all nights, Brigitte would answer the door. He pressed the bell and waited, hearing it echo in the cavernous marble entrance hall and stairwell.

Brigitte's voice in response sounded thick with smoking, and not a little anxious.

'Courvoisier,' he said.

There was a moment's hesitation, then she buzzed him in.

Patrick ignored the lift and took to the stairs. Something made him pause on the halfway landing. A scent? An instinct? He didn't know. He slipped the gun out of his waistband.

Brigitte was waiting for him at the open door, looking tired and worried.

'Everything OK?' he said quietly.

'She's gone.' Brigitte opened the door wide for him to enter.

Following her through, Patrick glanced round the empty room.

'What happened?'

'He got in. I'm not sure how. Maybe she let him. Anyway, she went with him.'

'Went with who?' Patrick said.

'He was Russian, big, very big.' Brigitte gave a description that matched Korskof.

Patrick was dumb-founded. How the hell had Chapayev found out where Camille was?

'Did Camille make any phone calls while she was here?' he asked.

Brigitte shook her head. 'I have no idea. I showed her to her room, then went back to mine. Later, I heard a noise and came through to find him here.' She shuddered at the memory. 'I asked her not to go, but she ignored me.'

Patrick stood for a moment, assimilating this news. Camille had taken his advice and come here. He remembered her terror when she'd viewed what Chapayev had done to Leon. Why would she willingly go with Korskof?

'You're sure he wasn't holding a gun on her?'

Brigitte raised her shoulders. 'If so, it wasn't visible.'

The woman was trembling. Patrick took her arm and urged her to sit.

'They must have followed her from the gunboat,' he said.

Brigitte looked distraught.

'Can I get you a brandy?'

She shook her head and found a cigarette pack on a nearby table. Fumbling it open, she extracted one and lit it.

'I've been trying to call you since it happened.' Her hand shook as she raised the cheroot to her lips.

'I'm sorry.' Patrick sat down beside her, waiting while she took her first draw. As she exhaled, he told her why he was here. 'Marie Elise has been avenged.'

Brigitte met his steady gaze, and for a moment he saw pleasure in her eyes.

'And what of this girl, monsieur? What is to happen to her?'

Patrick had no idea, but he said what he hoped was true. 'She works for Chapayev. I think they want to speak to her, not kill her.'

'I hope so.' Brigitte blew out a cloud of smoke.

'When I leave, call Moreaux,' Patrick told her. 'Tell him you had a visitor in the shape of a Russian. Tell him about Camille and that you are worried for her safety.'

Brigitte was surprised by his suggestion. 'Is that wise?'

Patrick nodded. 'Just don't mention me. Say Camille called you and asked to stay over, because she was afraid of someone. Naturally you agreed, after what had happened to Marie. Explain that a Russian man arrived and persuaded Camille to go with him. You're not totally sure it was of her own free will. Lieutenant Moreaux will be forced to investigate.'

A little colour had come back into her cheeks. 'OK.'

He stood up. 'I'll say goodbye then.'

'I take it you won't be needing the services of Hibiscus again?'

'You've done enough. Leave it to Moreaux now.'

She rose to see him out, her back steely straight once more. Korskof had unnerved but not defeated Madame Lacroix.

He retraced his steps through the empty streets. It would soon be dawn. He dispensed with his original plan to catch some sleep at the Chanteclair and headed back to the garage.

It was only a matter of hours since he'd driven this road, yet so much had happened. He wondered what Chapayev was doing, thinking and planning. He'd been beaten at the gaming tables by Chevalier, taken for a fool over the diamonds, and lost his diver. He would be well past anger. Revenge would be foremost in his mind. That and retrieving his goods.

As he took the bend at full speed in the middle of the empty road, Patrick could imagine the Russian's hatred. Most of it now focused on him, he hoped. He had purposefully deflected it from Angele, but may have inadvertently steered it towards Camille. Her turning up at *Les Trois Soeurs* had been unforeseen and unfortunate, because he still wasn't sure which side she was on. He had chosen to believe her fear and sent her to Brigitte. If she hadn't been afraid, why go there in the first place? To fool him? Or to hide from Chapayev?

He entered Le Dramont and slowed down. Instead of driving directly to the restaurant, he headed left into the criss-crossing of villas, having no desire to alert Jean Paul or Angele to his visit. His headlamps off, he used the security lights of the villas and the faint rays of dawn to light his way, eventually reaching a small rocky cove east of the Île d'Or.

A path from here wound its way around the headland, sometimes high above the water, at other places close to the shore. The final stretch lay along the beach in front of a small camp site and from there into the grounds of the restaurant.

Pleased to find the door to Angele's cabin locked, he headed round the back, and retrieved the extra key he'd planted beneath a stone. As he retraced his steps, a figure appeared from nowhere, propelling him to the ground with a thud that forced the air from his lungs. As he threw himself to the right, his attacker landed beside him. In a parallel motion, his gun and Jean Paul's knife met each other's chests, their eyes locked in combat.

'*Putain!*' Patrick spoke in relief as much as anger.

Jean Paul's list of expletives was more extensive. He finished them off by calling Patrick a '*Salope*' and pronouncing that he might have killed him.

Patrick slipped his gun back in his waistband. 'That's why I gave her to you to protect.'

They observed one another, anger and adrenaline still bristling their looks.

'Anyone apart from me?'

'No,' confirmed Jean Paul.

'Good. I'll come see you later.'

Dismissed, Jean Paul disappeared as quickly as he'd arrived.

Patrick slid the key in the lock and went inside. The fracas had apparently gone unnoticed by Angele, who lay fast asleep, the cover thrown back, the curve of her full breasts and slender body exposed. Patrick contemplated her for a moment, then taking off his clothes, slipped in beside her. As she started into wakefulness, he pressed his lips on hers to silence her cry.

He hadn't intended to fall asleep afterwards, but the night dive, the champagne and the extended poker game had taken their toll. When he awoke two hours later, Angele was already up and dressed.

'Jean Paul has ordered us to come to the kitchen. He says you'll be hungry.'

Jean Paul was right. Having satisfied a need for sex and sleep, hunger was next in line. Patrick told Angele to go on ahead, took a sixty-second shower and dressed.

On entry, Patrick smelled coffee and much more besides. A freshly baked baguette sat on the table, still warm to the touch. The French never indulged in a cooked breakfast. *Le petit dejeuner* meant what it said. Appetite was reserved for lunch.

In this instance Jean Paul had made an exception, depositing a plate in front of Patrick that would have happily graced a British breakfast table. Eggs, bacon, *saucisse de Toulouse*, mushrooms, tomatoes and an added steak for good measure. Angele appraised the offering and decided she would prefer her breakfast French style. Patrick got stuck in.

He had no idea how ravenous he'd been, until he'd cleared the plate.

Jean Paul, well satisfied, poured him a coffee. Patrick sat back, content. A glance at Angele suggested she wished to talk in private, so he motioned her to take their coffee outside.

It was one of those mornings on the Côte d'Azur that convinces you that heaven exists. The sun shone from an unblemished sky. A slight breeze intermittently ruffled the Mediterranean pines that surrounded the bay, releasing their scent. The sea glistened with joy.

And Marie Elise's killer had met his end.

Patrick did not relish death, but in this case he made an exception.

Angele was studying him. 'Where did you go last night?'

'The casino, where I arranged for Chapayev to lose a large sum of money.'

'But he is still alive?' she snapped at him.

'Yes, and in much better health than Leon.'

'What do you mean?' she asked suspiciously.

Patrick drank some coffee to keep her waiting. 'Chapayev deposited Leon at *Les Trois Soeurs* last night. Poor bastard won't be having sex for a while.'

A number of emotions crossed Angele's face, but sympathy wasn't one of them. She swore under her breath. 'I knew I couldn't trust him,' she said.

'So you had him hide what, exactly?'

She shrugged. 'A worthless necklace I left there during the filming.'

'So what's in the location you gave me?' he said as though he didn't know.

She was trying to read his expression and having difficulty. She decided to go back to what she did best. Patrick felt her foot nestle in his groin and begin to rub it. He let it stay there for a moment, then pushed his chair back. Her foot dropped heavily to the ground. She drew it back and, rubbing her ankle, eyed him cautiously.

'You gave me the location of the pearl, but not the diamonds,' he said.

Angele's shock at his announcement was evident, before she swiftly recovered. 'Diamonds!' she gave a 'poof' sound. 'What diamonds?' She had resorted to French in her desire to appear truthful.

Patrick interrupted her 'I don't know anything about diamonds' speech.

'Chapayev wants the stones back and is prepared to kill to get them. Leon is lucky to be alive. As are you.' *As am I*, he thought, but didn't say.

Patrick realized by her expression that she wasn't yet prepared to talk about any diamonds, so he extracted the black pearl from his pocket and laid it on the table in front of her. She immediately scooped it up, a covetous smile on her face.

Glancing out to sea, Patrick registered that Stephen's boat had arrived and dropped anchor west of the Île d'Or. On deck, a group of divers were already gearing up. If Chapayev hadn't retrieved the Swede's body by now, someone else was about to.

He contemplated calling Stephen, but decided against it. He'd asked him to take his group there this morning, without giving him a reason, aware that the less Stephen knew the better.

Angele had followed his gaze. 'What's going on?' she said, her eyes bright with interest.

'Someone's about to find hidden treasure.'

Half an hour later, the police launch arrived, suggesting Chapayev hadn't removed the body during the night. Maybe he was confident the Swede couldn't be traced back to the *Heavenly Princess*. Or he intended denying knowledge of the night dive. Alternatively, he believed he already had Lieutenant Moreaux in his pocket.

That particular thought disturbed Patrick. He didn't like Moreaux, but the lieutenant had his moral code, much like himself, and being subject to the whim of the Russian didn't fit with that. Moreaux was self-serving, but he was Cannois.

Angele watched fascinated as the body was brought up. 'Who is it?' she said excitedly.

Patrick shook his head. It was better she didn't know.

'So,' he said. 'If you want me to rid you of Chapayev, I need to know where the diamonds are.'

Seeing a body rise from the deep had given her confidence in him, but she wasn't sure yet.

'If I tell you, how do I know you won't double-cross me?'

'You don't. You'll just have to trust me.'

Trust wasn't a concept Angele was familiar with, or else she'd tried it and it had backfired badly. She contemplated this. 'How will you sell the diamonds?'

'I have my contacts.'

She rose and went inside, returning with a bottle of wine and two glasses.

Patrick accepted a glass, and she clinked hers to his.

'To freedom from Chapayev.'

Patrick could toast to that.

She drank hers down, and then she told him.

FIFTEEN

Moreaux's call came as he drove back from Le Dramont. Patrick had been expecting it. They would be in this together, despite their differences. He and Moreaux. It seemed inevitable, although Patrick would have wished it differently.

Moreaux's voice resembled Brigitte's, thick with cigarette smoke.

'Brigitte called.' He laid an emphasis on the 'g' and made it almost guttural, like a German might. Moreaux sounded upset, if such a thing were possible.

Patrick wondered if he'd been wrong and what lay between Moreaux and Brigitte was more than just sex.

'We need to talk,' Patrick said.

There was a moment when Moreaux evaluated the offer. 'Yes,' he conceded.

'Tonight,' Patrick said. 'La Castre.'

Le Suquet would be up at the castle courtyard en masse, celebrating the end of the film festival. There would be bands and local wine and several hundred inhabitants, young and old and all ages in between. The courtyard at La Castre was where every Le Suquet celebration took place and tonight was no exception.

Festival yachts and local boats of all sizes would sail into the old port, or anchor in the bay, to watch the festival finale firework display. Cannes would celebrate its place in world cinema. Hollywood would be there. The *Heavenly Princess* would be there too. It was a perfect time and place for the game to come to its conclusion.

Patrick continued before Moreaux could voice an opinion. 'The fireworks begin at ten. I'll meet you in the church at nine thirty.'

Moreaux didn't answer immediately, but Patrick could almost hear his brain go into overdrive.

'I'll be there,' Moreaux said finally, then rang off.

You and who else, Patrick thought as he drove the Ferrari like a red bullet through the intervening towns. The situation was delicate. Success would mean justice of a kind. Failure might mean death. He thought of Angele's empty kisses and fake passion. He thought of Marie Elise's genuine smile, smeared by chocolate and the cold lips that smile had become.

When he entered Cannes, he was met with evidence of its preparations for that evening. Entrance via the shore road was restricted. Boulevard Jean Hibert was set to close shortly and become a parking space from which to view tonight's firework display. He cut up through Le Suquet and was lucky to find a spot on Rue Louis Perissol. He would require the car later and was unlikely to escape Cannes via the normal route. From here he had more of a chance.

The Chanteclair appeared deserted, its clientele, apart from Oscar, still making movie deals. Pascal and Preben were eating in the courtyard, a dedicated Oscar under the table awaiting anything that might drop his way.

Pascal darted Patrick a worried look, like a mother about to lose a child. Oscar was affectionate, but in a manner that suggested he had food on his mind. Begging, Patrick realized, had become a way of life, a habit Oscar would have to be dissuaded from when he returned to *Les Trois Soeurs*.

'What's happened?' Pascal said, a little worried.

'Nothing important,' Patrick said. 'Are you going up to the fireworks tonight?'

Pascal threw Preben a look. 'Perhaps, but not with Oscar,' he stated categorically. They both awaited his response.

'I'll be busy tonight,' Patrick said. 'I'd be grateful if Oscar stays here.'

Pascal couldn't contain his pleasure. 'Of course.'

Patrick went up to his room. It smelled of whisky and sleep. He threw open the shutters and turned on the shower. Under its needle-sharp power, he contemplated what the night would bring.

Definitely fireworks, but what else?

Washed and dressed, he poured a whisky and held it up to the light. The world was in that glass. Time and patience, place and identity. There wasn't another drink like it on the planet. There would never be another woman like Marie Elise.

He savoured the whisky's warmth and flavour as it coursed through his chest and veins. Whatever happened tonight, he was looking forward to it.

Patrick wondered if Moreaux felt the same.

He headed downstairs and settled himself at the table outside the circle of plants. The air was still, the muffled sound of Cannes like a distant drum beat. Patrick remained there as evening fell, the whisky bottle and glass before him.

Pascal brought him food, but Patrick hardly tasted it. Death seemed to court him from the shadows. He had faced death before, many times, often by choice. He regarded death as an adversary, one who sought to out-manoeuvre and vanquish him. Just like Chapayev.

But neither death nor Chapayev had defeated him yet.

Darkness descended as he made the necessary calls. His table stood in the shadow of the back wall of number 10 Rue Forville. Above him, a washing line was pulled in. From open windows came the sounds of Cannes residents at their evening meal. Glancing up at the Chanteclair, he saw a couple in an embrace, never thinking they were visible to him or those in the flats above.

He rose as the clock on La Castre signalled the quarter hour. Neither Pascal, Preben or Oscar were to be seen, although there was a light behind the shutters of their small sitting room.

He went by Rue Panisse. Angele had given him a key and Patrick used it to enter, finding the room empty, a sleeping bag in the corner next to half-eaten food and an empty bottle of wine. The pillow had blood on it, which wasn't fresh.

Patrick had the distinct impression that Leon had flown, and for good. Angele had betrayed him with the necklace and Chapayev had been a further incentive to disappear. Patrick was glad. He didn't want Leon on his conscience.

He glanced at his mobile. Stephen had been trying to get a hold of him since he'd discovered treasure off the Île d'Or. Getting no response, he'd finally sent a text, imploring Patrick to get in touch. Patrick deleted the message. As far as he was concerned, Stephen and Colm had now played their part.

Crowds were making their way up the hill. Families with young children in prams; grandmothers and teenagers. The older residents were keen to get a seat as near the battlements as possible. The blue metal chairs, specially brought in for the occasion, were already filling up.

A stage had been set up with its back to the castle. It was deserted at the moment, but a DJ was playing a series of French ballad singers. Patrick checked the crowds, but there was no sign of Moreaux's iron-grey head, although there were at least four Police Municipale officers with their smart dark-blue uniforms.

He turned and exited by the vaulted opening in the clock tower. The double doors of the church stood open. Mass was over, but a trickle of the faithful remained inside, in silence or in prayer, before the high altar with its seventeenth-century virgin, the Vierge Couronnée, holding a ship's anchor.

Patrick moved into the shadows.

Korskof was the first to arrive. How he had come to know of the meeting, Patrick had already guessed. Korskof stood uncertain at the door, accustoming himself to the dim light. Patrick watched surprised as, with a glance at the high altar, the Russian bodyguard made a quick sign of the cross.

Next to appear was Moreaux. The lieutenant approached the Russian and a few words were spoken which Patrick couldn't hear, although he was pretty certain their discussion involved his whereabouts.

Both turned when Brigitte and Chevalier appeared at the door together. Brigitte hesitated, but Chevalier took her arm and led her inside and straight up to Moreaux.

Brigitte pointed at the Russian. 'This is the man who broke into my apartment, Lieutenant Moreaux,' she said in a ringing voice. 'And took Camille Ager away at gunpoint.'

All eyes in the church were now on the tableau. Muttering began, and grew louder. The Russian's eyes darted round as the interested parties began to move towards them. Patrick had the terrible thought that Korskof would produce his gun, even in that public place.

It seemed that Moreaux had had the same thought. With a wave of his hand, his backup materialized. Two figures rose from prayer, their guns discreetly at the ready.

It was over in moments.

Korskof was escorted from the church, the mix of tourists and worshippers stunned by what had just taken place. Chevalier was the last to leave. Following Moreaux out, he stopped and glanced back. This time, Patrick did show himself, just long enough to give him the thumbs-up. Chevalier nodded in return.

Patrick chose a different route out of the church.

Moving swiftly through the maze of side passages, he exited by a small door on to Rue de la Castre. This side of the castle was deserted. He walked swiftly downhill, pondering Moreaux's next move. The lieutenant had had no alternative but to arrest Korskof. He would hold him, but for how long? The policeman's inscrutable expression when he'd first seen Korskof had given nothing away.

Patrick had no idea, as yet, which side – or sides – Moreaux was on.

It would have been impossible to leave the harbour by water. It was jam-packed with boats, both large and small, in serried rows like sardines in a tin. Just off the lighthouse was no better, the larger yachts filling the bay almost as far as Sainte Marguerite. The display would begin when the appropriate official deemed it was dark enough, ten o'clock being merely a guideline.

Music drifted from the battlements in competition with that being played over loudspeakers on Le Pantiero. The display would be set to a chosen piece of music, something soaring and significant, the two locations trying to synchronize the accompaniment, but not always succeeding.

Patrick headed along the Quai Laubeuf, whose concrete curve stretched far out into the bay. It was a tricky passage, because of the numbers encamped there to view the spectacle, but it was still faster than swimming round the headland.

He moved down on to the rocks at the end and stripped off, much to the amusement of two young women, who'd settled down to watch the show. They screamed their encouragement as he dived into the water.

Patrick struck out strongly. He'd already plotted a route to the *Heavenly Princess*, but care would be needed moving among the rows of partying boats. He was yards from the black yacht when the first explosion of light occurred, making his approach all the easier. The small group assembled on the sky deck had eyes only for the firework display.

Pulling himself on to the metal platform, he headed up the steps and made his way, without challenge, to the laundry cupboard he'd used to change in before. A basket held dirty linen, due to go ashore for cleaning. Patrick rifled through and found a waiter's outfit that fitted, just.

This time he didn't intend to serve.

The various decks were deserted, and even the kitchen was empty, everyone outside taking in the show. The noise was deafening, a mixture of distorted music, bangs, pops and whooshes, the sky a kaleidoscope of colour.

Angele's revelation as to the whereabouts of the diamonds had given him food for thought. Her plan that Leon might be the one to retrieve them had failed. Patrick's appearance on the scene had in fact been her lifesaver. He wondered what she would have done if he hadn't shown up, then remembered her earlier disguise and realized she'd had every intention of coming back for them herself. Patrick couldn't help but admire her courage.

He made his way to her cabin. This time he found the door locked. Patrick stood for a moment listening for anyone approaching, before he extracted the key Angele had given him. Once inside, he re-locked the door, then approached the wardrobe.

The last time he'd been in here, he'd simply flicked through the contents, coming to the conclusion that they were Angele's and that he had found her room. Now he took more care, praying that Angele had been right when she'd assured him that Chapayev would never find or even think of her hiding place for his precious diamonds.

'He thought I was a stupid woman,' she'd said, 'because I let him do whatever he wanted. When all the time he was the stupid one.'

The item of clothing she'd described was a floor-length blue silk evening dress, low-backed with a bustle fashioned in the shape of a rose. Patrick located it eventually, hanging at the rear, behind a rail of daytime clothes.

As he extracted it, the moving silk emitted a scent that was definitely Angele's.

He stared at the dress for a moment, excitement causing his heart to up its tempo, then he tore off the rose-shaped bustle.

And there was the treasure, just as Angele had said it would be.

A small black felt bag, safely tucked inside the rose. Patrick extracted it and discarded the rose.

Drawing open the cord, Patrick tipped the contents into his palm. The sight of the sparkling stones caused him to catch his breath. He knew enough about diamonds to be sure those that glittered in his palm were worth a tidy sum.

There were at least twenty of them, premium cut to maximize their brilliance, beautifully clear and colourless. At a guess, they were a mixture of two and three carat. What the current value of the diamonds would be, Patrick had no idea, but certainly considerably more than the black pearl.

He carefully poured them back in the bag and put the bag in his pocket, then crossed to the door and listened. There was no sound of movement in the corridor, the only noise being the intermittent bangs and explosions from above. Checking his watch, Patrick estimated the fireworks had approximately ten minutes more to run. It was time to make his move.

He exited, re-locked the door and made his way to the sky deck.

A small group stood by the harbour side railing, their eyes on the exploding colourful sky. Patrick made out Chapayev's heavyset figure surrounded by an assortment of young, pretty women. Camille Ager wasn't among them. Patrick checked the sky deck for Chapayev's backup and spotted a man hovering in the shadows. Less imposing than Korskof, he looked a little nervous, as though he'd just been promoted in Korskof's absence ashore. It was difficult to tell in the intermittent light, but Patrick assumed he was carrying a weapon under the smart suit.

Having appraised the situation, Patrick stepped into view.

One of the women turned and looked at him, wondering why a tall man in a waiter's uniform should wear such an expression. Patrick ignored her and called out Chapayev's name, saying it correctly in Russian.

Chapayev's head shot round. To say he was surprised to find Patrick there was an understatement.

'What do you want?' he said.

'We need to talk,' Patrick said in Russian. He indicated the minder. 'Alone,' he added firmly.

The two men eyeballed one another, before Patrick turned and swiftly headed downstairs, making the assumption that Chapayev would follow, with or without his minder. Taking the route to the stern, Patrick opened the gate designed to keep passengers out, then took up a position in the shadows.

If his plan was to work he needed the Russian here, and alone.

Chapayev wasn't far behind, his breathing laboured as he came down the last set of steps and into the stern.

As Patrick heard the gate open and clang shut again, a shower of sparklers lit up the sky. In the silvery light, he saw Chapayev wave upwards and guessed that, contrary to his command, the Russian had placed his minder on duty on the deck above.

'Courvoisier?' he shouted, his voice almost drowned in the soaring music as the display beat its way towards a climax.

Patrick stepped into the light.

'Get rid of the minder, or I sprinkle the diamonds over the side.' Patrick held the small black bag up for Chapayev to see.

When there was no response, Patrick said, 'Angele hid them in a dress. She said you were so stupid you would never look there.'

The goading did the trick. The Russian had decided not to take a chance. He barked an order into the shadows. There was a shuffling sound in response. Either the minder had moved away, or else he'd just taken up a different position. Patrick suspected the latter was true.

The two men regarded one another in silence, as Patrick attempted to interpret Chapayev's expression. There had been time enough for the Russian to be informed of Korskof's arrest, which wouldn't improve his feelings towards Patrick. Neither would the death of the Swede, the still-missing pearl or the large sum of money he'd lost in the casino.

Patrick ran his eyes over the big body, identifying a well-concealed lump under his jacket that was surely his weapon. At the same time, he considered just how far away Chapayev's henchman had gone.

'Monsieur de Courvoisier.' Chapayev attempted to speak above the sound of the overhead extravaganza. 'You were expected at La Castre.'

'As I said, I only deal with you.'

Chapayev shrugged. 'And here I am. So, you have brought me my diamonds?'

Patrick held out the bag.

Chapayev reached for it eagerly and Patrick gave it up without resistance. He watched as the Russian dribbled some of the contents into his palm. In the exploding light of the fireworks, the diamonds glistened and sparkled. Chapayev studied them greedily for a moment, then he slipped the bag in his pocket and looked at Patrick.

'What is your price?' he asked in Russian.

Patrick knew exactly what Chapayev was thinking. He had the diamonds. All he had to do was shout and Patrick would leave, or he would be captured. What was the catch?

'Camille Ager is no longer in your debt and neither is Angele Valette,' Patrick said.

Chapayev contemplated this.

'Debts should be paid,' he said, as though this was unfortunate, but necessary.

His hand moved towards his gun.

Anticipating this, Patrick launched himself at the Russian, propelling him into the gate. He grunted as the impact of the bar on his lower back sent breath from his lungs, but he had reached the gun. Patrick heard the crack as it went off and felt the bullet slice his right arm just below the shoulder.

He caught Chapayev's wrist and heaved him round to face the sea rail, forcing his hand up his back. The Russian bellowed in pain, his feet slithering on the slippery deck. He dropped the gun and it skittered across the deck just out of reach. The music was rising to a crescendo, each note exploding in a series of bangs followed by a shower of riotous colour. An eruption of Russian expletives also peppered the air, followed by an order to shoot.

Patrick ducked as the first attempt ricocheted off the railing and flew into the night. The henchman was well positioned and a second shot would likely hit home. Patrick jerked Chapayev's arm further up his back, eliciting a squeal of pain, then suddenly released it and swung him round, placing himself between the Russian and the railing.

Free of Patrick's arm hold, Chapayev regained his balance.

The second shot rang out from above. This one zipped past Patrick's head. The marksman was good. Too good, and probably using night vision. Patrick encircled the Russian with his arms, using him as a shield. Patrick stretched himself to his full height, then threw himself backwards over the rail with all the somersaulting strength he would use in a dive.

Chapayev's feet lifted clear of the deck.

Their combined bodies balanced briefly on the top rail before tipping. Patrick let go his hold as they descended, Chapayev's arms flailing. When he hit the water a fraction of a second before Chapayev, Patrick had already taken a deep breath.

Chapayev had not.

In a mad panic he grabbed for Patrick and they descended into the depths together. Patrick tried to free himself but it was no use; fear had made Chapayev frantic, the last of his air escaping his unhealthy lungs like a car tyre rapidly deflating. His eyes popped white with terror, yet one hand still clutched at his pocket to prevent any attempt by Patrick to retrieve the diamonds.

Patrick's feet touched the bottom, stirring up a cloud of sand to choke them. In the resulting darkness he could no longer see Chapayev's face, but he could hear him.

The Russian had used up his meagre supply of air and was now breathing salt water.

Patrick kicked upward, trying to pull the Russian with him, knowing he had very little time, but Chapayev had become a dead weight, his massive girth acting like an anchor. It was useless. He should simply release him and take back the diamonds, but if Chapayev drowned, Korskof would be out for revenge, and not just on Patrick. Angele and Camille would be also on his list.

His own lungs heaving, Patrick secured Chapayev round the shoulders and kicked upwards.

His head broke the surface to meet the roving beams of search-lights. A shout in Russian was followed by a ping as a bullet hit the water near him. Patrick bellowed back that Chapayev was with him, and the shooter stopped.

Feet clattered down the metal steps. Patrick heaved the Russian's head and shoulders on to the diving platform and, taking a deep breath, submerged again. As he swam under the yacht, a chorus of yacht horns sounded in deafening unison, showing the marine audience's appreciation of the fireworks.

They would hoot like this for at least twenty minutes, as the yachts left their moorings in a great exodus, churning up the dark waters of the bay.

Metres away now from the *Heavenly Princess*, Patrick took a quick glance back. Standing by the railing, looking in his direction, was a tall figure in a smart grey suit. The African man from the dinner party had seen him leave.

SIXTEEN

The return journey was nerve-wracking. No one was looking out for a swimmer mad enough to weave their way through a flotilla of moving yachts. The first bullet had caught his arm just below the shoulder. He was pretty sure it was a surface injury, but knew it was impeding his ability to swim. Speed wasn't important, although avoiding propeller blades was.

Eventually he drew within sight of his diving spot and was relieved to see his two female fans had already left. He trod water while he pulled off the waiter's uniform and stuffed it among the large rocks that made up the foundations of the Quai Laubeuf. Then he pulled himself clear of the water.

The path along the *quai* was thick with people leaving their vantage points and heading for their cars. Patrick did his best to negotiate his way through, eventually taking to the rocky outpoint east of the curved swimming bay. From there he dropped on to the sand and made for the beach shower. He stood under it long enough to remove the salt, knowing he had a change of clothes in the boot of the car.

Checking the Quai Saint Pierre he spotted two policeman standing next to *Les Trois Soeurs*. It was just as well he hadn't planned to go there to shower and change, or the Chanteclair either. No doubt Moreaux would also have someone watching the hotel.

He slid into the car's leather driving seat, still wearing his wet shorts. His plan to avoid the snarl-up on the shore road paid off. As he departed Le Suquet by the back route, the yacht horns honking their pleasure were replaced by departing cars voicing their annoyance at the inevitable traffic jam.

He eventually met the shore road beyond the body of traffic and accelerated, overtaking wherever he could. Since all the cars were headed out of town, it was relatively easy. As he drew nearer to Le Dramont, he speeded up even more, adrenaline still flooding his veins.

Parking in the upper car park, Patrick dried himself and got dressed, before composing himself to walk down through the trees to the restaurant. As he neared the building, he called out to Jean Paul, not wishing a re-enactment of his previous nocturnal visit.

Jean Paul, Joanne and Angele were sitting out on the deck. In the soft lantern light, Angele looked extraordinarily beautiful. Patrick remembered the first time he had seen her. How he had been reminded of an angel caught in the exploding bulb of a camera.

She rose and came running towards him. He could smell her excitement and her need. Desire for power and wealth had the same scent as lust. She kissed him. A long, lingering kiss that would have swept him off his feet, if it had been someone other than Angele bestowing it. Yet his loins reacted of their own free will. Angele detected this and pressed herself closer.

Patrick considered whether he would tell her about the diamonds before or after they had sex.

Jean Paul waved him over to the table. 'Sit. I'll fetch more wine. Have you eaten?'

It seemed a lifetime ago that Pascal had brought food into the courtyard for him. Patrick couldn't even remember if he'd eaten any of it. Jean Paul took his silence as a 'no' and disappeared inside to fetch him a plate, which brought a scowl to Angele's face.

Patrick ignored her silent protest and took a seat. The night was still and filled with fragrance, pine and the sea, and something tasty warming in the kitchen.

Jean Paul appeared with a bottle of red. 'Suitable for a celebration,' he said.

Patrick nodded and accepted a glass. The wine was dry and full of flavour. He settled down to eat the plate of food Jean Paul had set before him. This time the casserole was rabbit, flavoured with wine and herbs. It seemed pertinent, somehow.

Hunger overtook him and it wasn't until he wiped the plate with the last of the bread that he fully acknowledged that the atmosphere round the table was less cordial than it had been on previous occasions.

Angele's enthusiastic greeting had been replaced by a sullen look. Joanne kept exchanging glances with Jean Paul, who, it seemed, was waiting until Patrick finished his meal before saying something.

'We had some excitement here after you left,' he finally said.

Patrick looked to Jean Paul in concern. 'Really, what?'

'Angele had a visitor.'

'Who?' Patrick directed his sharp question at Angele.

She pouted, then answered defensively, 'Leon, if you must know.'

After Korskof, it was the last name Patrick wanted to hear.

'How did he know where to find you?' Patrick said worriedly.

Angele moved from little-girl pout to attack mode. 'I told him.'

Jean Paul's muttered expletive voiced exactly what Patrick was thinking.

'What happened?' Patrick said, trying to stay calm.

'He wanted to see me in person, to know that I was safe, and to ask about his passport so he can leave Cannes.' Angele directed him an innocent, big-eyed look.

Lying, like acting, Patrick realized, was second nature to Angele.

He rose and, taking her firmly by the arm, led her towards the cabin. Once out of sight of Jean Paul, she gave a little sob, as though she was upset, rather than annoyed at being found out. When this didn't work, she resumed her petulant air.

'You shouldn't have told Jean Paul to spy on me.'

Patrick didn't answer as he unlocked the door and threw it open. The air that escaped was stuffy and smelled of sex, which meant Leon had got more than just information on his visit. Patrick was surprised he'd been up to the job, considering the damage done to his genitals by Chapayev.

He pulled Angele inside and slammed the door shut.

'What exactly did you tell Leon?' he said.

She hesitated, deciding how she should deliver her next line. 'That I was sorry Chapayev had hurt him.'

'Did you mention the pearl?'

She shook her head. 'And he doesn't know anything about the diamonds.'

He wondered what line she had fed Leon about the worthless necklace; what she had said about the pearl, and about his role in all of this.

'Get your things,' he said. 'We're leaving.'

Her beautiful eyes widened. 'Now? I thought you would . . .'

'Would what?'

She glared at him. 'I thought you would show me the diamonds.'

He paused before answering. 'I gave them back to Chapayev.'

Her look was incredulous. 'What?'

Realizing by his expression that he was telling the truth, Angele flew at him, nails outstretched. He caught her wrists before they reached his face, and she let loose a string of expletives that were new, even to him. Patrick waited until she paused for breath.

'It was the only way to get Chapayev, and Moreaux, off your back,' he said firmly.

She studied him. He knew she was imagining he still had the diamonds. That he planned to double-cross her and keep them for himself.

His mobile rang. Patrick released her and looked at the screen. It was Moreaux.

'Lieutenant Moreaux.'

Patrick listened in silence to Moreaux's message, rewriting his plan for the rest of the night as he did so. When Moreaux finished, Patrick said, 'I'll be there in forty-five minutes,' and rang off.

Angele's eyes narrowed. 'What did the policeman want?'

'Change of plan. You'll leave in the morning,' Patrick said.

'What about you?' she shouted at Patrick's retreating back.

Patrick didn't answer.

His old comrade in arms was back in the kitchen, taking his anger out on his pots. When Patrick entered, Jean Paul told him exactly what he thought of Madamoiselle Angele Valette. Patrick agreed with him. By bringing Leon here, she had endangered Jean Paul and Joanne. But the fault lay with him. He shouldn't have involved Jean Paul in the first place.

His apology was met with silence, then a shrug.

'I have enemies of my own,' Jean Paul reminded him.

Patrick reached in his pocket. 'Are you still planning that extension to the kitchen?'

'When I have the money.'

Patrick passed him a small fold of cloth. Jean Paul opened it and gave a long low whistle at the diamond nestling inside.

'I need one last favour,' Patrick said. 'Can you put Angele on the first train to Monte Carlo in the morning?'

'With pleasure.' Jean Paul smiled at the thought. 'Anything else?'

'I spent last evening here with you and Joanne.'

Jean Paul nodded. 'What time did you arrive?'

Patrick did a quick calculation. Chevalier would vouch for his presence in the church at nine thirty. 'Just after ten,' he said.

'When we ate rabbit with a good red out on the deck.'

'With Joanne and Angele,' Patrick added.

Jean Paul raised an eyebrow.

'I want Moreaux to know she's been staying here.'

Jean Paul shrugged. Whatever Patrick decided, he would go along with.

'I take it I'm on guard duty again tonight?'

Patrick nodded. Moreaux had indicated on the phone that Korskof had been let go. Apparently, Camille Ager had come forward and testified that she'd let him into Madame Lacroix's apartment and had gone with him willingly. There were therefore no charges. Moreaux's tone had been deadpan, but Patrick recognized it as a warning of a kind, for which he was grateful to the detective.

Angele was sitting outside the cabin, smoking when he returned. She darted him a poisonous look on approach, which Patrick ignored.

'Jean Paul will put you on the seven-thirty train to Monte Carlo tomorrow morning.' He wrote down a phone number and handed it to her. 'Ask for Jacques and tell him I sent you. He will buy the pearl. After that, go and see Lieutenant Moreaux. Tell him you were exhausted by the festival and went to ground here with Jean Paul to get away from the pressure.'

She considered this for a moment.

'What if Moreaux asks about the pearl?'

'Tell him you have no idea where it is. That you changed in your room, where you left the dress and the pearl. Then you left the yacht with Leon. You're a good actress. I'm sure you'll be able to convince him that you're telling the truth.'

Angele's expression suggested that she had no doubt of her ability on that score.

'And Chapayev?' she said.

'He won't bother you any more.'

Patrick departed before Angele could challenge him on that.

SEVENTEEN

Moreaux's black car sat next to *Les Trois Soeurs*. As Patrick approached, smoke drifted from the open driver's window and he caught the scent of Moreaux's trademark cheroot. Another pleasure the detective shared with Brigitte.

The officers who had been on duty earlier had disappeared. It was just the two of them. Something that suited Patrick, and obviously Moreaux.

Moreaux got out of the car and they stood for a moment, yards apart, eyeing one another.

'Lieutenant Moreaux.'

'Courvoisier.' Moreaux said the name with a sigh, indicating Patrick was causing him problems, as well as depriving him of sleep.

'Would you like to come aboard?'

Moreaux acquiesced and Patrick lowered the walkway, hoping there wasn't an additional welcoming committee waiting inside.

He offered Moreaux a drink, craving one himself. Moreaux asked for a whisky and Patrick poured two of the same malt he'd enjoyed earlier at the Chanteclair. They agreed to sit down. Moreaux looked tired, and not a little puzzled. Patrick waited for him to go first. He had no idea whether Chapayev had survived or not, or what that meant regarding the diamonds. He also didn't know what story was circulating about the death of the Swede.

Moreaux took his time, savouring the whisky. It brought a little colour to his pale cheeks, but only for a moment.

'Chevalier tells me you were in the church tonight.'

'I was.'

'Yet you failed to reveal yourself.'

'My presence seemed unnecessary.'

Moreaux considered this.

'Mademoiselle Ager dropped the charges.'

'Because Chapayev is blackmailing her.' Patrick watched Moreaux closely as he said the Russian's name, but could discern no change in his expression.

'Really? How?'

'He invested money in her business. Now he wants it back with substantial interest.'

Moreaux sampled the whisky again. 'Her diamond business?'

Here was the first indication that Moreaux knew something of the diamonds. Patrick waited for more.

'Perhaps the situation with Mademoiselle Ager has been resolved,' Moreaux said quietly.

'What makes you think that?'

'The *Heavenly Princess* has left port.'

'What?' Patrick couldn't hide his surprise. He hadn't checked for the distinctive lights of the big black yacht as he'd approached Le Vieux Port; he had been too intent on looking for Moreaux's car.

'You didn't know?' Moreaux was fishing, but he wasn't going to catch anything.

'I didn't,' Patrick said honestly, although whether the yacht had left with Chapayev dead or alive on board was something he definitely wanted to establish.

'But that wasn't the reason I asked to speak with you,' Moreaux continued. 'I would like you to identify a body.'

'What body?' Patrick said cautiously.

'A diver. Your friend the Irishman found him caught in a fishing line off the Île d'Or. We think he may be the Swedish national who was with Marie Clermand the night she died.'

Patrick was silent for a moment. Did this mean Moreaux was unaware of the Swede's involvement with Chapayev? Or was he merely bluffing?

'I only glimpsed him at the restaurant. It was Marie Elise who caught my eye.'

'Nevertheless . . .' Moreaux finished his whisky. 'How is Oscar? I believe he was quite badly hurt that night?'

Patrick bit his tongue, remembering his story of the bitch in heat.

'Pascal found him on the point with a head injury. He's lucky to be alive.'

'As are we all,' said Moreaux as though he meant it. He rose. 'I will expect you at the morgue at ten o'clock.'

Patrick watched the car drive away. Moreaux was an expert at gleaning information whether he asked questions or not. Not for the first time he thought Moreaux was wasted in the police force and should be working for the intelligence services.

Patrick took a seat on the upper deck to mull over what had just happened. If Chapayev was dead, it seemed his death hadn't been reported to the authorities, which would suit Moreaux very well. The lieutenant did not relish spending police time and resources on the wandering rich and often criminal fraternity who chose to visit Cannes.

If Moreaux was in any way involved with Chapayev personally, then it seemed their business was complete. Moreaux had played his hand well. Whatever the lieutenant had learned during their interview, he had certainly given nothing away.

The air was cool and fresh after the warm cabin. He was tired and the thought of sleeping in his own bed tonight was a welcome one. The clock in La Castre struck four. Le Marché would soon be in full swing, local fishermen including François would chug out past *Les Trois Soeurs* on their way to their fishing grounds. Patrick went inside, calling Oscar to bed, before remembering he wasn't there.

He woke again at eight, as refreshed as it was possible to be on four hours' sleep. A shower helped, plus a fresh pot of coffee and a croissant from the nearby bakery. He took his coffee out on deck. Today he would bring Oscar home. Pascal would be devastated, of course, but maybe he could lighten his distress by offering to loan him Oscar on occasion. It would be cheaper than boarding him with the vet, although, with the various titbits Oscar was receiving at the Chanteclair, weight gain might be a problem.

Patrick stood for a moment, surveying the west bay. The yachts which had sailed in to watch the fireworks had all departed, including, he could now see for himself, the *Heavenly Princess*. The harbour too seemed remarkably empty after last night's packed rows of smaller boats. With the end of the film festival, Cannes was returning to normal, for a while at least.

He had slept with his gun to hand. The revelation that the Russian's yacht had sailed hadn't succeeded in making Patrick sleep easy. Chapayev dead or alive, there was no way of knowing what the outcome of last night's events would be. And there was also the question of Korskof. Had he departed with the yacht? Or had he been left on shore to ensure that all debts were repaid?

Patrick finished his coffee and set off for the Chanteclair, where Pascal had a queue of festival attendees waiting to check out. This suited Patrick very well. There could be no histrionics in front of guests. He waved at Pascal and indicated he was taking Oscar for a walk, then headed back out of the courtyard, Oscar trotting at his heels.

The dog's scar was pink but looked nicely healed and Oscar had a spring in his step, which boded well for his recovery. Patrick walked him along the Quai Saint Pierre, and re-boarded *Les Trois Soeurs*. If Oscar's last occasion there brought back bad memories, he didn't show it, rushing round the boat, sniffing and squeaking with pleasure. The dog was glad to be home. And Patrick was glad to have him there.

Eventually he joined Patrick on deck. Patrick ruffled his ears, a gesture Oscar was particularly fond of, then put him on guard while he set out to view the body in the morgue.

He took the route along the pedestrian Rue Meynadier, which was already busy with local shoppers reclaiming their town after the festival. As the railway station came into view, Patrick wondered if Angele had caught the train to Monte Carlo as ordered, and had made contact with Jacques. Jean Paul hadn't been in touch, so Patrick assumed all was well for the moment, although he doubted that he'd heard the last of Angele Valette.

Crossing the busy Place du 18 Juin, Patrick climbed the steps of the Police Nationale headquarters.

Moreaux came down for him as soon as the officer on reception made the call. He looked a little less tired, although Patrick guessed by the hard line of his mouth that the lieutenant was annoyed about something. He acknowledged Patrick with a curt nod and indicated he should follow him.

They took the lift down to the basement in silence. It was the first time Patrick had been in the morgue, but it brought no surprises, and he had seen much worse in West Africa. The smell of decomposition was evident, despite the disinfectant, but it didn't bother him. You never got used to the scent of death, but you could learn to mask it over time.

The Swede was lying on a metal gurney. The post-mortem over, he had been neatly sewn together again. The fishing line having been entangled with his tanks, there were no external marks on his body apart from the incisions made by the pathologist to allow him to investigate the internal organs.

Studying the face of Marie's killer, for a moment Patrick recalled the eyes behind the mask as the Swede had struggled for air. Patrick felt no qualms about Gustafson's death. If the Swede had taken a dive buddy with him, he might well be alive. Marie Elise had had no such luxury.

'Is this the man you saw with Marie Clermand?' Moreaux said.

'It is.'

'We have evidence which leads us to believe he was her killer.'

At least the police had worked that one out.

'So I'm out of the frame?'

'For her murder at least,' Moreaux said, ominously.

He led Patrick from the room. On the other side of the metal doors, the air was much sweeter.

'I'd like to ask you a few questions,' Moreaux said.

'Of course.'

They adjourned to an upper room, where Moreaux had coffee brought in. No tape was set to record them and no one else sat in on the interview. Patrick glanced about, checking to see if there was any evidence of cameras and found none. Whatever was going to be said in here, was for their ears only.

They each drank some coffee.

'I had a call from Angele Valette, the missing starlet.' Moreaux put his espresso cup down. 'It seems she has been staying at Le Dramont at Jean Paul Suchet's place.' He paused. 'But then you would know that, since you had dinner with them there last evening.'

At least Angele had done something he'd asked her to.

When Patrick acknowledged that this was correct, Moreaux continued. 'Madamoiselle Valette was relieved to learn the *Heavenly Princess* had sailed without her. It seems Chapayev was a very demanding employer.'

When Patrick offered no comment on this, Moreaux went on. 'So, after the incident at the church . . .' He waited for Patrick.

'I drove to Le Dramont, where I was when you called.'

'And when the diver died?'

The question, slipped in, almost caught Patrick off guard.

'When was that?'

Moreaux gave him the time Stephen's boat had appeared off the Île d'Or.

Patrick met his gaze squarely. 'I spent the night with Mademoiselle Valette. We had breakfast together outside and noticed the activity on the water.'

'And yet you weren't curious to find out what it was about?'

'I had other things on my mind. Mainly Mademoiselle Valette.' Patrick smiled. The truth was, the memory of that particular night was a very good one.

Moreaux sat back in his chair, and extracting a cheroot from his cigarette case, lit up.

A waft of blue smoke filled the air between them. The 'no smoking' sign was obviously not intended for Moreaux.

'So,' he said. 'Am I to take it that you and Madamoiselle Valette are an item?'

Patrick shook his head. 'Sadly no, Angele is headed for Hollywood. I remain here in Cannes.'

Moreaux assumed a disappointed air, whether for Patrick's loss of the lovely Angele, or for the fact that he intended staying on in Cannes, he didn't divulge.

Moreaux pushed his cup away. It seemed the interview was at an end. Patrick should have felt relieved, but didn't.

'Is that all?' he said.

Moreaux inclined his head to indicate there was something else.

'I thought you would like to know that we have released Marie Clermand's body for burial. Brigitte is organizing the funeral. She's being laid to rest tomorrow at Cimetière du Grand Jas. Mass is at the Chapelle de la Misericorde at ten.'

Patrick found himself unable to reply for a moment.

'Thank you for telling me,' he finally managed to say.

Moreaux nodded as though, at least on this, they were in agreement.

On the walk back along Rue Meynadier, Patrick called Chevalier and they agreed to meet for lunch. It seemed a long time since they had eaten together in Le Pistou. On this occasion, Chevalier suggested Los Faroles, which suited Patrick. He wanted to ask if Fritz had any news of Leon.

There was an air of relief on Rue Saint Antoine. The tables were out, but the madness that had existed during the film festival had dissipated. The French were back, the American voices depleted, a more studied enjoyment of the food replacing the frantic deal-making.

He passed the restaurant where he had last seen Marie Elise. He believed now that she had come to the gunboat the night she died, to tell him more of her conversation with Angele, perhaps even to warn him of the danger Chapayev posed.

The Russian had seen Marie as a threat, an inconvenience or simply a way to remove Patrick, by framing him for her death. Had Patrick arrived minutes later, he would have been caught red-handed with Marie's body. The swiftness of Moreaux's arrival had been testament to that.

Chevalier was already seated outside Los Faroles when Patrick arrived. His friend had discarded the formal jacket and was wearing a brightly checked long-sleeved shirt with a primrose silk cravat. When he glanced up, the neatly trimmed and waxed moustache glistened in the May sunshine. Chevalier rose to plant a kiss on each of Patrick's cheeks. His own cheek was smooth as a baby's and his cologne smelled as delicate.

'I have already ordered the catch of the day.'

Patrick nodded and joined him. There were two glasses and a half bottle of red on the table. Chevalier poured them each a glass.

'The Russian's yacht has departed,' Chevalier offered, 'and with it my sale on the villa,' he said with a sigh.

'I'm truly sorry about that.'

Chevalier shrugged. 'No matter. Cannes already smells sweeter.'

On that note, Patrick said, 'I've just come from the morgue.'

Chevalier raised an eyebrow. 'Really, why?'

'Lieutenant Moreaux asked me to identify the diver found off the Île d'Or as the man I saw Marie Elise with the night she died.'

Chevalier took a sip of his wine. 'At least Moreaux got that right.' He muttered a popular Le Suquet curse. 'Brigitte is unhappy that he let the Russian's sidekick go.'

'Moreaux had no choice, unless you can persuade Camille to press charges.'

Chevalier shook his head. 'Whatever arrangement she has with Chapayev frightens her too much.' He eyed Patrick. 'Do you know what hold he has over her?'

'None,' Patrick said. 'Her debt has been repaid.'

He passed Chevalier a fold of cloth. 'A little something for your trouble and the loss of a sale on Villa Astrid. Although the thought of Chapayev's presence in the house of my ancestors was a little hard to take.' Patrick smiled.

Chevalier cast him a quizzical look, placed the cloth on his knee and discreetly unfolded it.

Inside was the second of the three diamonds Patrick had removed from the bag. Chevalier had risked his money in the casino and lost a good sale to help. He deserved it.

Chevalier smiled in astonishment, then re-folded the cloth and slipped it into his top pocket.

'*Mon Dieu*. So this was never about the black pearl?'

'It was, and it wasn't,' Patrick said.

'It is over, I hope?'

'So do I,' Patrick said with relish, although he wouldn't have placed a bet on it.

Chevalier waited for a moment. 'You know the details of the funeral?'

Patrick nodded. 'Moreaux told me.'

They were prevented from discussing this further by the arrival of the food, which turned out to be sea bass, caught that morning by François, around the time that Patrick had fallen gratefully into bed.

When they'd finished their meal, Fritz removed their plates, brought them coffee and pulled up a chair.

'Leon's about. He's been asking for credit in various places, insisting he's coming into money.' Fritz raised an enquiring eyebrow at Patrick.

Patrick contemplated the news. Contrary to his hopes that Leon had left town, it seemed that he and Angele had got together again. Patrick wondered what story she had spun him, to keep him on the leash. Did Leon know that Angele had the pearl? Did he have any idea what had happened to the diamonds, if he even knew about the diamonds in the first place?

'Sounds like Leon,' he said, non-committal.

Chevalier threw him a look, but Patrick's expression indicated there was nothing more to say on the matter. Patrick finished his coffee and, without looking at the bill, put down thirty euros.

'I'll see you tomorrow,' he told Chevalier, 'at the funeral.'

EIGHTEEN

Oscar was waiting on deck when he got back. Patrick whistled to him and he jumped ashore without the aid of the walkway. They strode along Le Vieux Port in the May sunshine, passing diners lingering after lunch on the quayside restaurants. The beach next to the harbour held a smattering of bathers, most of whom were grouped next to the eastern rocks and looked as though they were members of Cannes' elderly swim club.

Patrick turned left on to the walkway that led out to the point. Oscar was ecstatic at being free of pain and rushed along, checking out smells, marking his territory at every available opportunity and generally enjoying life. When they reached the point, Patrick stripped to his swim shorts, told Oscar to stand guard and dived in.

The route this time was free of traffic. He had aligned the *Heavenly Princess*'s mooring with three onshore locations. It wasn't difficult to line them up again. Once there he took a deep breath and dived. By his reckoning Chapayev had had four to six minutes from the moment he entered the water. They'd struggled together for at least two of those. There was always a chance that Chapayev's body had sunk down again before they got to him, and pulling him up, for anyone but an expert swimmer, would have been almost impossible. Korskof hadn't been on board, and Patrick had no idea who would be in charge if Chapayev was dead – then he recalled the African he'd seen standing on deck. Would he now be in charge of operations?

Patrick sunk slowly downwards, turning as he did so, checking in all directions. The darkness of last night had been replaced by a watery light that exposed the ocean floor as rippled sand covered by clumps of sea grass. He swam around, checking for an outcrop of rocks, a difference in depth, but there was nowhere Chapayev's body could have sunk to. There was always the chance that the movement of the departing yachts had shifted it. If so it would reappear on the surface twelve hours from now, but somehow Patrick didn't think that would happen.

He rose and broke the surface, convinced now that Chapayev had been taken back on board, maybe even alive. If so, then he'd ordered the *Heavenly Princess* to depart. Did that mean he'd decided to cut his losses now that he had the diamonds back?

Oscar was sitting like a sentinel, awaiting his return. He yelped in pleasure when Patrick appeared out of the water and he felt a rush of pleasure that he and the dog were back together again. He didn't bother with the beach shower but headed straight back to *Les Trois Soeurs*. The bathroom was no longer taboo. Marie Elise's death had been repaid, although he still had to face her funeral.

As he walked back to the gunboat, he contemplated turning up only for the burial. He wasn't religious and the Sunday ten o'clock Mass at the Chapelle de la Misericorde was traditionally said in Latin. He immediately felt bad at the thought. Brigitte had known Marie Elise better than he had ever hoped to. If Brigitte believed that's what Marie would have wanted, he should be there.

He dropped the walkway and Oscar happily scampered aboard, dispensing with any concerns Patrick might have about unwelcome visitors. He allowed himself a moment to consider that it might all be over, as Chevalier had said, although he knew from experience that that was rarely the case.

For the first time since Camille Ager had walked his way, the evening was his own. He contemplated how he might use it. He could go to the casino, but didn't feel in the mood. He would have to visit Pascal some time, admit to taking his (their) dog back, which would be traumatic and might be better left till tomorrow. He wondered if Pascal knew about the funeral and decided the news would travel fast in Le Suquet; he had no need to deliver it personally.

He showered off the salt and changed his clothes, then made himself a martini and took it out on deck to watch the world go by.

The majority of his jobs didn't involve either violence or death. They were predominantly low key, and involved sorting out clients' personal or financial problems. He usually charged his rich clients large sums of money for his help. Locals often repaid him in kind, like Jean Paul.

That's why he had come to Cannes, he reminded himself. To leave his past behind, although this particular job had left him unsure if he still wanted to do that.

He finished the martini then called Astoux et Brun and booked a table for one for seven o'clock. He'd bought the shellfish platter from there the night he'd invited Marie to dinner on *Les Trois Soeurs* and it seemed appropriate.

Smartly dressed, he departed the boat at six, ordering Oscar to stay on board. The dog settled himself on the top deck under the awning, facing the *quai*, upright, alert and full of self-importance. Turning left, Patrick made his way up the steps on to Rue Georges Clémenceau, and from there to Leon's building. The same woman answered the intercom and, perhaps remembering his previous generosity, let him in immediately. He found her waiting at the open door of her apartment, the TV blasting in Arabic in the background.

Patrick asked if Leon was at home. She nodded, which surprised him.

'He's drunk,' she said in guttural French.

Patrick slipped her twenty euros and she unlocked Leon's door for him.

The room stank of stale wine. There were six empty bottles next to the bed where Leon lay snoring, his face an ugly mass of yellow and blue bruising. He was curled like an infant, his hands protectively cradling his crotch.

Patrick put a hand on his shoulder and shook him, gently at first. When that didn't work, he shouted Leon's name in his ear. Consciousness came suddenly. Leon sprang up, reaching below his pillow. Patrick caught the hand before it could rescue the gun and removed it himself.

Leon tried to focus, fear clouding his eyes.

'Bastard,' he said, recognizing Patrick.

'You're lucky it's only me.'

Patrick stood back to allow Leon to come fully to his senses, then handed him his passport. Leon took it, suspicion filling his face.

'You need to get out of Cannes,' Patrick told him.

'And you're going to make me?' Leon sneered.

'I take it you don't mind meeting Korskof again?'

Leon swung his feet on to the floor, the action bringing a grimace of pain.

'The yacht's gone,' he said defiantly.

'More than likely it's just moved along the coast. And there's no guarantee that Korskof is on it.'

'Then it's you who should be worried,' Leon retorted.

'My advice is to get out of Cannes. Try Monaco, that's where

Angele is. She's selling the pearl. Some of that money should be yours.' He tossed Leon the gun. 'And keep an eye on your back.'

He exited then, shutting the door firmly behind him, silently wishing Leon good luck.

Astoux et Brun was barely three-quarters full, which showed that Cannes was recovering from festival fever. He chose a table near the thoroughfare, happier to view the passing human traffic than sit alone near the back. The tray of shellfish, when it appeared, looked similar in content to the one he'd purchased for Marie. By the response of the waiter who delivered it, the word of her impending funeral had spread.

Patrick accepted the half bottle of white wine 'on the house', which turned out to be very good, and set about eating. He took his time over the selection, remembering Marie's delicate fingers as she'd prised open a langoustine, and her laughter when he'd told her that the Scots' name for the tiny *bigorneau* was winkles or whelks. He completed his homage meal with a selection of cheeses from Le Marché served with coffee, then paid his bill and left.

The evening was balmy and surprisingly quiet for Cannes. He re-enacted the stroll he'd taken with Marie, pausing to sit on a bench and watch the *boules* players near the carousel. The click of the balls on the cool night air seemed to anchor his thoughts.

He didn't normally get personally involved in cases. It was better to operate alone. To *be* alone. This case had only reinforced that belief.

Rising, he made his way to Bijou Magique. He had eaten early and the shops were still open, to catch the late-evening trade. When Patrick entered, the same young woman stood behind the counter and cast him an anxious glance.

'Is Camille here?' he said.

There was a moment's hesitation, then she disappeared into the back shop. Two minutes later, Camille Ager appeared. She looked pale, her hand fluttering against her dress like a nervous butterfly.

'Can we talk?' he said.

She nodded. The girl had re-emerged behind her and Camille told her to close up at nine as normal, before following Patrick out.

Walking alongside Camille, he realized how tall she was. Tall and beautiful and very apprehensive. Patrick didn't relish making her so uncomfortable. Whatever had happened between her and Chapayev, the Russian had definitely held the upper hand.

Patrick opened the proceedings as soon as they were clear of the shop.

'The *Heavenly Princess* has left Cannes,' he told her.

She started as though she hadn't known. 'Chapayev has gone?' she said.

'The yacht departed last night at the end of the fireworks.'

She looked puzzled, as though he had just told her that Alice had gone down the rabbit hole.

Patrick decided to elaborate. 'I gave back the diamonds Angele stole, on the understanding that Chapayev leave both you and Angele alone.'

She came to a halt and cast him a worried glance. 'I thought Angele took the black pearl?'

'She did, but she also stole twenty diamonds probably destined for your shop.'

Her face paled at the thought. 'Chapayev never said.'

'He didn't need to. You were frightened enough by the pearl.'

They had reached Rue Félix Faure and the Hôtel Splendid. Patrick led her to a table out front. She acquiesced, sinking gratefully into a seat. The waiter was there almost immediately and Patrick ordered two glasses of champagne.

'Tell me about Angele,' he said, when the waiter had left.

Camille looked sad and thoughtful. 'We didn't meet until I was fifteen and she twelve. Even then she was beautiful and difficult to manage. My stepfather called her his fallen angel. She was the daughter of his previous lover, so we are not related, not by blood, but we did spend a little time together, because of the various relationships of our parents.' She gave a Gallic shrug. 'Back then, we thought we were bohemian. Now, I know we were just pawns, caught up by the sexual relationships of our parents and step-parents.' She paused. 'My stepfather left us soon after and created yet another family, so my contact with Angele ended. I had no idea what had happened to her until she appeared in Cannes with Chapayev.'

'He knew of the connection between you?'

'I don't think she ever told him. But it didn't matter. Chapayev already had me in his grip.'

'How?'

'I came here with nothing. I had some of the skills required by Madame Lacroix, but not enough. I had a little money saved because I wanted to open a shop, but I needed more. I met

Chapayev at a party. He had money to invest. I took it.' She paused. 'I soon found out how many strings were attached.' She dipped her head to avoid Patrick's eyes. 'Then he told me about Angele. How she had left, taking the pearl. If I didn't help him find her and bring her back . . .'

'And you came to me?'

'He made me come to you.'

'When I challenged Angele, she denied you were her half-sister,' Patrick said.

Camille gave a small smile. 'It's easy to lie when you think your life depends on it.'

'Has she been in touch?'

She shook her head.

'What about Chapayev?'

'Not since Korskof was set free.'

Which was good news.

'If Chapayev, or anyone connected with him, makes contact, you should tell Lieutenant Moreaux. He knows you were being blackmailed.'

'But . . .'

'Chapayev has his diamonds. You have your shop. Moreaux will make sure you keep it.'

For the first time he saw what might be joy in her eyes.

'How can I thank you?'

He thought for a moment. 'There are two rings in your window. One silver, one gold.'

'The lovers' moon and stars.'

'I suggest you give them to Moreaux as a gift. I'm sure his wife will be pleased.'

Patrick left her then to return to the shop, wishing he could be sure that his plan had in fact worked.

NINETEEN

Arriving next morning at the paved square by the Chapelle de la Misericorde, Patrick found it thick with mourners. He recognized many of the staff from the nearby restaurants, a variety of Suquet residents including Pascal and Preben, Veronique from Le P'tit Zinc and many of the marketeers.

Chevalier looked resplendent in a dark-grey silk suit and red tie; Moreaux was sombre in black; but no one could match Madame Lacroix and her colourful cortege of beautiful young women, there to say goodbye to one of their own.

He and Camille took their place just behind the Hibiscus contingent. Brigitte observed his entry with a sharp eye and bestowed a nod. The coffin standing at the altar was dark ebony, the roses that adorned it blood red. It seemed impossible that it should contain something as beautiful as Marie Elise.

The service was conducted in Latin. Unfamiliar with the workings of any church, Patrick followed Brigitte's lead, but found himself discomfited by words he didn't understand and music that brought him no sense of peace.

Afterwards they all filed out into bright May sunshine and Patrick led Camille to the car. The Cimetière du Grand Jas occupied a nine-hectare terraced site just off Avenue de Grasse. He had never buried anyone there, but had visited it when he first came to Cannes, and been amazed at how little it resembled the grey windswept graveyards of his home.

They drove there in silence. He knew Camille was upset and still blaming herself in some way for Marie Elise's death. He hadn't revealed the meeting between Marie Elise and Angele on the *Heavenly Princess*. The one that had probably sealed her fate. Patrick did so now.

When he'd finished, Camille looked round at him.

'You think Chapayev recorded that conversation?'

'I'm sure of it. Nothing you could have done would have saved her.'

His words seemed to give Camille comfort. She placed her hand over his for a moment on the steering wheel.

Patrick didn't approach the graveside, but chose to watch from further up the hill. The Cimetière du Grand Jas was a suitable last resting place for Marie Elise. Stunningly beautiful and classical in form, it overlooked the sparkling blue waters of the bay.

The graveside service was brief. Patrick noted Brigitte's slight figure in black, Moreaux beside her, the way she raised her veil for one last look before the first shovel of earth was thrown on the ebony coffin.

At this point Patrick turned and walked back to the parked Ferrari to wait for Camille.

The funeral party was adjourning to the Hôtel Splendid for lunch but Patrick had no wish to join them. Camille came to tell him she'd arranged to go there with Chevalier. Patrick was relieved by this. He needed to forget what he had just witnessed, and driving fast and far would help him do that.

He took the A8 westward, running high above the coast, before turning north on a minor road towards the town of Bagnols-en-Forêt. This was one of the areas he liked to walk in, but today he was happier driving, negotiating the empty hillside roads like a race track.

Even now, he knew he didn't fully understand what had happened. There were still too many questions as yet unanswered. Perhaps they never would be.

As he drove like a maniac, he saw again Marie's smile as she spoke to the Swedish man in the restaurant. Why had she met him, if he wasn't a client? Had she sought him out after seeing him on board the *Heavenly Princess* the night of the launch party? Had she done so to try and discover what, if anything, he knew about Angele?

And what of Moreaux? Who had signalled to Korskof that he, Patrick, would be at the church the night of the fireworks? Did Moreaux do it in order to draw Korskof there, with the intention of arresting him? Or was his intention to pick up Patrick?

He thought again of Chapayev. Relived their moments together below the water and Chapayev's frantic efforts to hang on to him, at the same time showing his desperation not to give up his precious diamonds. Patrick wondered whether he had made a mistake in not letting Chapayev drown, and taking back the diamonds.

In the past, that's exactly what he would have done.

Maybe he was growing soft in his retirement. Maybe jobs involving unpaid rent and messy business deals in and around Le

Suquet were no longer enough for him. At that point the memory of the gilt-edged invitation returned to mock him.

Patrick hit the accelerator even harder.

The next corner he took close to the edge. The following one even closer. The blood sang in his veins the closer he got to disaster. It was a feeling he recognized and knew he had missed.

Then he heard the sound of blades above him.

The helicopter hung there, black, with the distinctive red logo of Chapayev's company emblazoned on its side.

He had been right. The game wasn't over yet.

Patrick tried to remember where the road he was on led to. One thing he did know: it didn't lead to civilization. Continuing on in this manner was a mistake. He needed to get out of sight, or among people, neither of which was possible the way he was heading.

There had been no pot shots so far, but he had no doubt there would be. If Korskof was up there, he would have his sights trained on the car. Their best solution for the irritant that Patrick had become was to cause an accident which sent him over the edge into the steep valley below. No bullet wounds, no evidence of an attack.

Just a man, crazed by loss, taking a bend too fast.

As though reading his mind, the helicopter dropped lower. Patrick prepared himself for the inevitable. A bullet to the brain, or a bullet to a tyre.

They say you see your life flash before you at such moments. He didn't see his life; only the dead faces of the two women whose deaths he felt responsible for.

Then he swerved.

The bullet hit the rock wall to the left of the car. The echo of it splintered his hearing for a moment. Now he knew. They would kill him and not care whether it looked like an accident. Men like Chapayev thought they were powerful enough to defy the law. They had done that already in the place of their birth. Why should the South of France be any different? Moreaux had known that and had studiously avoided the Police Nationale wasting resources trying to bring to justice a man who had the power, influence and money to make that almost impossible.

But Patrick had no such thoughts. He owed nothing, and to no one.

He slowed suddenly, the brakes meeting the tyres in a frantic smell of burning rubber. The car skewed, leaving a film of black on the road to witness his abrupt halt. In seconds he was at a standstill, and out of the car.

The helicopter took longer to react to what was happening below.

Patrick used the time to get among the red rocks. If they wanted him, they would have to come and get him.

The helicopter hovered as though trying to scent its prey. Whoever was inside couldn't see him and wasn't about to waste bullets on the rocks; instead they decided to take their anger out on the car.

An onslaught of bullets hit the Ferrari, pinging death on the metal work, tearing at the handsome leather. Patrick watched as the deluge reduced the car to a beaten body, like Leon's when they'd thrown him on to the deck of *Les Trois Soeurs*.

Patrick swore in French, which was much more satisfying than in English and much more colourful.

Now he knew their plan.

The car was out of action, so they would find somewhere to land the helicopter and come for him on foot. They had the fire power, and he didn't think Korskof would be alone.

Patrick checked his mobile, but knew before he did so what the result would be. They were in the middle of the Estérel Mountains and there was no signal.

TWENTY

Lieutenant Martin Moreaux watched as Courvoisier's car took off at high speed, guessing he was heading out of town. The man's prowess behind the wheel was legendary, as was his liking for speed. It seemed obvious that Courvoisier's current emotional state demanded he get in the Ferrari and drive as fast as possible.

Moreaux could, of course, prevent this, by sending the traffic cops after him to pull him over, but he didn't fear for other road users, although he did have some concerns about Courvoisier himself. Their earlier meeting had given Moreaux some cause for thought. The unreported case of the missing black pearl had grown to include the 'accidental' death of a diver, who not only worked for Chapayev, but was also implicated in the murder of Marie Clermand. Add to that Brigitte's dismay at Korskof, yet another employee of Chapayev, being set free, and it had become clear to Moreaux that all his efforts to contain the situation had failed.

Courvoisier had told a number of lies, one of them being that he hadn't been aboard the gunboat the night Marie had died. Moreaux was aware of this, but had chosen not to follow it up. He didn't believe Courvoisier to be her killer, plus the anonymous call had been a little convenient. The death of the diver also left some questions unanswered. One being why he was diving there alone in the first place. Moreaux suspected it had a great deal to do with the pearl and Mademoiselle Valette.

Angele Valette was a fine actress, perhaps a little too good. She was also an extremely alluring creature, and was able to make good use of such attributes. Moreaux smiled as he contemplated how even someone of his age and experience had reacted to Mademoiselle Valette's advances.

He'd now come to the conclusion that she had been staying with the Suchets at Le Dramont, but not for the reason she'd given. That particular bird had now been seen flying about Monaco, sent there by Courvoisier no doubt, to sell either the pearl or, intriguingly, a set of diamonds.

Which is what he suspected this had all been about.

He paused in his thoughts as Brigitte approached, stiff-backed as always, but with her veil replaced to cover her distress. Moreaux felt her sorrow and was moved by it.

'Where is Courvoisier?' she asked.

Moreaux explained about his abrupt departure.

She glanced towards the upper reaches of the graveyard near the road.

'I'm sure I saw Korskof up there.'

Moreaux patted her arm reassuringly. 'The *Heavenly Princess* has left port. Korskof will be on it.'

Brigitte lifted her veil so that he could see the anger in her eyes. 'He's free to go where he pleases, because you let the bastard go, despite what I told you.'

'Camille Ager wouldn't press charges.'

'Because she was scared of him. Even I could see that.' Brigitte dropped her veil in disgust.

'I have to make a call, then I'll come on to the Splendid,' Moreaux offered.

Brigitte didn't acknowledge his response, but instead strode away to rejoin the crowd of mourners moving towards the gate, suggesting Moreaux was definitely in her bad books.

This business with Courvoisier was causing too many problems, he decided, and not only in his public life.

Moreaux removed himself to a quiet spot outside the departing throng. His first move was to try calling Courvoisier, but he got the voicemail service. Either Courvoisier was already high in the hills and therefore out of range, or he wasn't breaking the law by answering his phone while driving, even if he was exceeding the speed limit.

Moreaux made a second call, this time to the traffic police. He wanted to know where the red Ferrari was and quickly. If Courvoisier had been foolish enough to acquire diamonds Chapayev believed were his, then his life might well be at stake. His third call was to the coastguard with a request to find the exact whereabouts of the *Heavenly Princess*.

Moreaux ended the call and swore eloquently.

Patrick de Courvoisier was a thorn in his side. One he could well do without.

TWENTY-ONE

Patrick stayed under cover, hoping to hear the beat of the blades retreating. Instead they grew louder and he suddenly understood why. The helicopter had been ordered to land on the road. There was simply nowhere else close by that they could set down. They were taking a chance. The road was one hairpin bend after another. It was remote, but that didn't mean there were no cars. Farm vehicles and small trucks used it too. If one came round a corner at even a slow pace, it would plough into the helicopter.

Patrick took a look to make sure his guess was right. The helicopter was hovering just above and to the right of the Ferrari, as Korskof and another man dropped to the ground. Both were armed. The second guy looked like the minder who'd taken a potshot at Patrick just before he'd somersaulted overboard with Chapayev. The two men made a dash for the shelter of the rock face as the helicopter shielded them, then it rose and headed west.

Patrick set about calculating the odds he was facing. Firstly, his mobile wasn't working, but neither would theirs be. On the plus side, he knew these mountains, and they didn't. The odds stacked against him, however, were substantial. He felt at his waistband automatically, already knowing he wasn't carrying his weapon. You didn't take a gun to a funeral – although maybe you should if the deceased had been murdered. So it was two against one, and they had the firepower and were obviously intent on using it, as witnessed by the wreck that had been his car.

That thought made him angry, but it was a cold and calculating anger, which would serve his purpose. He checked out his position. It wasn't perfect but he did have the advantage of being above them, and with a clear view of the rocks below. The danger would be if one of them managed to circle round unnoticed behind him.

He took a moment to look for any recognizable landmarks. By the speed and timing of his journey, he estimated he was somewhere in the vicinity of the Blavet Gorges, where the rocky riverbed of the Blavet passed alongside sheer cliffs. At the base of the cliff lay the grotto of Mureron, an opening twenty metres deep, created when a chunk of rhyolite rock had collapsed. It wasn't the only cave in the area: the red rock was riddled with them. The lower slopes were also home to a thick forest of oak trees which could provide excellent cover if only he could reach them.

Decision made, Patrick did the opposite to what was expected. Instead of heading upwards, he began to move back towards the road, while intermittently tossing a pebble in the other direction. He fooled them just long enough to cross the road. As he threw himself over the edge he'd earlier courted with the Ferrari, the first bullet skiffed the rock beside him. Patrick kept on going, half-running, half-sliding downwards, while intermittently getting below or behind one of the larger rocks. Bullets were becoming plentiful, but he was in more danger of being hit by a ricochet than by a well-aimed attempt.

Here the odds against him increased, but he was playing for higher stakes. He could already see the trees. Once among them, he had a chance. That thought kept him careering downwards, sending intermittent showers of red stones before him, trusting to luck that he wouldn't break a leg before reaching his destination.

Metres from the first trees, he broke into a straight run. Down here out of the sun, the shadows were long, the visibility poor. He might just make it.

He didn't.

The shot was perfectly aimed to bring him down. His left leg gave way and he crumpled.

A voice barked in Russian. 'If you try to get up, I'll shoot the right one as well.'

Patrick stayed exactly where he was. Had Korskof been alone, he might have tried to bring him down. Once on the ground, the odds would have been more evenly matched. But there were two of them. Patrick decided to conserve his strength.

It seemed the intention had not been to kill, but to capture him.

A foot caught him in the groin and flipped him over and Patrick was staring up into Korskof's face. The Russian was sweating like a pig, his bulk more suited to beating his opponents to a pulp than chasing them through the Estérel Mountains. The other guy looked as nervous as he had been on the yacht. His eyes kept darting about, as though he expected help for Patrick to appear miraculously from behind a rock.

'Now you get up,' Korskof barked.

The bullet had entered just above Patrick's left knee. The wound was bleeding but not badly, the pain still dulled by the adrenaline and fury that continued to course through him. Nevertheless, Patrick did his utmost to convince Korskof that he was both in agony and unable to walk. If they planned to get him to the road, he wasn't going to make it easy for them. Calling him all manner of names normally used against women, Korskof and his sidekick dragged Patrick to his feet.

His determination not to aid the move in any fashion slowed them down considerably. Patrick guessed that either the helicopter would return or there was a vehicle on its way. But there was always a chance that a car would come round the road and, seeing the trashed Ferrari, decide to find out what had happened.

It was a hope, but a small one.

Climbing back up the steep slope was a lot harder than running down it. Korskof's lungs didn't sound any healthier than Chapayev's. The other guy was slimmer and fitter and took the brunt of Patrick's attempts to slow them down. As luck would have it, nothing did come by on the road, so his plan failed.

He was dragged unceremoniously over the lip of the hill and thrown down by the roadside. Korskof proceeded to go through his pockets. He located and removed his mobile, which he threw down and stamped on, before kicking the remains over the edge.

Then the two men had a conversation in low voices, but definitely not in Russian. Patrick took a guess at Chechen, which he had no knowledge of apart from an occasional word. Minutes later, a car arrived. It was the one Patrick had seen parked outside the Villa Astrid. He was dumped into the boot and the lid slammed shut.

Shortly afterwards, by the forward and reverse movements, the sound of grinding and the thumps, he guessed the Ferrari was being helped over the edge to topple down the rocks.

Then they were off, at much the same speed he'd been driving before.

The trip took around forty minutes, according to the lit dial of his watch. Judging by the directions taken, they'd wound their way down to the main coast road, then turned left, which suggested he was headed back towards Cannes, although being in the boot was disorientating and he couldn't be sure. Patrick was assuming he was on his way to the black yacht, which, as he had suggested to Leon, could simply have moved further along the coast.

Moreaux had shown no inclination to follow the *Heavenly Princess* outside his jurisdiction. The detective was glad to see the back of the black yacht. Why involve the Police Nationale with Chapayev any more than necessary? Besides, Moreaux – as far as Patrick was aware – knew nothing about the incident on board regarding Patrick, the diamonds and Chapayev. He would have no wish to come looking for trouble.

Therefore, Patrick was in this alone.

As the car rumbled on, he considered why they should want him alive and came up with three good reasons. They wanted to know the whereabouts of the black pearl. They'd counted the diamonds and discovered three were missing. They just wanted to kill him slowly. Or all three put together.

As Chapayev had said: debts must be repaid and it seemed Patrick was on his way to pay his.

The car finally came to a halt. Just prior to this, he'd judged by the change in sound that they'd entered a building of some sort. He heard the occupants of the car get out, three by his estimation. Minutes later, the boot was opened.

Patrick blinked in the sudden electric light and tried to focus – in vain as it turned out, for a cloth bag was immediately pulled over his head before he had a chance to check out his surroundings, or who the third member of the trio was.

Hauled out of the boot, he slumped to the ground and made no attempt to get up. The weaker they thought he was, the better. Korskof reiterated his litany of Russian abuse and hauled Patrick to his feet. The smell of fuel and lack of fresh air suggested they were in a lockup of some kind, but he thought he could make out the lapping of water. Then he heard the chug of an approaching motorboat and decided he was in a covered jetty, probably below one of the isolated luxury villas that dotted the coast around Cannes.

Patrick expected to be shoved into the approaching motorboat, but instead he was hustled up a flight of stone steps. He counted twenty-two. A door was opened and he was met by a different quality of air, suggesting that he might well be in the basement of a house.

Another flight of stairs followed, then another, but this time they were carpeted and the scent was of luxury. The final flight were wooden and bare, after which he was propelled into a room, and pushed briskly down on a wooden chair. His hands were wrenched behind his back and tied firmly together, his feet fettered to the legs.

Korskof's last action before he left the room was to punch Patrick hard in the stomach. Patrick had already braced himself, expecting some act of violence, so it wasn't unexpected, but it was, he thought, a harbinger of what was to come.

Sitting in the dark, his breathing hampered by the bag, his earlier feeling of disorientation returned. He'd made some effort to free his hands, but plastic tie tags were extremely difficult to remove. As for his feet, taking off his shoes had proved no help at all. Both ankles were tightly secured.

His next move was to take the chair in small steps towards what he hoped would prove to be a wall. Every small jump backwards seemed to echo in what he suspected was an empty attic room. Whatever noise they could discern from below, it didn't seem to concern them. No one appeared. The door remained shut.

Finally reaching the wall, Patrick tipped himself back against it, his plan being to ease the tie tags off the chair legs and at least set his feet free. It was a worthy idea but harder in the execution than the planning, and it didn't take into account the jarring effect on the bullet wound in the back of his leg. Persistence eventually paid off. His feet freed, he contemplated his next move.

As far as he was aware his hands were tied together but not to the chair, the back of which was relatively high and wide. There was a chance he could work himself free in two possible ways. Abruptly, which might result in a dislocated shoulder, or slowly, which might need more time than he had.

Patrick decided to go for speed.

His first effort left him gasping and still firmly attached to the chair.

The next time he rose slowly to his full height. The weight of the chair was now in his favour. Patrick stretched his body upwards and the chair slipped down a little more. Bracing himself he extended his shoulders as far as possible, without them exiting their sockets.

His determination paid off. The chair dropped with a clatter and he was free of it, but still hampered by his lack of vision and his firmly tied hands, and surely his time alone was running out.

He made his way round the room looking for anything metal that might be used to help free his hands. En route he bumped into a table and a radiator, neither of which offered any help. Then he found the fireplace.

The grate was small with a tiled surround. Cannes winters could be cold, particularly in the hills and close to the sea – hence his own winter stays at the Chanteclair. The newer houses generally had central heating, but the older villas and town houses sometimes used wood fires.

Patrick sat down, back to the grate, and eased his wrists over the metal grill.

He had barely begun the sawing back and forth when footsteps approached the door. There was no time to locate the chair. No time to sit back down and pretend he was attached.

The door opened and two sets of footsteps entered.

There was a moment's silence as the scene before them was absorbed, then Chapayev told Korskof in Russian just what an idiot he was.

TWENTY-TWO

Chevalier was regarding Moreaux with some consternation. The two men were seated on the terrace of the Hôtel Splendid, each with a glass of wine in his hand, while waiters brought round plates of small delicacies, and passersby stopped to stare at the youth and beauty of the female guests at a funeral. Madame Lacroix's girls were stunning when viewed individually; as a group they caused mouths to fall open, and young male waiters to lose their wits entirely.

'I need to know the truth,' Moreaux repeated.

'Seldom do we need to know the whole truth,' Chevalier said. 'We need only know what is necessary.'

It could have been himself speaking, which only irritated Moreaux more. He decided to say exactly what he was thinking, for once.

'I believe Courvoisier to be in danger.'

'From whom?'

'Vasily Chapayev.'

Chevalier gave a small laugh. 'Then you have only just woken up, Lieutenant Moreaux.'

Moreaux accepted this well-aimed and deserved jibe, as Chevalier went on. 'Your job, as I see it, is to protect your fellow Suquetans. Marie Elise was one of us, as is Brigitte, as now is Courvoisier. Instead, you appear to prefer courting favour with rich and powerful Russians who use Cannes as their playground.'

Moreaux smiled. 'Unlike those who sell them our houses and welcome them into our casinos,' he hit back.

Chevalier chose this moment to savour his wine.

'Diamonds,' Moreaux said. 'Does Courvoisier have diamonds belonging to Chapayev?'

Chevalier's hand rose involuntarily to his tie, which was fastened with a diamond pin.

'Ah,' Moreaux said. 'Purchased from Camille Ager's shop, I presume? The shop that she opened with the aid of Chapayev's money.'

When Chevalier failed to respond, Moreaux continued. 'If Courvoisier is your friend then you will help me locate him, before Chapayev does.'

'Courvoisier prefers to work alone.'

When Moreaux swore under his breath, Chevalier continued. 'Why do you think he's in trouble now?'

'Because Korskof was seen leaving the graveyard shortly after him.'

That declaration caused a change of heart in Chevalier.

The story that he now told was an interesting one and answered some of Moreaux's questions. Coupled with Angele's story and that of Camille Ager, it appeared to match Moreaux's own train of thought. Chapayev was using Moreaux's patch to launder diamonds.

It was inconvenient and extremely irritating and had certainly caused the death of at least one of Cannes' citizens, but Chapayev was a force to be reckoned with. The dinner party had been designed to show Moreaux just how much influence and power the Russian already exerted in Cannes. Perhaps it had even been a warning that he should stay well clear.

That thought had entered his head before, but Moreaux was a man who often played sides off against each other, thus avoiding bloodshed and keeping the peace. In this instance, he decided that he had kept the peace for long enough.

He rose and wished Chevalier a good afternoon.

'What are you planning to do?' Chevalier asked.

'Sometimes it is better to only know what is necessary,' Moreaux threw back at him.

Just then Moreaux's mobile rang. He took the call. 'Where?' he barked after listening for a few moments. 'I'm on my way.'

Moreaux then left, ignoring Chevalier's enquiry as to the subject of the call.

TWENTY-THREE

Sunlight filtered through the small attic window, beyond which was a glimpse of blue sky.

Since they'd removed the bag from his head, Patrick had concentrated on that one spot, imagining himself outside, looking up, free and unrestrained.

He was well practised in the technique of dissociation. The ability to disconnect from unpleasant physical and mental experiences had proved his salvation on a number of occasions such as this. Unfortunately, dissociation had also become a habit, creating havoc in his personal life.

He was aware that Chapayev stood before him. He was aware that he was speaking, but Patrick had no interest in what was being said. He was more conscious of Korskof's proximity, because at times the Russian's henchman's actions brought Patrick back abruptly from that place outside himself.

A shadow blocked the light as Korskof moved into position once again. As a result, Patrick's mind filtered back into his body.

'You saved my life, Monsieur de Courvoisier. A sign of weakness.'

Patrick tried to return to his patch of sky.

'You also stole three diamonds, and of course the black pearl, which I would like returned. Where is my property?'

Patrick waited for the blow to fall. This time it didn't, although Korskof itched to dispense one. The conversation so far had been one-sided.

Patrick had refused to say anything until they'd removed the bag from his head and he could look Chapayev briefly in the eye. The Russian had appeared none the worse for his dice with a watery death. The popping eyes had gone, the water-filled lungs no longer gasping. He'd appeared no prettier, however, and no less greedy.

'Where are the remaining diamonds?' Chapayev repeated.

It was time, Patrick decided, to respond.

'I gave them to Lieutenant Moreaux. You should expect a visit soon to question you regarding their origins, and your connection to the death of Marie Clermand.'

It was worth his return, if only to observe Chapayev's expression at his announcement. The discomfort, quickly masked, suggested Moreaux wasn't entirely in the Russian's pay, which gave Patrick some cause for hope.

Chapayev was studying him with undisguised hostility. Had Patrick been in the Russian's shoes he would, at this moment, be considering how much pleasure he would get from disposing of Patrick, and how easy that would be.

No one had seen him brought here. He could be killed and dumped at sea or buried in the garden of the villa. The chances were his body would never be found, or would be washed up in another jurisdiction far from Cannes.

'I also told Lieutenant Moreaux that you were blackmailing Camille Ager,' Patrick added for good measure.

'You have been busy.' Chapayev gave a small, unpleasant smile. 'I think it's time we retired you.'

Chapayev turned on his heel.

'I should have left you down there to feed the fish,' Patrick called after him.

'You will soon wish you had.'

It was a war of words Patrick could never win, but it felt good to try.

The door slammed shut behind Chapayev and silence fell. A heavy brooding silence, filled with malice. Korskof's hatred advanced before him in waves. Patrick felt it beat against his body, a warning of the physical abuse that was yet to come.

Korskof stripped off the smart suit jacket, then the pristine shirt, to reveal his upper body, which was almost completely covered with tattoos. Patrick recognized a few of them, especially the Russian prison tattoos. Korskof had been a busy man in his youth.

The tattoos didn't bother Patrick. He had his own scars, not tattooed on his chest, but in his mind and his heart, and he didn't wear them as a badge of honour.

Patrick said this now in Russian, challenging Korskof to fight him, man to man, with honour. Hitting a tied-up man, Patrick said, was like hitting a woman, or a child. That was the work of a coward.

Sensing a slight change in the Russian's demeanour, he kept at it.

'No man fights like a woman,' he said, using some of the derogatory words the Russian had spat at him earlier. 'Kill me like a man.'

Maybe he had hit a nerve, or maybe Korskof just fancied some fun. After all, Patrick didn't look much of an opponent. He could barely stand and had already taken a fair beating. Or maybe the Russian fancied a longer match than he would get with Patrick sitting down and tied up.

There wasn't much fun in pummelling a corpse.

Korskof came over and, going round behind Patrick, cut his bindings.

'Get up,' the Russian ordered.

Patrick gave his legs the same command and waited for them to obey. Finally they did.

Korskof kicked the chair away, just as Patrick's body considered making use of it again. The Russian was circling him, licking his lips, planning his first move. Patrick continued to play the injured soldier. He *was* injured, but he was now free and he intended staying that way.

The room was small – bare apart from a table in one corner and the south-facing window. The patch of blue sky was still there, under which would be a glistening sea. Patrick imagined dropping into that water, how good it would feel against his hot seared skin, how peaceful and quiet it would be below the surface.

The Russian, growing impatient, was coming at him, bellowing like a bull.

Patrick sidestepped him so quickly he hardly noticed the move himself. His body had been hammered, but his instinct and reflexes still worked. The move buzzed his brain cells, sending them into quick-fire motion. He felt a surge of something. Adrenaline, fury, hate. What he couldn't achieve with his body, he would have to do with his brain.

The Russian came at him again, his weight as much a hindrance as an advantage. Patrick took up a stance and kicked. His right foot met Korskof directly in the groin. The impact was as unexpected as the movement. Korskof bent over in shock and instant agony.

Patrick quickly swivelled and kicked again, reaching high between the legs, but this time from the back. The Russian went down, groaning, but he wouldn't be down for long.

Patrick grasped the thick neck between his hands. He had a moment in which to break it and he didn't hesitate. Quickly releasing the head one way, he snapped it back the other. The Russian's body relaxed, collapsing outwards and downwards like a pool of water. There was no blood, or outward evidence of death, but it was there in that room, all the same.

Patrick made for the door, his left leg suddenly dragging. If he was challenged now, he had nothing left to give. On the other side of the door, all was quiet. He crept down the stairs, still shoeless and silent.

The carpeted stairs were even better. He paused at the bottom, listening for sounds from the villa, but heard nothing, apart from the quiet tick of an ornamental clock. He had a choice now. Exit on to the terrace and try to reach the road or sea from there, or make his way into the basement from whence he'd come.

The choice wasn't good either way, but a need to get into water as quickly as possible made him make for the basement stairs. Fairly certain now that Korskof had been left to deal with him alone, Patrick emerged into a cave hewn from the red Estérel rock. The motor boat he'd heard arrive as he'd been bundled up the stairs was no longer there.

Three carved stone steps led into the water. Patrick stripped down to his shorts and lowered himself in. The water felt icily cold against his skin. This, he decided, was what heaven would be like.

The strength that had helped him fight Korskof, and got him down the stairs, drained from him now. He floated, and with the slightest of efforts, helped the water take him. Outside, the brightness of the sun was blinding. He glanced about, recognizing the distant craggy outline of the golden island where the Swede had lost his life.

Patrick flipped on to his back and lay weightless, staring up at the blue sky, trying to reinhabit his body and his mind, while knowing he had reawakened a part of him that he'd hoped to vanquish.

TWENTY-FOUR

Containing Courvoisier would always be a problem, should he be alive and remain in Cannes, Moreaux mused as the police car wound its way up to the scene of the 'accident'. He did not like usurpers on his patch, but Moreaux had to admit that Le Limier had proved useful on occasion, plus the inhabitants of Le Suquet had grown to accept him.

He had therefore no wish to see Courvoisier dead.

As regards Chapayev, he was definitely the outsider, and one who thought his money could buy just about everything. The Russian needed to be shown his place, and soon.

The *Heavenly Princess* had been located anchored off Monaco. Moreaux's sources told him that Chapayev had gone there in search of Angele Valette, and no doubt the pearl. It appeared obvious to Moreaux that the Russian didn't know when to cut his losses.

Camille Ager's recent statement had given him enough ground to detain the Russian for blackmail and suspected diamond smuggling. That would involve bringing the *Heavenly Princess* into port; a tricky and expensive business, which would alert his superiors to what had been going on under his watch. The murder of a beautiful woman during the film festival had been unfortunate, bringing the press down on Cannes, giving the world the impression that Moreaux's city was not a safe place to visit, even during the biggest movie festival in the world. The Swede's death had been declared accidental, and since he'd been implicated in Marie Clermand's murder, that case was now closed, but it still left a bad taste.

Moreaux extracted a cheroot, lit it and took a long draw, exhaling his anger and distaste at the latest episode in the story – Courvoisier's car found in the hills west of Cannes, bullet riddled, its owner missing. Chapayev, he decided, had gone too far this time, and must pay the price. The next thing he knew the papers would be talking about Russian gangsters taking over Cannes.

It was time to reassert his authority, but in a manner that deflected both the attention of his superiors and of the media, and which removed Chapayev from under his feet.

By the time the police car had reached the spot where the Ferrari had been found, Moreaux had formulated the beginnings of a plan.

He made his way carefully down through the rocks towards the red shape that had been Courvoisier's pride and joy. Moreaux had admired the car on a number of occasions and felt anger at its destruction, but he was more enraged at the thought that whoever had done this should imagine they could get away with it.

Speaking with the forensic team currently examining the vehicle, Moreaux learned that there were no bloodstains present inside the car, and therefore it was unlikely that anyone had been in the Ferrari when it had been fired on, or when it had gone over the edge. Moreaux allowed himself a small smile at that news, because it suggested to him that Courvoisier was alive, at least two to three hours ago.

Whether that was now the case was another matter.

Moreaux made his way back to the road. From that vantage point he could see the swathe of searching officers strung out along the slope below. If Courvoisier had escaped, where would he have headed? The hills were filled with places to hide. Caves, deep and numerous, peppered the red rock.

Le Limier knew these mountains well. If he'd escaped his attackers he would be currently making his way back to civilization and a mobile signal. Alternatively, he'd been caught, or disposed of somewhere close by. Moreaux didn't see them carting Courvoisier's remains too far, so they'd be located soon, if they were here.

The area where the car had gone over the edge had been cordoned off. A couple of forensics were studying the area in detail, lifting tyre impressions, photographing and taking samples. A discussion with one of them, a woman, revealed that the evidence suggested the Ferrari had been shoved off the road by something bigger.

'A truck?' Moreaux suggested.

'More likely a big black car by the paint scrapings we've recovered. The tyre tracks are fairly distinctive, so we should be able to match for model.'

So, whoever had come for Courvoisier had been a little careless with the traces they'd left behind. Still, if Brigitte hadn't spotted Korskof leaving the graveyard, they would never have been looking for Courvoisier in the first place. As Chevalier had said, Le Limier liked to work alone and wasn't in the habit of revealing where he was going, or for what purpose.

'We have also located drops of blood, on the gravel close to the tyre tracks,' she added.

'Which means?' he asked curtly.

'Someone was hurt, but not while they were in the Ferrari.'

Moreaux silently wished that it was Courvoisier who had been the one to inflict the damage.

Back in his car, he ordered the driver to take him to Cannes, specifically to the Vieux Port. It was time to take another look at *Les Trois Soeurs*.

Once on the main road, a mobile signal appeared and his phone started ringing. The first call was from Brigitte. It wasn't a habit of hers to contact him, under any circumstances, and certainly not on this number. Because of this Moreaux answered immediately.

Brigitte's voice was strained when she spoke.

'Have you found Courvoisier?'

Moreaux wasn't keen to divulge information and certainly not news that would upset Brigitte further.

'We're looking for him, but he isn't a man who chooses to be found, when that suits him.'

There was a short pause. 'What of Korskof?' Brigitte's voice cracked on the name.

'He hasn't been seen,' Moreaux said, which was true.

'I remembered something. I think Chapayev has a villa west of the Île d'Or. He rang once from there, demanding an escort one night to have dinner with him.' Brigitte hesitated. 'I didn't like his tone, so I told him all the girls were engaged.'

Moreaux asked if she remembered the name of the villa.

There was a short silence, while she tried. 'Les Sylphides, I think.'

As soon as she rang off, Moreaux used his mobile to do a search on the name. Three possibilities came up, two of which were termed 'luxury' and one 'exclusive'. The exclusive one was on a rocky promontory, with a jetty. It sat just east of the Île d'Or.

Had Moreaux been a man prone to exhibit joy, he would have cheered. Instead he gave curt instructions to the driver to turn the car and head west.

TWENTY-FIVE

Patrick was swimming, or at least attempting to. Fortunately the current was flowing in the direction he wanted to go. Had it been otherwise, he would never have made it this far.

He had stopped periodically to float, when the willpower and energy to continue had deserted him. On at least two such occasions, he'd suddenly come to, as his mouth filled with water, having sunk below the surface in a stupor.

But he was almost there, he told himself. The tower on the Île d'Or was getting closer; the rocks on which it stood were reddened by the setting sun. He was aware that by making for Jean Paul's place he was placing his friend in danger again, but promised himself that he would spend so little time there that it wouldn't pose a problem.

Rounding the final rocky headland, he spotted the pebble beach of the camp site and the patch of sand that lay beyond it. Not trusting his left leg enough to try walking across the stones, he made for the sand instead. Floating as far inshore as possible, Patrick then attempted to stand.

As he hauled his body from the cushioning water, the feeling of weightlessness evaporated and was replaced by pain, so shocking that he groaned out loud. Forcing his feet to move, he staggered up the beach.

Patrick was relieved to find the restaurant terrace deserted. In the failing light it might not be obvious what state he was in, but he had no wish to scare any visitors Jean Paul might have. Having negotiated the beach, he tackled the two flights of wooden steps that led to the restaurant. Fortunately Jean Paul had provided a rail.

Now out of the water, his body had taken to excessive shivering in the cool night air, which made his ascent even trickier. Had he not felt so bad, Patrick might have laughed at the image he presented. Relief at being alive and being here compensated for everything.

A peel of laughter came from the kitchen. Jean Paul was relating a story which Joanne found amusing. Patrick, not wishing to walk in on that scene, sat down abruptly at one of the outside tables.

Reacting to the sound of movement on the terrace, Patrick heard

Jean Paul order Joanne to stay put while he went to investigate. Moments later, he appeared in the doorway.

Patrick called to his friend in Cannois, hoping Jean Paul would recognize his voice.

Jean Paul came quickly forward. In the light from the doorway, Patrick's condition was reflected in his friend's eyes. There then followed a litany of curses and threats of retaliation that would have started World War Three.

Patrick interrupted him. 'Can I come inside?'

'*Mon Dieu*. Of course.'

Patrick waved away Jean Paul's helping hand, and rose to his feet again. This time his legs remembered their job.

'I could use a stiff drink. Whisky, if you have it.'

Moments later, he was seated by the stove, a blanket round his shoulders, with a large glass of malt whisky in his hand. The warmth of the room enveloped him like a woman's body.

Patrick gulped down the whisky and held out the glass to be refilled.

Joanne urged him to have some food first, but Patrick wanted nothing but whisky inside him, dulling the pain. The third glass brought the inner glow he sought.

'I'll take some food now,' he told a worried Joanne.

She ladled out a bowl of thick soup and sat it next to him on the stove, handing him a wad of bread. Patrick ate hungrily, finishing both soup and bread in minutes. He had a second bowl, then a third, the rich mix of meat and vegetables bringing both sustenance and warmth.

Eventually he ceased, replete for the moment.

Jean Paul, meanwhile, had sat nearby in silence, although fury furled his brow.

He now asked in guttural French what bastard had done this to Patrick.

'Korskof,' Patrick replied. 'At Chapayev's command.'

'Then both will die,' Jean Paul said.

Patrick shook his head. 'You and Joanne are not to be involved.' He shifted a little in the seat. 'Although there's one more thing I need you to do for me.'

'Anything,' Jean Paul said with gusto.

The operation took place on the kitchen table. Jean Paul had served in Algeria and knew the importance of a well-stocked medical kit. He also didn't trust doctors in general, and the French health service in particular.

Patrick took advantage of another whisky, was then arranged face down, and given a local anaesthetic. His wound, though painful, hadn't greatly prevented walking, despite his performance on the mountain. Patrick was convinced the bullet hadn't penetrated far, or may even have exited.

The first scenario turned out to be the case.

Jean Paul extracted it without too much difficulty, made some reassuring sounds featuring the words 'flesh wound', and applied a dressing.

He then turned Patrick over, helped him sit up, and cleaned and patched up the rest of him, after which he handed him two capsules and another glass of whisky.

'These will kill the pain.'

'But not put me to sleep, I hope?'

Jean Paul shook his head.

'Good, because I need to make a phone call.'

TWENTY-SIX

Then double gates of Les Sylphides were firmly shut. Moreaux had expected no less, although he had hoped the motor launch he'd ordered from Cannes would be approaching the jetty below, if not already, then very soon.

He stepped out of the vehicle and lit a cheroot.

He suspected Chapayev had already flown this nest. His main reason for coming here was to check for Courvoisier. It wasn't a long journey from where he had disappeared. Had they removed him alive from the mountain, this would have been the place to bring him.

The only reason he could think of for Chapayev keeping Courvoisier alive was to locate his diamonds. How the Russian would extract the information he wanted was something he had no wish to speculate on.

He made a call, establishing that the motor launch had docked at the jetty and someone was on their way to open the gate. According to the officer, the villa looked deserted, and they'd had access to it via the basement jetty. Moreaux ordered them to await his arrival before exploring any further.

Minutes later, the gates swung open and Moreaux and the police car entered.

The villa had extensive grounds, which included most of the promontory on which it stood. As reported, there were no vehicles in the drive, and the place looked abandoned. Moreaux approached the front door, which had been opened for him, and stepped inside.

The air of opulence immediately offended him, not because of its richness, but because it smelled of Russian money. An ornate clock ticked in the large reception area, bringing an air of timeless serenity, which matched the antique furniture seen through the open doors.

Moreaux ordered his men to examine the ground floor and took himself upstairs.

Interrogations did not take place in such luxurious surroundings. As in the police station, they took place behind locked doors, where the sounds of distress could not be heard. The second storey consisted of a variety of bedrooms and accompanying bathrooms. Moreaux left these to his men and ventured further.

A set of wooden stairs took him to the attic.

There were three doors off the landing, all of them firmly shut.

Moreaux opened the first to find a cupboard, the second a sparsely furnished bedroom, which left the third. He stood outside for a moment. Had he been a religious man, he would have prayed. As he wasn't, he uttered a curse as he opened the door.

The first thing that hit him was the smell – a mixture of vomit, sweat, urine and human excrement. The draught from the open door caused a cloud of flies to rise and buzz furiously before settling again on the open eyes of the figure on the floor. Moreaux took in the chair and the wall behind where blood splatters had painted a picture of what had taken place in this room.

Moreaux felt bile rise in his throat, and fought it back down as he established that the body on the floor was not that of Courvoisier, but of Korskof.

TWENTY-SEVEN

Moreaux was standing on the jetty, considering his next move, when the phone call came. Studying the unknown number on the screen, he considered whether to answer. Thinking it might be Brigitte, he did so.

He didn't recognize Courvoisier's voice at first, or perhaps he thought he was speaking with the dead.

'Courvoisier?' he said, to make sure.

'Lieutenant Moreaux.' The voice now took on the faintly mocking tone that was the norm for their conversations.

A sense of something like relief washed over Moreaux.

'I thought you were dead,' he said.

'Sorry to disappoint you.'

Moreaux didn't deny disappointment, but said instead, 'We need to talk.'

'I agree.'

'Where, exactly?'

'I will be waiting in the car park at Le Dramont thirty minutes from now.'

As Moreaux rang off, the setting sun broke through a thin film of dark cloud. In the distance, he could make out the Île d'Or. All roads, it seemed, led back to the place where the Swede had died.

If Courvoisier was in the vicinity of Le Dramont, he was less than fifteen minutes by car from the villa and the body in the attic. A closer inspection had revealed that Korskof's neck had been broken. Not an easy thing to achieve on a man his size. Whoever had snapped that thick neck had known exactly how to do it. Which suggested it was not the first time they'd carried out such a manoeuvre.

The jigsaw that was his image of Patrick de Courvoisier just had another piece fitted. It was not a pretty picture, but it was a more admirable one, in Moreaux's eyes, than that fashioned from Korskof or Chapayev.

The team from the mountain would come here next. Korskof's body would have to be examined and then taken to the morgue. It

was important that this unfortunate sequence of events came briskly
to an end, and life in Cannes got back to normal.

Perhaps it would take the combined forces of himself and
Courvoisier to achieve this.

Jean Paul insisted on driving Patrick up the hill at least. Patrick
agreed, but only on the condition that he dropped him and immediately drove back down.

'I do not trust Moreaux,' Jean Paul argued.

'Neither do I,' Patrick agreed, 'but in this case, I have little
choice.'

Jean Paul expressed his distrust even further through a selection
of choice phrases. 'I have seen his type before, in the army. They
look only to their own interests.'

'In this case, I believe, our interests are the same.' Even as he
said it, Patrick hoped that was true.

As the lights of the jeep wound their way back down the hill,
Patrick revisited his plan. If he could trust Moreaux, it might work.
If it did, it was to the advantage of both of them, provided Moreaux
valued a quiet life and a return to normality.

If, instead, Moreaux had his eyes on a hefty pension and early
retirement, then Patrick might well end up dead, or behind bars. To
reassure himself, he thought of Brigitte. Perhaps she knew Moreaux
better than Patrick did, or better even than Moreaux did himself.
Patrick could only hope that was true.

Patrick stepped behind the landing craft as a set of headlights
slowed on the road, then swung left into the car park. He watched
as the car drew up some metres away and doused its lights. Moreaux
obviously thought he was there first, which was to Patrick's
advantage.

He waited, checking to make sure Moreaux was in fact the only
occupant. Then he heard the window roll down, saw the striking
match and caught the familiar scent of Moreaux's cheroot.

Patrick moved as swiftly as he could to the car, opened the
passenger door and slid inside.

'Like a shadow, as always.' Moreaux turned to look at Patrick.
After a moment he reached up and switched on the inside light.
Now he could see Patrick's face in all its glory. He flicked the light
off again.

'That was your blood on the walls of Les Sylphides?'

Patrick contrived to sound puzzled. 'I don't know what you're talking about.'

Moreaux took a draw on his cheroot. 'Then where did you get the injuries?'

'Someone took a pot shot at the Ferrari up near Blavet Gorges. I pulled up and got out. I managed to make the trees.'

Moreaux smiled. 'And from there to here?'

'Yes.'

'Who patched you up?'

'A friend.'

Moreaux turned his gaze downhill. 'Ah, Jean Paul, who also helped Angele Valette, I believe.'

Patrick remained silent.

'Brigitte saw Korskof leave the graveyard just after you,' Moreaux said.

Patrick understood now why the car had been found.

'So we must presume it was he who fired on you.'

'Probably,' Patrick conceded.

'He won't be doing that again,' Moreaux said. 'Korskof's dead. Someone broke his neck.'

Patrick stared out the window, remembering the snap and relishing it.

'I intend to visit Chapayev's yacht,' Moreaux went on. 'I would like you to come with me.'

This was the moment Patrick had been dreading. He was about to be handed over to the Russian, in payment of what? A debt? Or a hefty pension and early retirement? Jean Paul had been right. Moreaux wasn't to be trusted.

'Why would I do that?' Patrick said coldly.

'Because I intend to arrest him, but I need your help in convincing him otherwise.'

TWENTY-EIGHT

Moreaux drove Patrick back to the gunboat. They travelled in silence, having discussed the plan in full. Patrick wasn't persuaded they were on the same side, and Moreaux made no attempt to convince him.

Moreaux's reason for taking Chapayev into custody was clear. The Russian had overstepped the mark and had to be curtailed from inflicting further damage, which was in both their interests. Patrick agreed, but wasn't sure that the plan to achieve this would come out in his favour.

Yet he had to admit, if only to himself, that he could not do it alone.

They arrived back around midnight. The Irish bar was in full swing, the remainder of the *quai* quiet. Patrick checked the outside crowd for Stephen, before exiting the car. He had no wish to engage his friend in conversation or to offer any explanation for the damage to his face, or for that matter the rest of his body.

Pulling down the walkway, he heard Oscar's joyful snuffled bark. Patrick took some time over the small dog, noting that someone had put food and water aboard for him. He guessed Pascal, and was grateful the dog hadn't been simply removed in his absence.

He took Oscar below, fixed himself a drink and sat down on the leather couch.

He would sleep on Moreaux's proposal. If he decided he didn't want to accept it, then he would have to leave Cannes, and swiftly. Moreaux would no doubt feel it necessary to question him about Korskof's death. He had intimated as much during their lengthy and circular conversation.

If Moreaux chose not to apprehend Chapayev, the Russian would not give up on Patrick once he discovered Korskof was dead, and Patrick alive.

Debts must be repaid being his motto.

'Mine too,' thought Patrick as he stretched out on the couch, rather than drag himself into the bedroom and a proper bed.

He woke as the early morning light found the portholes. The

warmth on his face was pleasant and he strove to enjoy that moment before wakening fully and facing the day. This time standing had become easier. He put on the coffee pot, but chose not to venture out for fresh croissants, and made a cooked breakfast instead. He ate first, then went through to the bathroom to wash and take a good look at the damage.

Viewing himself in the full-length mirror, he took stock. He didn't care how bad he looked, but he did care if he thought his body wasn't up to the job ahead. The wound in his leg had knitted well together. Jean Paul had been correct when he'd declared it superficial. The nick in his arm from the earlier bullet wound sustained on board the *Heavenly Princess* looked fine. There was a great deal of bruising on his upper body, but most of the blood splattering in that room had come from head cuts, particularly one to the back of his head.

Jean Paul had patched him up well. He still resembled a boxer who'd gone too many rounds, but he was free, unfettered and could look at the sky any time he wanted. Patrick dressed and returned to the galley where he poured another coffee, added a tot of whisky to it and swallowed two painkillers of sufficient strength to let him believe he endured no pain.

Then he and Oscar went out on deck.

Patrick chose a seat at the stern looking out over the marina to await Moreaux's call. The dive boat had already departed and with it any concerns he'd had about meeting Stephen. Moreaux had indicated that both Chevalier and Brigitte were worried at his disappearance, but he hadn't told either of them about finding the Ferrari. Word would get out soon enough that the car was his, but they had a small window of time, at least.

'The less people know, the easier it will be to resume normal life,' Moreaux had said with conviction.

Patrick wondered if he would ever be able to resume normal life as he had known it here on the gunboat, in Cannes, whatever happened.

Moreaux called him at ten on the alternative mobile number Patrick had given him, and arranged to pick him up shortly for their journey to Monaco.

Moreaux was a skilled driver, with a liking for speed similar to his own. It wasn't the only similarity. They differed in age, and a liking for cheroots, but Patrick recognized something of himself in the stern countenance of the man who sat beside him.

Moreaux was a serving policeman, and as such had to be seen to uphold the law, but that did not mean he always did. Moreaux made his decisions based on what served Moreaux, his welfare and his own moral code. And as in Patrick's previous occupation, personal morality was often at odds with the requirements of the job.

Patrick found it interesting that Monaco should be the location of the end game. Sold as a luxurious destination for the rich, it was little more than a concrete jungle of high-value real estate, a tax haven for the super rich, squashed into two square kilometres. Beauty it had none, except perhaps for the palace gardens, which was the image most often used to attract the tourists.

Moreaux headed for the harbour, parking in a reserved spot. Patrick wondered just how often the lieutenant visited the place. That wasn't the only surprise, as Moreaux indicated Patrick should follow him down a walkway to a speedboat that bore the name *Michelle*. It seemed the rumours surrounding the wealth of Moreaux's wife might well be true. Or else, Moreaux had an extra income from somewhere.

Moreaux made no attempt to explain, just informed Patrick that the black yacht was anchored in the bay and that Chapayev was expecting him. Patrick wasn't sure whether his use of the word 'him' rather than 'them' should cause him concern, or bring relief.

The journey out there took twenty minutes, during which Patrick visited the toilet. Once inside he checked on the knife he carried, as well as his gun, retrieved from *Les Trois Soeurs*. He wanted to be ready for all eventualities, of which he feared there were many.

Whatever Moreaux decided to do, Patrick had his own itinerary.

As he resurfaced, Moreaux was already drawing alongside the platform. He secured the motorboat and jumped out, indicating Patrick should follow. Patrick climbed out more gingerly, having no wish to reveal what state he was really in.

There was no waiting reception for them on the lower deck. Moreaux strode ahead as though he knew this boat well and was welcome aboard it. For a man who had only been here once for dinner, he appeared a little too knowledgeable.

Chapayev awaited them in the stateroom.

He greeted Moreaux as 'Lieutenant' and wished him good day. His attitude was affable with not the remotest indication that he was nonplussed by their appearance. He then turned his attention to Patrick.

'I see my part-time waiter has returned.'

'From the dead,' Patrick said.

'I, too, have had a brush with death,' Chapayev reminded him.

There was a moment's standoff before Moreaux took charge.

'We found your man Korskof in a villa called Les Sylphides. His neck was broken.'

This was news to Chapayev by the look on his face. His eyes darted from Moreaux to Patrick and back again, suspicion blossoming.

He was reassured by Moreaux's next remark.

'We believe this man was responsible for his death.'

Patrick's hand was already reaching for his gun, but Moreaux was faster. Patrick felt the press of metal in his side.

'As agreed, I hand over Courvoisier on the understanding that your interest in Cannes and its inhabitants is at an end.'

Chapayev smiled. 'I have a lot invested as you know. It would make us both the poorer, I think.'

'Nevertheless, that was the deal,' Moreaux said.

Patrick's brain was in overdrive. This was similar to the plan Moreaux had outlined, but sufficiently different to make him worried. Very worried.

'And what of Courvoisier's disappearance?' Chapayev said.

'Le Limier comes and goes. All of Cannes knows that. Except on this occasion he will not return.'

Chapayev was growing more relaxed by the moment.

'There is the little matter of the three diamonds he still has in his possession.'

'They are forfeit,' Moreaux said.

'And the black pearl?' Chapayev said, looking to Patrick.

'You indicated it had been recovered,' Moreaux said.

Now this was news to Patrick.

As though on cue, the far door of the stateroom opened and a woman walked in. She was dressed in dark-blue silk, the pearl hanging round her neck. Angele was as beautiful as ever, although her eyes had the look of someone heavily sedated.

'Ah, Angele. Look who has come to visit us.'

If she recognized Patrick, Angele didn't show it. Chapayev caught her and drew her to him, cradling her in the crook of his arm. His big hand rose up to catch her breast. If his grip was painful, she didn't register it, her pupils big with whatever substance she'd chosen to take, or he had administered.

'The movie has done very well. It is going to make Angele a star,' he told them.

Moreaux seemed unaffected by Angele's appearance and Patrick wondered whether he'd known all along that she would be there.

'So,' Chapayev said. 'It is time to make a decision, Lieutenant. All those dignitaries you mingled with on the *Heavenly Princess*. How would they react if you ban me from Cannes? He paused for a moment to allow time for his words to sink in. 'There is, of course, an alternative solution. We dispose of Monsieur de Courvoisier. You return to your police station and life continues as normal.'

As Moreaux appeared to contemplate this, Patrick felt the pressure of the barrel lessen on his side, while Moreaux muttered something in Cannois.

Patrick took him at his word and slipped his hand in his pocket, just as Chapayev sensed a change in Moreaux's demeanour. He pulled Angele in front of him as the gun which was pressed in Patrick's side was raised to point at Chapayev.

The sequence of movements all took place in a matter of seconds.

Angele, too drugged to figure out what was happening, stared at them with startled eyes, like someone disturbed in their sleep.

'Don't be a fool, Lieutenant. If you take me in, I will implicate you. Your career will be over. If we let him go, Courvoisier will do the same.'

Patrick eased his hand into his pocket to clasp his weapon of choice. The UK-SFK knife hadn't seen the light of day since he'd arrived in Cannes, but fitted as well in his hand as it had always done.

'You have no choice, Lieutenant,' Chapayev was saying. 'You cannot kill me and get away with it. Come, let us both dispose of this nuisance, and continue as normal.'

Sensing Moreaux's hesitation, Chapayev levelled his gun at the policeman's head as a figure appeared in the doorway. It was henchman number two, armed and ready to finish the conversation in whatever way Chapayev wanted it to go.

Patrick had waited long enough.

The speed and accuracy of the throw was as soundless as it was deadly. The thin-edged blade embedded itself firmly between Chapayev's eyes, just as his gun went off. The bullet skiffed Moreaux's cheek as he threw himself sideways and let off a volley towards the doorway. For a moment the stateroom resounded to Angele's screams and the thud of bullets burying themselves in the walls.

Then it was over.

Patrick, his gun out now, surveyed the damage. The gunman had taken a shot in the chest that didn't appear fatal. Chapayev lay on his back, staring upwards in startled death. Angele, released from Chapayev's arms, curled on the ground beside his body, weeping silently.

Patrick moved swiftly, first to remove his knife from Chapayev's brain, then to block both doors to the stateroom in preparation for the next onslaught. Just then he heard the deafening scream of a police siren, followed by another, as two launches swept into view.

He crossed to Moreaux and helped the policeman to his feet.

'Who are they coming for?' Patrick said, still unsure how this would end.

'Not for you, Courvoisier,' Moreaux said with a grim smile.

TWENTY-NINE

The rain came on as they left the marina, falling in torrents as they met the race track route used in the Grand Prix. Steep concrete walls rose on either side of them, channelling the downpour on to the road surface, reminding Patrick of racing along a storm drain in Los Angeles.

Moreaux drove at speed, surface water flying from his wheels, his flashing blue light causing drivers to give way before them.

Patrick sensed the adrenaline running through the policeman's veins, recognizing the same in himself. They had both faced death and survived. Life could never taste sweeter than it did at such a moment.

They were back in Cannes in record time. Moreaux drew up alongside *Les Trois Soeurs*, light still flashing, causing all the lunch-time drinkers outside the Irish bar to stare at them. A few more emerged to see what was going on, but thankfully Stephen wasn't among them.

When Patrick climbed out of the car, Moreaux immediately took off without a word of farewell. During the return journey the policeman had said nothing. The silence between them had been as full as a conversation.

Moreaux had seen the knife. Had witnessed Patrick use it. Moreaux now knew more about him than Patrick would ever have willingly volunteered.

Patrick had been present at the conversation between Moreaux and Chapayev. He now knew more about the policeman than Moreaux would be comfortable with. It would have been better for Moreaux had Patrick died during the incident.

Both had had secrets revealed that should have remained hidden, and both were now in one another's debt.

And debts always have to be repaid, Patrick thought, as he climbed aboard the gunboat and greeted his excited little dog.

THIRTY

Later that evening, showered and changed, his wounds treated via the medical kit, Patrick took a stroll to Le P'tit Zinc with Oscar, hoping to catch Chevalier at his aperitif.

Chevalier wasn't there, but Moreaux was, with a glass of red wine in front of him.

'Ah, Courvoisier. I see you have recovered from being shot at.'

'Thanks to you.'

Moreaux indicated that he should sit.

'Your assailant has been apprehended, the one that was left alive. He will face prison for attacking a lone driver in our beautiful Provence countryside.' Moreaux assumed a deeply offended expression. '*Naturellement*, the story will not be reported on. We do not want to scare away the tourists from Cannes or Blavet Gorges.'

Moreaux went on: 'My men tell me you drive very fast, too fast for those country roads. Speed can kill, Courvoisier.' He gave a thin-lipped smile.

'I owe you one, Moreaux.'

The lieutenant acknowledged this with a small nod and reached for his glass. The gold ring from Bijou Magique suited him well. Patrick wondered which of his women was wearing its mate.

'I am sorry that Chapayev died,' Moreaux continued.

'Really?' Patrick kept his voice even.

'Had he not, I would have charged him with smuggling diamonds.' Moreaux shrugged. 'However, we have picked up his accomplice. A Mr Jacob Haruna, a Nigerian with interests in Zimbabwe. He was on board the *Heavenly Princess*. You may have seen him and his wife at the dinner party where you were serving as a waiter.'

'It was an interesting party.'

Moreaux nodded. 'If I were you, I would not mention the names of the other guests. They are important people and would not want their names mixed up with a Russian diamond smuggler.'

Patrick was rescued from commenting further by the arrival of Veronique with a glass of red wine, which she plonked down in front of him. Patrick had been planning to order something else, but decided by Veronique's expression it was better not to.

Oscar had moved to sit beside Moreaux, who was ruffling his ears, just the way Oscar liked it.

'I do not like people who are cruel to dogs,' Moreaux said firmly.

Patrick couldn't agree more.

'What of Angele?' Patrick said.

'Free to pursue her movie career, which will go very well, I believe.' He raised an eyebrow at Patrick.

A few minutes later they heard the roar of Chevalier's motorbike in Rue de la Misericorde. Chevalier looked decidedly pleased with himself as he approached them after parking it. Tonight he was dressed in cream with a blue silk cravat, fastened with a delicate diamond pin. Patrick was pleased to see the diamond had been put to good use. He glanced at Moreaux to see if he had noticed it.

Moreaux indicated his new ring. 'Madamoiselle Ager stocks such pretty items, don't you think?'

Without asking, Veronique arrived carrying a third glass of red and a selection of hors d'œuvre.

Chevalier smiled his thanks, then raised his glass.

'Gentlemen, shall we have a toast?'

'To Le Suquet,' Patrick suggested.

'To Le Suquet,' the two men chorused.

Oscar barked his approval, while Veronique allowed a smile to fleetingly pass her lips before heading back inside.

A sense of peace descended on Patrick on his walk back along the *quai*.

Perhaps life had returned to normal as Moreaux had indicated. He hoped so.

He pulled down the walkway and stepped aboard. Oscar was immediately in attack mode, his hackles rising, a low growl in his throat. Patrick put a hand on his head to silence him. The scent when he opened the cabin door was not of a female, but of an expensive male cologne.

A suited man sat on the leather sofa, a whisky glass on the coffee table alongside the bottle of Islay malt. It was a face Patrick had hoped never to have to look on again.

'Ah, Courvoisier. You surface at last.' The voice was clipped and confident to the point of arrogance.

'What do you want?' Patrick said coldly.

'You did not answer our invitation,' the voice said in mild surprise.

'I tore it up.'

The thin face narrowed even further, the lips a mere line.

'That is unfortunate. We wish you to accept.'

'You mean you order me to.'

'I would not presume . . .'

Patrick cut him off. 'I do not intend to return for any reason.'

His visitor looked nonplussed, but only for a brief moment. 'I understand you've got into some local difficulty. A Russian national, killed on a yacht with a UK-SFK knife, which, I believe, belongs to us.' He raised an enquiring eyebrow.

Patrick thought back to his recent meeting with Moreaux. Was this how Moreaux planned to remove Patrick from his patch?

He held open the cabin door. 'I'd like you to leave. Now.'

Oscar, hearing his tone, growled menacingly and bared his teeth.

His visitor rose, nodded and exited, with the final words: 'We will expect you at the Garden Party on the twenty-fifth of June. Come to the diplomatic tent at two p.m.'

CPSIA information can be obtained at www.ICGtesting.com
Printed in the USA
BVOW07s2004151114

375077BV00001B/2/P

9 781847 515155